AN
ENGLISH
GENTLEMAN

AN
ENGLISH
GENTLEMAN

SKY GILBERT

Cormorant Books

Canada Council for the Arts **Conseil des Arts du Canada** ONTARIO ARTS COUNCIL CONSEIL DES ARTS DE L'ONTARIO

The publisher gratefully acknowledges the support of the Canada Council for the Arts and the Ontario Arts Council for its publishing program. We acknowledge the financial support of the Government of Canada through the Book Publishing Industry Development Program (BPIDP) for our publishing activities.

Printed and bound in Canada

NATIONAL LIBRARY OF CANADA CATALOGUING IN PUBLICATION

Gilbert, Sky
An English gentleman: a novel/Sky Gilbert.

ISBN 1-896951-55-4

I. Title.

PS8563.I4743E64 2003   C813'.54   C2003-904231-6

Cover and text Design: Tannice Goddard/
Soul Oasis Networking
Cover image: Dolores Pitcher
Author Photo: David Hawe
Printer: Friesens

CORMORANT BOOKS INC.
215 SPADINA AVENUE, STUDIO 230, TORONTO, ON CANADA M5T 2C7
www.cormorantbooks.com

For Ian

At this moment Wendy was grand. "These are my last words, dear boys," she said firmly. "I feel that I have a message to you from your real mothers, and it is this: 'We hope our sons will die like English gentlemen.'"

— J.M. BARRIE, *PETER PAN*

PREFACE

This book has a very strange history. Manny Masters dedicated it to me. I'm not going to tell you that it's a dangerous book, or evil, or that you shouldn't read it until you're twenty-one. I'm only twenty-five. I wrote part of it (a very small part, at the end). I agree with what Manny says. This is an important document. You might want to read it for that reason. You might learn something from it.

Don't be put off by Manny. Just think of this book as an entertaining mystery, about people in a faraway time and place who are very different from you. The strange thing about this story is that — even though the incidents really happened — it's still a fairy tale.

Alan Peche
December 20, 2002

INTRODUCTION

by Manny Masters

Any journalistic report on a factual incident sometimes tells less about the actual incident than about the journalist himself.

In 1921, not long after the official end to the First World War, the following two reports appeared in London newspapers, each cataloguing the same incident.

The first report accompanied a picture of a bathing pool, and the picture of a boy.

> Sandford Pool, Oxford, where Mr. Michael Llewelyn Davies (inset) and Mr. Rupert Buxton, both undergraduates, were drowned while bathing. The bodies were recovered yesterday. Mr. Davies was one of James Barrie's five adopted sons.

The second report was considerably more baroque.

> There is something of the wistful pathos of some of his own imaginings in the tragedy which has darkened the home of Sir James Barrie. Almost the first remark of friends, on hearing of

the death of the adopted son of the dramatist today, was "What a terrible blow for Sir James!" The young men, Mr. Michael Llewelyn Davies and Mr. Rupert E.V. Buxton were drowned near Sandford bathing pool, Oxford, yesterday. The two undergraduates were inseparable companions. Mr. Davies was only 20 and Mr. Buxton was 22. The original of Peter Pan was named George and was killed in action in March 1915. Now both boys who are most closely associated with the fashioning of Peter Pan are dead. One recalls the words of Peter himself, "To die would be an awfully big adventure."

Whether the first report is simply the truth and the second merely poetic conjecture, sheds little light on this, my book. For the last thing I am interested in is poetry, or conjecture, or romance. Instead, I offer a solution to a mystery, long shrouded in a veil of ignorance.

To answer the question you have not yet posed (but will), why did I write this book?

The answer is twofold: because a) I found them; b) I have a responsibility.

Perhaps "a" is not completely accurate. I did not actually find them (the story of their discovery is fascinating, if apocryphal) but they are now mine; they rest in my ownership. Because they are mine, it is my responsibility to bring them to the world. But more than that, because they are so tender, so intimate, so incredibly revealing, they constitute something of a revelation, a revelation about a lost time and way of life. But as such, if uncovered by the wrong hands, if read in the wrong way, they might prove to be damaging. They are a very dangerous thing. Of course, it's a presumption on my part that I hold the "truth" about them. Well then, let me make that presumption. What else can any writer, worth his or her salt, propose to do?

If you are wondering what "them" is, the answer is that they are the lost letters which passed between James Barrie and Michael Llewelyn Davies from 1905 to 1921. The letters between a loving father and his adopted son.

To call these letters "lost" is somewhat romantic, because I think they were, in fact, hidden.

The first question which might come to mind, especially if you are a scholar, is — why I might chose to write about them as casually as this? For this book (and I am unapologetic about it) consists of the letters themselves, my (what might seem to some) personal and possibly irrelevant (or even objectionable) commentary, and scant footnotes.

Well, now that the letters are revealed, I will leave the scholarship to someone else. At one time, I was a bona-fide scholar. Perhaps that pretension will contribute to this work, or perhaps it may not. I leave it to you to judge. If footnotes annoy you, then you may forgo reading the few I have been unable to resist supplying. In other words, my notations (they are not, technically, footnotes) are not absolutely necessary to understand the documents to follow. Many of us, of course, have experienced the nightmare of wading through Joyce's *Ulysses* footnote*less.* One needs a signpost, a lighthouse in the dark, to avoid a wreck on those sharp, daunting literary rocks. Alternatively, some may have experienced the irritation of happily motoring through a novel by the abundantly annotated Virginia Woolf, only to be confronted with an asterisk after every proper name, when pursuit of the little star merely produces the startling revelation that Winchester, is, in fact, a district of London (what a surprise). There will be none of that nonsense here; only the most obscure or confusing references will be annotated. (Old habits die hard, and old scholars never die — they simply feel the urge to *clarify* — yet again — some vital point, *unto extinction*.)

6 | You see, it was my brief foray into the academic arena that was the genesis of this discovery. Or more accurately, it was in pursuit of a career as a scholar that I discovered these letters. But, it was due to circumstance, my own personality, and the personality of others (or particularly, one special other, a kind of behemoth of scholarship) that I decided to leave the scholarly world for the world of the real.

These letters are much more important than mere "primary sources." They are so beautiful, and so tragic, that it would not do them, or the world, justice to let them loose, like so many lethal butterflies, replete with their alluring poison so tempting to an unsuspecting world.

For these letters have changed my life.

God willing, they may also change yours.

BACKGROUND

        The story of James Barrie (the author of *Peter Pan*) and the Llewelyn Davies boys has been told, with a very particular point of view, in Andrew Birkin's carefully researched *J.M. Barrie and the Lost Boys*. I do not wish to discuss the merits and demerits of his book here. There is much to find objectionable in it — much that is not scholarship, much that might be called opinion or perhaps innuendo. But at this time I wish merely to acquaint you with the some of the details of James Barrie's relationship with the Llewelyn Davies boys. If you wish for more facts than I provide here, you should consult the Birkin book.

        James Barrie, the Scottish author, met Sylvia du Maurier (daughter of actor Gerald du Maurier and granddaughter of writer George du Maurier) in the late 1890s and quickly became enamoured of her. That is to say, he did not so much fall in love with her, as desire her for a friend. From all accounts, Miss du Maurier was a sweet, beautiful, charming woman, full of creativity, motherliness, and fun. She married a handsome, kind barrister named Arthur Llewelyn Davies, and their fruitful union produced five boys between 1893 and 1903: George, Jack, Peter, Michael, and Nico. The boys, like their parents, were attractive and charming creatures. James Barrie resided near the family in London and soon found that, due to his friendship with Sylvia, he was to accompany them on their walks through Kensington Gardens. It was from these walks, and because of his participation in various games with the boys, that Barrie was inspired to write *Peter Pan*: the leading character of which was variously claimed to be based on the oldest boy George, and the second-youngest boy Michael. But this blissful friendship between the successful playwright and the Llewelyn Davies family took a tragic turn in 1907. That year, Arthur Llewelyn Davies died after a brief illness, and his wife Sylvia followed him three years later. The boys were left with only a nanny, Mary, to care for them. In 1910, James Barrie adopted all five orphans. Barrie raised the boys and watched each of them march off to Eton, then Oxford, and in the case of the three eldest — George, Jack, and Peter — to war. George, a young man by all accounts as sweet and handsome as his father, died in The Great War in 1915. Peter, Jack, and Nico all grew to adulthood. Michael, as noted in the news items quoted in the introduction, drowned in a bathing pool in 1921. Peter committed suicide by throwing himself under a train in 1960.

Many were especially struck by the mysterious and unexpected death of Michael, since the statue of Peter Pan, which still stands to this day in Kensington Gardens, was in fact, modelled from a photograph of him.

During the years of the loving father/son relationship between James Barrie and Michael Llewelyn Davies many letters travelled back and forth. Michael was often separated from his adoptive father, specifically when off at Eton and Oxford. According to Michael's brother Peter, there were some 2,000 letters. (If this seems like a large number, it should be remembered that Michael was Barrie's favourite.)

Until recently, all of these letters were thought to be lost. Or more accurately, destroyed.

Fifty-six of these letters are now in my possession.

MY STORY

Who am I? On the one hand, it doesn't matter at all. On the other, it matters very much. These are my letters, this is my "spin" on the letters, this is my story. If you are to come to any independent judgment about my presentation of these letters, then it's important you know something about me.

Let's start with the facts. I am forty-seven years old, and I am a teacher at Robert Kennedy High School, in Manhattan. I am unmarried, Jewish, I alive alone, and I am homosexual. I live four blocks away from my mother (whom I visit regularly). I live two blocks away from my school. My apartment is technically a one-bedroom apartment, but in actual fact it has four large rooms, a loft bed, a bathroom and a kitchen. I have lived in this apartment for seventeen years. I pay $525 a month rent. In New York City. It is the year 2002.

I suppose you might call me a typical New York Jewish homosexual. Yes, alright, I love show tunes. I never miss a Sondheim opening. Bernadette Peters makes me shiver. I am an aficionado. For instance, I own a recording of Barbara Cook singing songs from *The Grass Harp*, a musical based on Truman Capote's novel of the same name. The lyrics are by Kenward Elmslie (who, if you don't happen to know it, is a brilliant lyricist). Of course I have the original cast recording of *I Can Get It For You Wholesale*. And of course, once a month I listen to *Miss Marmelstein* just to remind myself that life is worth living, and that Barbara Streisand was once brilliant.

12 | We won't discuss her recent accomplishments.

Life, of course, would not be worth living if Ethel Merman had never sung "Make It Another Old Fashioned, Please" or if Mary Louise Wilson had not outshone Miss Liza Minelli by belting "The Flame" with such hilarious passion in *Flora The Red Menace*, which, for those of you too young and too naive to know about such things, was actually a musical comedy about a young girl's joyous conversion to communism. (Only in the early 1960s!) There is no pleasure quite like listening to Cole Porter's filthy ode to the plumbing profession, called, quite simply "Plumbing", unless it is eating Ray's Pizza (something Woody Allen and I have in common) or a real New York bagel with any cream cheese other than "Philadelphia."

My tastes also run to classical: Verdi (one can't help but love him), Rachmaninoff, Donizetti, Rossini, and a smidgen of Poulenc (when I'm feeling avant-garde).

My favourite restaurant is Café Lalo (it's right across the street), which — for those of you who have been living in a geodesic igloo in the Arctic for the past few years — is the café where Tom Hanks met Meg Ryan in *You've Got Mail*. There is something silent, seductive, and hypnotizing about a fall evening at Café Lalo, as one sits, nursing a murderously strong espresso between tactfully greying stockbrokers and their jewel-encrusted wives, watching the lights in the trees sway gently in the autumn breeze, and waiting until just the right young man walks by.

No one ever visits the Café Lalo for the desserts.

I am a member of every museum, but of course I never go. Now and then I have to visit The Frick and just sit in front of "The Polish Rider" because, well, it's an important thing to do.

I visit my mother every Sunday and, yes, she is a typical Jewish mother. All she does is complain and I can't keep up with her ailments. She is unmercifully clinging, an ever-changing adolescent in the casing of an eighty-year-old. She still wears layers of heavy pancake makeup and false eyelashes — and that's just to take out the trash. She fights all the time with her neighbours, her landlord, her sisters, and the owner of the local delicatessen. Nothing is ever right. All she wants to do is listen to Steve and Edie on the record player and talk to me, in gory detail, of the slow and yet persistent disintegration of her body. I know more about the insides of an aging woman's body than most gynecologists. For me she is a trial but also the heroine of her own real-life dramas. I don't care in the slightest if people think that I have a mother fixation or that I lavish more attention on her than I do on my best friends. My mother is my best friend. I don't mind telling you that. She listens to everything I have to tell her. She doesn't always approve. But she listens. And she adores me, asking nothing in return, other than that I turn up on Sundays and bring some bagels with me.

I love my job. My students are a constant challenge and a constant trial, but they are my students and I wouldn't trade them for anything in the world. Most of them are black and this touches my heart. Robert Kennedy holds a certain resonance for them (as he does for me, I must admit) and though most of them come from unpromising inner-city backgrounds, there is a distinct possibility that they will all become doctors and lawyers if they just apply themselves.

I have a wonderful job which I love, a ridiculously cheap apartment in downtown Manhattan, and I can walk to work. By all sensible measurements of human fulfillment, my life is complete. If I were not to be a happy man, I would have only myself to blame.

And yet, I am not.

For, of course, I am bitter.

And what am I bitter about?

Love.

If you've been reading my little résumé with anything approximating interest, then you might easily note that there's something missing: the perfect boyfriend, the live-in lover, even the occasional fuck. (If I may be so frank.)

For I am celibate.

Celibate, I might add, by choice. My physiognomy is not horrific. I have no obvious external disfiguration; my back is lacking a hump. My prick is perfectly adequate and my body sags as much as a forty-seven-year-old's body might. Actually, I'm in pretty good shape. I'm what some might call "handsome." I'm smart, articulate, and cheerful. I don't have a temper, I don't smell, or fart inappropriately or too often. I'm good company. I love music, art, and (you guessed it) long walks in the country. I would make some man a perfect husband. (Or wife.) My taste does not run to the inordinately young or handsome. I have not the curse of yearning beyond my station. And yet, romance eludes me. Why?

I'm not sure. But I have the good sense not to blame myself. There is always circumstance. But it seems to me that to blame circumstance is to be sentenced to death by a court of fools. No one specific person is actually responsible for my celibate condition (though there is *one* candidate who may be eligible for the lion's share of the blame). No, I hold men in general responsible for my celibacy.

Or more specifically, homosexuals.

To say that I am bitter about the homosexual community would be an understatement. For those of you who are not familiar with what is erroneously called the "gay" community, let me fill you in. It is not very gay at all.

The most obvious example of the ridiculous injustice of queer life is that, by all rights, I should be married to a sweet man by now and curled up with him by the fire this very minute. (Yes, my apartment has two fireplaces and the one in the bedroom actually works). No one can say that I haven't tried. I will spare you the gruesome details. Maybe the best way to describe my love life and the reasons for my forlorn condition, is to describe what I'm not.

I'm not my best friend, Ronnie Connaught.

Ronnie, of course, has several advantages over me. Though I am not by any means unattractive, Ronnie has, ever since his long-lost days as a pretty boy, been considered "a catch" (although no one has ever "caught" him). A catch, in the homosexual world, is quite a few notches above "not unattractive."

Ronnie is forty-three years old, although one would never know it. He doesn't look at day over thirty-five. He has all of the original full head of blond hair that the Lord blessed him with, and skin (through another blessing from above) that is marvellously unwrinkled, though persistent smiling and an army of tanning machines have wreaked havoc on the corners of his eyes. (The corners of the eyes never lie.) His body is firm and toned, and the cleft between his prominent pectoral muscles is always on display in the *v* of his pastel shirts. I have never had the privilege of viewing Ronnie's penis, but by all accounts (his own) it is of normal size but of prodigious beauty. And, as Ronnie says, "I certainly know how to use it." Ronnie is very popular in the bars, and bathhouses, and occasionally, he attends the ever popular circuit parties which have risen to prominence since the advent of AIDS. Apparently, the trick at these parties is to ingest an inordinate number of drugs (Special K — a cat tranquilizer — E or ecstasy, and crystal meth being the odds-on favourites) which helps one endure the omnipresent, pounding, unmelodious music. At a key point in the evening (usually about 3:30 a.m.) one disrobes down to one's see-through or otherwise negligible underwear. Then comes the passionate screwing at the party itself, or in the hotel rooms, or in the hotel-room whirlpools, or all three. Ronnie has travelled, with a couple of his younger companions, to Palm Springs for the White Party, to Montreal for the Black and Blue Party and to Atlanta for some party or other that involves whitewater rafting.

I relate these details about Ronnie with some scorn, but I don't wish to be judgmental, for most certainly each has his own life and makes his own choices. Perhaps, if I had been luckier, (or unluckier) I would be Ronnie Connaught. Of course, I have not always taken the differences between us so philosophically. When we met (at teacher's college, for Ronnie is a high-school teacher too) it irked me beyond comprehension that he would be so consistently in demand. In those dark days, when I was still doing the bar scene, I would accompany him, like the ugly step-sister of yore, to Charlie's or Ty's. And always the inevitable happened: a predatory young man bought him a drink, and the two ended up chatting, and before you could say "Screw me slowly, please" they would be off. I was left at the bar, alone, eyeing the quickly dwindling opportunities for passion, which, by the end of the night, had narrowed themselves down to the fattest man in the bar, the oldest man in the bar, the bartender, a far too persistent, very stoned hooker, and my own right hand. Countless nights, I would walk home, desolate and lonely, to my only solitary consolation: masturbation. (I still masturbate to this day. Several times a day. It doesn't hurt anyone, and I find I'm my own best partner in some ways.)

What is it about Ronnie that draws them, like bees to honey? Well certainly, in New York City, there's always been something about being blond. Surrounded by so many Blacks, Latinos, and Jews, to be blond is something of a cachet. Ronnie has often told me stories of his visits to the Latino bars, where the bevy of oiled, medallioned, dark-eyed passion flowers parted for his entrance, not unlike the Red Sea for Moses. For years I tortured myself, standing in front of the mirror and grabbing fistfuls of my flabby stomach, making ill-conceived and immediately betrayed promises to attend the gym. Once I even dyed my hair blond. I looked grotesque, and it almost gave my mother a heart attack.

Thankfully, I have stopped questioning my own attractiveness and my own very worthiness, as it were. Why is Ronnie the fairy princess, and I the ugly stepsister? It may be the happenstance of precipitant effects: his blond hair and great body and flashing smile. But if that is true, then is the world merely superficial?

The most troubling revelation of nearly thirty years of adult life (ten of which were spent competing as a commodity in the homosexual marketplace) is that the homosexual marketplace is, indeed, superficial. It is about nothing more than the feeling of the moment, the drug of the week, and most importantly, the orgasm of the night. For those of us who think, who ponder life's complexities, who perhaps will forever carry around the baby fat of our human vulnerability, there is simply no hope in this brash, inhuman, cruel competition.

If I was heartless, I could console myself with the knowledge that Ronnie is HIV positive. I would not, however, take his tragedy as my boon. Let me just say, however, that it does makes sense. Part of Ronnie's thrill was (and still is) unsafe sex. He has played Russian roulette with his life, and if he is forced to ingest a medical regimen of up to sixty-five pills a day as a result, then he has only himself to blame.

There is another ignoble fact; Ronnie, for all the last thirty years of being the most popular boy on the block, has never had a live-in boyfriend, and never had a relationship which lasted longer than three months. Ronnie claims that this solitary life is not a problem. He claims that as a Sagittarian, he is an eternal bachelor. He claims that his popularity, his bar-and-bath-and-party hopping, his friends and his teaching are all he needs to keep him happy.

Could this be true? Is any human being really happy without a partner?

I don't think so. And there are moments when I have seen Ronnie eyeing the perfect couples, at AIDS benefits and Pride marches, with envy. I know that Ronnie too feels loneliness and is not as completely content as he appears. When I get him alone (for a few moments at cocktails on Saturday nights, before the meat market begins) he even says so. Not all gay men are superficial and entertaining sluts, charming and handsome professional best friends. There are those who have found Mr. Right and settled down in Yonkers or New Rochelle with their mates and equals. There are lawyer couples, and environmental-rights-activist couples, and teacher couples too. There are perfectly handsome homosexual couples with perfect jobs, and, it appears, perfect lives, who love each other, and sometimes adopt children.

Since I am a homosexual who rejects the promiscuity (unlike Ronnie Connaught) and who is a warm and loving man, why am I to be cursed (like Ronnie) with a solitary life?

Let me also say that, like the redoubtable Ronnie, I don't find it all doom and gloom. I am exceedingly happy with Barbara Streisand, my walks to work, my incredibly cheap apartment, and my visits to my mother. And, after all, I have my health. Many have less. The fact that romance has somehow eluded me I take as a circumstance of life, which must be accepted, like a facial tic, or a birthmark. Or arthritis. At first it seems unbearably painful, and then you come to understand that it's always with you, and it becomes just an ordinary part of a many-faceted existence.

To those female friends who enjoin me not to give up the search for the perfect man, I say, "I haven't." Of course, I adamantly refuse to prowl the streets, or the toilets, or don a towel and wander the popper-fragrance-infused bathhouse hallways. But on the other hand, there is always a twinkle in my eye, and a spring in my step. And I always smile at the young man at the flower shop, and at the tall, bespectacled boy who sits behind the information desk at

Barnes and Noble. (Yes, I happen to find his pimples endearing!) My energy is always present, and positive, and life-affirming. I realize that at my age, and with the deteriorating physique that accompanies it, these attributes have no hope at all of attracting love in the so-called gay world. So I am, for all intents and purposes, celibate.

Why am I telling you all this? Right now I feel like the inebriated soubrette from a 1930s movie, who has meandered on and on about the minute grotesqueries of her personal life, only to look up at the end of it all, through a fingerprint-spotted, lipstick-smeared whisky glass, and apologize for her baroque, embarrassing revelations. To be perfectly honest, I think that maybe I have told you about Ronnie Connaught only to highlight my own generosity and open-mindedness. That is to say, to compliment myself. For if I am to tell you of the discovery of these letters, I am also required to tell you about Leslie Sexton.

When it comes to Leslie Sexton, I am somewhat less generous than I have been about Ronnie Connaught. There is little love lost between myself and Leslie, and perhaps there was never any love at all. But then, I think I can say, without fear of contradiction, that he was not a loving person: he did not yearn for love, require it, or even feel its loss. I am not painting a distorted picture of Leslie when I describe him as somewhat of a monster.

I met Leslie in early 1984, which was a crucial time for both of us and for the homosexual community. It was the end of my youth (I was thirty) and also the end of my years of bar-hopping and ugly-stepsistering to Ronnie.

I was also frustrated with my job and harboured dreams of grandeur.

A LOST FRIEND

To call Leslie Sexton a "lost friend" is over-romanticizing what has, tragically, become a mundane detail of our homosexual lives. Leslie died of AIDS in 1993. Of course I don't mean in any way to trivialize his death. But, Leslie would have said that his own death was a trivial matter for him, and that it should have been too, for other people. Except for some of his most exceptional students, like myself, and his most exceptional "tricks," I suspect it made nary a ripple on anyone's emotional radar.

I met Leslie in, of all places, The Stud. The Stud, for those not familiar with New York homosexual watering holes, was at one time an extremely decadent place. Along with its sister bars, The Anvil and The Eagle, The Stud was where the serious practitioners of what we what now fashionably call "unsafe sex" would come to play. In other words, it was at these bars that the butchest and raunchiest men, adorned in leather regalia, would have group sex. They would perform various other perversions, including sado-masochistic sex, urinary acts, and other equally unmentionable things. How I ended up in this place, I do not know. I do know that I was at the end of some sort of emotional rope or other. I had been unceremoniously dumped by a handsome young thing. I can't remember who. It may have been someone that I met through an ad in the papers. I was very discouraged about love. At any rate, I found myself in the most dreadful, sleazy sex pit in town, very drunk, in a dark corner, and Leslie hauled out his prodigious prick and proceeded to wave it in my face, and well, the politest way to express what happened is to say that I did not resist.

A description of Leslie is, I suppose, necessary, though there is not much to say. He was extremely tall, and slender, and distinctly lacking a chin. Those who have participated in any sort of promiscuous sex will recognize this as the usual description of the well-endowed. God, in his infinite wisdom, has more often than not chosen to bless skinny, pigeon-chested, chinless individuals with an added bonus, what professional homosexuals will call the "dick-of-death." Leslie's was certainly that. Twelve inches long and as thick as a fat baby's arm. His body was phenomenally lean for a healthy person. (And Leslie was undeniably healthy in early 1984. Ever since 1986 I have been tested for AIDS every six months, like every responsible homosexual, and I have never tested HIV positive. In 1984, people were just beginning to practice what is known as safe sex. Leslie and I, in fact, didn't have safe sex — I know that for certain because I wasn't really aware of the procedures at the time — and yet Leslie's lethal virus was not passed on to me. So I can only assume he didn't have any infection.) Of Leslie's face, the less said the better. There was something elfin about it, but not in a Santa Clausish, or even in a Tolkienish sense. It was the face of a prematurely old person; one could easily imagine Leslie without teeth. Patchy black hair dotted his lack of chin (but was no help in covering it) and the hair on his head was long and black and tied in a braid (to testify to his outlaw status).

I cannot say that we immediately became fast friends. What I remember is that Leslie passed along his phone number after the deed was done, and for some reason (I can't imagine why, I'm not what those in the gay trade call a "size queen") I phoned him. I like to flatter myself by making the assumption that I called him because I noticed his intelligence during our first meeting. I know that might sound suspect — and somewhat after the fact — but intelligence is something that one can often read on a person, even from the most casual of encounters. Anyway, I somehow ended up in Leslie's living room, which was less a living room than a study. Leslie only had two rooms (he was somewhat less lucky in the apartment department than I). The one room was the typical pervert's bedroom (which I never accompanied him into; it frightened me). It was the largest part of the apartment, of course. It was probably intended to be the living room. It featured a gigantic leather-covered bed, the posts of which had leather straps attached with heavy chains, which could be utilized for restraining the, I assume, willing victim. There were mirrors on one wall, and on the ceiling. On another wall were a row of sexual "toys" which included dildos lined up in gradually increasing sizes — to the largest, which was very frightening and left even Leslie's prodigious member far behind. As well, there were all manner of harnesses, leather restraints, cock rings, lubricants, nipple/testicle torture devices, as well as paddles, riding crops and a vase full of cat-o'-nine-tails. The remaining two walls were scribbled with erotic drawings: cartoonish representations of men with gigantic ejaculating phalluses. I have no idea who made these original creations; it could have been Leslie. The room was always immaculately clean and neat. The kitchen (ironically) opened off this room, as did the bathroom, so I was forced to walk through it if I experienced a call of nature.

Leslie's living room, on the other hand, was extraordinarily messy. It was piled from bottom to top with books. Books everywhere. Books on shelves, books stacked on the floor, books on his desk. I remember that when I came to visit, books always had to be removed from chairs, and often simply dropped, unceremoniously, in a dusty heap on the floor. His desk was inordinately small, and piled high with papers. There were certain books in the room which had most certainly been put down in mid-read, never to be moved again, for months, or even years. I was always amazed to visit Leslie, and to find a book on, let's say, Victorian musical theatre opened casually at a certain page and lying on top of a column of tomes on an unused chair, only to return a month later to find the same book in exactly the same place, opened to exactly the same page. It was unnerving. There were two tall windows, which gazed down on what always seemed to be a wet and rainy street, with burgundy velvet curtains always partly drawn, and covered, like the furniture, with a thick layer of dust. The walls of Leslie's living room/study were covered, from top to bottom, with gold-framed, original photographs of Victorian and Edwardian actors in fancy dress. Mostly they were photos of stage productions — vast empty stages with only the requisite couch and chair — and two actors, one kneeling, say, and the other seated. Captioning each photo was an alluring stage direction ("She knelt before him, apoplectic . . .") or a quoted line from a play ("When you close that door, you leave my life forever!"). Leslie's favourite offering was Bengali tea, (usually served with freshly warmed cinnamon buns; it was a cinnamon orgy) and while he was in the kitchen fixing it, I would find myself wandering about the room reading the captions on the pictures. It seemed that I could never read all of them. Perhaps he changed the pictures, to suit his mood. Or perhaps there were so many that by the time I had viewed them all and started over again, I had forgotten the first.

The object that dominated the room, however, was very large | 25 photograph behind the desk, which — for Leslie almost always sat in his old, wooden swivel desk chair when we talked — always ended up framing Leslie. The photograph was of Gerald du Maurier, dressed as Captain Hook in Barrie's *Peter Pan*. Often, when we talked deep and long into the early hours of the morning, it seemed that Leslie had somehow become Captain Hook.

There was something very frightening about the photograph, even though it was simply just a picture of a middle-aged man dressed as a character in a children's play. By all accounts Gerald du Maurier was no slouch at the role of Hook. Not only was the part written for him by James Barrie, but du Maurier played it for many years until he was simply too exhausted to continue. The audience adored him to distraction, but the children, it was said, were truly frightened. His performance was said to be more than caricature, that his villainousness was excruciating, and his sadness before walking the plank was truly tear-inducing. Du Maurier was possessed by the role, and his fiendish eyes often haunted me long after leaving Leslie's apartment. I remember hurrying along, on the long walk home, my coat pulled tightly around my shoulders, and stopping once or twice, imagining footsteps behind me. Occasionally I would whirl around, imagining that I could see the malevolent pirate standing behind me, brandishing his sword. But of course, it would only be some drugged-out transsexual hooker, her impertinent heels making a staggering click-clack on the pavement.

Leslie himself was a little like Captain Hook. He was born in Deal, a seaport in southeastern England: his parents had owned a country house there, but had fallen into poverty before they died. He still had more than a faint touch of an accent; at times he sounded like the stereotypical upper-class twit. He had been something of an actor during his undergraduate days in London, but upon coming to America during the seventies (Leslie said, "I just followed the boys . . . they were all dancing in New York.") he ended up teaching drama at New York University. Leslie's specialty was Edwardian theatre and, more specifically, James Barrie. His doctoral thesis (which I read several times at his request) was entitled "Repellent Resonances: The Many Subtextual Meanings of Hook's Villainy" and was devoted to a strange quest. Leslie's obsession was to convince the world that Captain Hook was a gay figure, based on Oscar Wilde.

When he first told me of his theory I was amused and not a little bit skeptical. I remember on my first visit, Leslie, of course, tried to get me into his intimidating bedroom, but I refused, and what had started (this is so often the case in homosexual friendships) as a sexual association, became an intellectual one, as we realized that we had much in common. My specialty is English, and for ten years I have been the sponsor of the drama club at Robert Kennedy High. We were, I think justly, famous for the productions created there under my direction. (Famous, that is, among Manhattan schools.) My racially cross-cast production of

L'il Abner was quite the hit. When Leslie and I realized that we had quite a lot in common, we met monthly for Bengali tea, and to discuss theater.

Let me make it clear that we didn't always (in fact, hardly ever did we) agree. Leslie was a traditionalist about some things. For instance, he completely rejected the idea of racial cross casting. It was (and is) my contention that all productions, even those with the most specific racial, regional, or political content, can be racially cross cast. He claimed that audiences cannot see past the skin boundary. I responded with the idea that it is up to the director to lead audiences, not follow them. As usual, with Leslie, everything came down to sex, and as an elderly Brit, there was something colonial about his point of view. He viewed black men merely as bodies, I think; as sleek black-skinned orifices and projectiles, with their glistening asses and gigantic pricks created only for his pleasure. (Mapplethorpe photographs adorned Leslie's dildo table in the bedroom.) | 27

With Leslie, in fact, everything came down to sex. Early on, I tried to tell Leslie of my discomfort at playing the lonely stepsister to the dazzling Ronnie, but Leslie had nothing but scorn for my personal problems. When it came to discussing human emotion, Leslie pretty well didn't have time for it. He would laugh and say, "Do you wish then, to get fucked all the time, like Ronnie? Because if you do, then just go to the gym, and produce some pectoral muscles; or go the other direction, develop a beer gut, revel in your body hair, and attend the Bear Party nights at The Stud. There's a market for everything, my dear, and if you want to get laid, it's easily enough done. Sex is very democratic. If you were a hump-backed dwarf, there would be a market for you." Now this was easy enough for Leslie to chatter on about. After all, with his incredible endowment, everyone, cute boys, muscle men, whatever, would just fall to their knees in blind worship if they were lucky enough to get a peek at his largesse. I would explain to Leslie that I was looking for love. "Whatever for, my dear?" he would ask. "Sex is love. Every sexual act is an act of love. See Tennessee Williams." Eventually I stopped talking to him about my boyfriends, my bad dates, my failed ads in the gay newspapers.

28 |

Leslie was distinctly unsympathetic. I know it's not nice to speak ill of the dead, but this is just a fact. Only two things were important to Leslie: convincing the academic world that Captain Hook was a homosexual, and having as much sex as possible. Nothing else mattered. Because of his amazing appendage, his tricks would, naturally, become obsessed with him. If they managed to get his phone number (probably because they had some incredible physical attribute themselves) Leslie would have his way with them until he was bored, and then stop. In sado-masochistic lingo, Leslie was what is called a top. This made it doubly impossible to talk with him about romance. If I was nervous about phoning a boy and asked Leslie for advice, he would say, "What are you on about, darling? They should be begging to phone you. But don't let them. You phone them when you feel like it. Or not even that often. Make them desperate for you, never give them what they want, and they'll be at your feet!" I would explain that I didn't necessarily want someone at my feet, just someone to love, at which point Leslie would say, "Listening to you talk is sometimes just like listening to a Barry Manilow song." And so I would shut up.

So what was it that made me continue to visit this cold man?

The other side of Leslie, of course, was that he was brilliant and fascinating on one subject alone: *Peter Pan*. Though I didn't actually agree with most of his views, I was astounded by the sheer breadth of his knowledge. For instance, his outrageous and, I think, quite mad theory that Captain Hook was a gay character, formed the basis of an even more outrageous idea. I hope you're sitting down for this: James Barrie was a pederast. This of course, explains why it was difficult for Leslie to get anyone but a few | 29 looney academics to take him seriously.

To put Leslie's views on James Barrie in context, you might be interested in some of his other extreme views. Leslie actually believed that Shakespeare — the actor, the husband of Ann Hathaway — was not the bard of Stratford-upon-Avon but (you guessed it) a homosexual count named Edward de Vere. It didn't matter that de Vere died years before Shakespeare's final work, *The Tempest*, was supposed to be written. Leslie had an explanation for that too — *The Tempest* is, apparently, misdated. Leslie's craziness also leaked into his political ideas. He also believed that HIV was not the cause of AIDS. (When Leslie told me this, I thought for a moment that he was actually insane). According to Leslie, the whole thing is a conspiracy, and AIDS is just a name for a bunch of diseases that had been around for a long time. This means, of course, that Leslie never used condoms and proceeded to pump his infected sperm into a countless number of innocent asses. I know that this is unforgivable conduct. But one must keep in mind that it takes two to tango, and those who begged to have Leslie's unwrapped endowment plunged into them (as it were) were equally to blame. What was unforgivable though, considering his outrageous sexual behaviour, was that Leslie used to make light of men who turned up at our local bars looking ill. Occasionally I would meet Leslie in one of his favourite leather haunts (I didn't stay long; I usually claimed an early class and bolted before 11:00) and Leslie would quip, "Tch tch tch, that one's not looking too well, is she? Hmm . . . she'd better start drinking her carrot juice." Though I never bothered to research Leslie's mad theories, his bizarre opinions stimulated me. He could persuasively argue his outrageous points, and not without wit. It was, in short, a thrill to listen to him talk.

As a long time theater director and student of the dramatic arts, I found his outrageous hypothesis about Captain Hook and James Barrie fascinating. After all, it's true that Barrie was obsessed with the Llewelyn Davies boys, and later adopted them. He photographed them endlessly (sometimes in the nude) and certainly loved them to death. But that's where I part company with Leslie. It's a huge leap from claiming that Barrie loved the boys, or even loved them too much, to claiming that he had sex with them.

The first clue to Barrie's sexuality, Leslie believed, was to be found in the character of Captain Hook. Having decided that Barrie was a pederast, Leslie theorized that all of Barrie's homophobia, all his hatred of his own impulses, was sublimated into the character of the pirate. At first this idea may seem as wacky as Leslie's notions about AIDS or Shakespeare. But I must give the old man some credit; he had done his research. For instance Captain Hook was originally portrayed by Gerald du Maurier, the son of George du Maurier, who also happened to be, not so coincidentally, Michael Llewelyn Davies' real uncle. You see, Barrie's link with the five Llewelyn Davies boys was also theatrical, as Sylvia, Michael's mother, came from the theatrical and artistic du Maurier clan. George du Maurier was known primarily for his novels (*Trilby*, for instance), but was also a renowned cartoonist. During the late-nineteenth century, when Oscar Wilde was all the rage, George drew caricatures of Oscar Wilde that were featured in *Punch* and became the universally accepted image of the Victorian dandy. The elder du Maurier fuelled the controversy over Wilde's homosexuality with his censorious cartoons picturing Wilde, surrounded by statues of nude men and limp-wristed friends, sporting the requisite lily while all the time drawling "My dear" this and "My dear" that.*

| 31

Now, Leslie's contention was that by casting Gerald du Maurier in the role of Hook, Barrie was purposely calling up the image of

---

* Leslie's source for this information about du Maurier was a book by Denis Denisoff — *Aestheticism and Sexual Parody* 1840–1940 — one which Leslie was proud to discover, late in his life, and which he phoned me about, to my surprise, just before his death. It contains an essay on du Maurier's career as a Victorian novelist and cartoonist. Denisoff's essay is interesting, and offers ample proof for Leslie's theory. Indeed, the dandies portrayed in du Maurier's cartoons do, more often than not, resemble Oscar Wilde, and also consistently spout his aphorisms, including the celebrated aesthete's much-vaunted announcement that he wished to "live up" to his blue china. A close reading of the essay also accentuates the similarities that can be drawn between Hook and Wilde. Denisoff contends that George du Maurier viewed Wilde as the epitome of the pretentious, pseudo-artistic fraud. There is certainly some of this in Captain Hook, who speaks in a florid, pseudo-poetic vein. Where Mr. Denisoff goes overboard, however, is in suggesting that George du Maurier was actually a homosexual — someone who had experimented with what Denisoff calls "homosocial bonding" during his adventures as a young bohemian painter in Paris. Nowhere does Denisoff actually offer proof for this. The truth is that Denisoff has a bias; he is a "queer" intellectual out to prove that everyone important in history was of his ilk. I make this accusation with impunity, because Denisoff actually came out in a rather grim book of gay erotic stories, which he edited in the early 1990s (and which contains one of his fictions). The anthology, believe it or not, is entitled *Queeries*. It is a desultory tome, filled to the brim with stories that are pronouncedly pornographic and therefore not worthy of serious literary attention. I must admit that the title *Queeries* made me laugh. It reminded me of an embarrassing experience I had as a teenager with a clumsy acting teacher. The class was for young male actors, and after the teacher had finished a lecture, he inevitably asked if there were any "queries." Well, no one in that acting class ever raised his hand!

Oscar Wilde because Gerald's father had become identified with the aesthete. According to this line of reasoning, Captain Hook was yet another caricature of Oscar Wilde, only this time a living stage caricature, not a cartoon. According to Barrie himself, Hook is "a different class from his crew, a solitary among uncultured companions . . . In dress he apes the dandiacal . . . there is a touch of the feminine in Hook, as in all the greatest pirates . . ." For Leslie, these stage directions confirmed that Barrie was alluding to Oscar Wilde, the predominant feminine dandy of the period.

32 |

If I'm beginning to sound a little academic, it's for a good reason. Recalling this part of my life brings back a different vision of myself. You see, my friendship with Leslie, which began as a sexual encounter but soon morphed into cozy chats over Bengali tea, would have come to an abrupt halt if I hadn't had an ulterior motive. For as much as I found Leslie entertaining, I was appalled at his lack of essential humanity. But what made me return again and again to his cramped and claustrophobic rooms was the fact that I was, myself, considering an academic career.

I suppose this is one of the many side effects of a Jewish upbringing. Certainly my parents, and the parents of so many of my generation, harboured an obsession with education that often verged on the psychotic. My mother was terribly proud that I was a teacher, but she never stopped harping on one idea: "If you want to be a teacher, why not be the best there is?" "But I am," I would say, pointing to the Shelly Winters Award (a theatrical prize given out to the best play in the Manhattan High School Drama Competition), an award that my students had won many times. "No, I mean — be a professor!" I'd reply wearily, "I'll think about it, ma."

And I was thinking about it, because of Leslie. You see, for whatever reason, Leslie encouraged me to imagine that I was capable of a Master's Degree in Drama at New York University, and that I might actually someday become a PH.D. I don't know if he was truly impressed with my abilities, or if he still nurtured the faint hope of getting into my pants for a second time (which was not going to happen). I suppose it doesn't matter. Leslie encouraged me in my academic ambitions. I began to work with him on his theories, to develop theories of my own. Leslie's most exciting quest was to find the lost letters that had passed between J.M. Barrie and his adopted son, Michael.

|33

The letters present a unique literary conundrum. Barrie is arguably one of the most influential writers of the last century. *Peter Pan* is certainly one of the most popular plays of the modern era. It's been performed more than ten thousand times in England alone. It was made into a live-action film in 1924, a musical, a television feature, and a cartoon film, and has spawned countless revivals. Peter Pan's name has leant itself to a popular neurosis — the Peter Pan Complex — describing adult males who have difficulty adjusting to the responsibilities of adult life. This incredibly popular writer, who has had such a great influence on children of all ages for an entire century, had a strangely intimate relationship with his adopted son.

Michael's death is somewhat mysterious. Leslie classified Michael as homosexual and assumed that he had been molested by Barrie as a child. (Only Leslie didn't call it molestation, he called it "intergenerational love.") Leslie also assumed that the molestation, as it so often does in these incest situations, continued on into puberty. So Leslie's second big project (besides outing

Captain Hook) was to prove that Barrie and Michael were having sex together, and that Michael committed suicide because he was unable to handle the implications of his love for the friend he died with. Michael's obsession with Rupert E.V. Buxton was, according to Leslie, a threat to his romantic relationship with his adoptive father.

As bizarre as this theory might seem, there are some extant facts which back it up. Andrew Birkin's book quotes Nico, the youngest of the brothers: "I've always had something of a hunch that Michael's death was suicide . . . I'm apt to think — stressing think — that he was going through something of a homosexual phase."

Of course to Leslie this was no phase. He was convinced that Michael was a homosexual, for one reason and one reason only: because of his relationship with his adoptive father, James Barrie. But, even if Michael Llewelyn Davies was a homosexual who may have committed suicide because of his sexuality, does that necessarily mean that his adoptive father James Barrie is somehow implicated? I don't think so.

In fact, all we really do know for certain is that Michael and Barrie were terribly close. Obsessively so. Besides countless reports from people who knew them both, there are the two thousand letters sent between the two.

Letters which were supposedly destroyed.

The person who owned these letters, and *confessed* to destroying them, was Michael's older brother, Peter Llewelyn Davies. According to Birkin, Peter said that he burned them because they were "too much."

The phrase "too much" obsessed Leslie. I remember sitting

opposite him in his drafty room, waiting for the Bengali tea to steep. "Too much? And will you tell me what 'too much' means? What can it mean? Too much affection, perhaps? Or is it something more than that? Too much sex? Too much undying love? Were these letters maybe 'too much' because Barrie confessed his undying love for Michael in them, and pleaded with the boy to love him back? Were they the jealous letters of a spurned lover who, when confronted with his love object's obvious adoration of another, turned accusatory, vile, and irrational? Are these letters 'too much' because they show Barrie as he really was? A pederast? Is that what we're afraid of, the truth? And why should we be, since it's the truth, after all? Manny please, have some Bengali tea, and tell me in all honesty — and I use the term honesty with some irony here — why then should we tell the truth at all? Perhaps we should lie all the time? Or is that indeed what we do? Because we hate our own vile bodies so much because they can only remind of us of infection and death?"*

| 35

It was certainly something to think about. Add to this the fact that Leslie had unearthed letters from Barrie's friends which suggested that Barrie was less than cordial to most of Michael's

---

* Leslie's suspicions about Peter Llewelyn Davies' ulterior motives are supported by history. Beginning in 1945 and continuing until nine years before his suicide, Peter was compiling a very important book: the collected letters of the Llewelyn Davies family. He referred to the project, somewhat morbidly, as "The Morgue." Birkin, in a footnote to his book, reveals an interesting and rather suspicious fact, of which Leslie was acutely aware: something mysterious stopped Peter from completing what had clearly become his life's work. He collected all the family letters up until his brother George's death in 1915, and then, suddenly, he stopped. Since beginning this monumental job, Peter had claimed he initiated a process of incinerating the letters that he found inappropriate. This ritual became a habit which he couldn't seem to stop. He seemed driven to do so. The youngest Llewelyn Davies brother, Nico, thought Peter's feelings about these letters were peripherally related to his suicide.

male friends — well, Leslie figured that his theory was more or less confirmed. All he needed as proof positive of his thesis was to get his hands on those letters. The ones that Peter had supposedly burned.

Convinced that the letters still existed, Leslie set out to find them.

It was a difficult job. In 1987, Nicholas Llewelyn Davies (the youngest of Barrie's adopted sons) was a very old man — eighty-four years old. But Leslie was determined to find him. He knew that Nicholas, like his brother Peter, was involved in the book trade. Somehow, Leslie was able to contact Nicholas by mail, and told him that he was doing some sort of innocent research about *Peter Pan*. It was an insane idea. There was no reason to suspect that Nicholas would have the letters his brother claimed to have destroyed. So when Nicholas Llewelyn Davies replied favourably to his letter and said that he would be quite pleased to have Leslie come and visit, Leslie hopped on a plane and he was off to London.

I remember how impressed I was by his little trip. It was 1987 and the peak of my professional admiration for Leslie. Leslie had led me to believe my Master's thesis was going well. I was writing an essay on the Edwardian roots of Noël Coward's comedies. He had even promised to be the advisor for my dissertation. So basically, I was willing to support him with his research into James Barrie.

The postcards I received from London were very allusive and alluring. They seemed to be the tip of the iceberg of a fabulous time. "Caught a fleeting glimpse of Jean-Paul Gaultier in this sleazy little bar near Covent Garden. Apparently it's where he picks models and smuggles them back to France. Some appalling little *modele* was after moi, and I neatly avoided him. Lots of fun to be had there at the ruins in the park. No luck with Peter yet. Yours, Sexly." He always signed his postcards in this manner. "Sexly" was a bastardized abbreviation for Leslie Sexton, something you got when you squashed the two words together.

It was an irritating habit.

Another postcard read: "Visited Foucault's grave the other day. Still can't believe we lost him so soon! I wish he'd been around to hear the news about AIDS — that it doesn't exist I mean. Only one day in Paris dahhlling! Missed *La Tour Eiffel, quel dommage*, but caught the Key West Baths. Peter still recalcitrant. Hope Noël's going well . . . xxx Sexly."

| 37

You see, Leslie had known Foucault. Apparently they'd had an affair when Leslie was teaching in London and Foucault was touring the local nightspots there. I had asked him about Foucault many times, but Leslie was very close-mouthed — which seemed to me to prove he must have actually known the man. Name-droppers brag about the people they've screwed. That wasn't Leslie. Leslie only bragged about the tricks with humungous equipment or with a humungous capacity to take on his. It made perfect sense to me that he'd hung around with Foucault, and his secretiveness caused me to fantasize that they'd had a serious affair; perhaps it was the closest Leslie came to true love.

When Leslie arrived home, he called me, and casually left a message that the prized letters were in his possession. God knows how long he'd been in New York. Finally he invited me over to view them.

I arrived at his place at around ten one March evening. (It was his preferred time. He always left me by midnight to go on his sleazy prowls.) It was foggy and the curtains were drawn. When I knocked on the door he called from the kitchen, "*Entrez*, my dear!" And so I did. He made me sit alone for a couple of minutes. There was a candle on his desk, which was uncharacteristic. It frightened me; what if he were to knock it over and burn the precious letters? (For a second time, it would seem.) I could hear him humming in the other room. Which was very strange, for Leslie. When he entered, carrying steaming Bengali tea on a silver tray, I knew that this was a very important evening.

38 |

Leslie's long hair, which was usually in a braid, had been let loose and was flowing over his shoulders. It gave him the appearance of an old matron about to go off to bed, except that he was dressed from head to toe in leather. And at the same time there was the incongruity: why all this lovely long girlish hair? How picturesque and yet how out of place on this homely old man.

At first he talked about his tricks, of course. Of the orgy at the ruin. Of the boy in the bathhouse in Paris with the five rings in his penis, of the boy that he'd met in The Tate Gallery, with "an enormous capacity! Absolutely phenomenal! The spanking I gave him, I'm sure he couldn't sit down for days!"

I listened politely and smiled, as I always did with Leslie. I could see he was enjoying his little game. It was a typical sado-masochistic tactic: withholding the anticipated pleasure. Finally I couldn't bear it any longer. I didn't care about his silly game. I asked him about the letters.

"What letters . . . you mean my postcards?"

He said that. I certainly can't remember everything he said. But he actually did say that.

"No. The J.M. Barrie and Michael Llewelyn Davies letters."

"Oh, of course, those." And he pulled a pack of letters from between two books. They were tied with gold ribbon. They seemed to glisten in the candlelight. "Here they are, my dear."

I knew that he wasn't going to let me touch them, but I wanted to devour them, read everyone one. "Well, do they confirm your theories? Was James Barrie a pederast? Was he his adopted son's lover?"

"But of course, my dear."

Well, now I couldn't resist. "Please may I —"

He moved them out of my reach.

"All in due time, my good man. All in good time."

"But —"

"These are magical letters my boy. Quite magical. To open them, to touch them, to read them — you must be ready! Soon . . . soon it will be time."

I couldn't believe it. He put the letters away. He put them in a drawer in his desk, locked the drawer, and then put the key on a chain he always kept around his neck. I was very frustrated, but I assumed this was all part of his little game. I was sure he wanted to tell me about the circumstances of their discovery. So I asked him.

"Monsieur Nicholas Llewelyn Davies was much recalcitrant. Very much the gentleman. Very much guarding the memory; the lion guarding the throne, as it were. Wouldn't hear a word spoken against Sir James, of course. I think that my leather gear and queen-like demeanor quite put him off at first. But of course I kept the dirty words to a bare minimum, spoke, in fact, only in polite words of three syllables and flattered the memory of James Barrie end-lessly, and quite honestly. Because as you know — and this is no lie — *that play* is famous justly because it touches everything very secret and frightening and precious. We both know that. I think, finally, he understood that I loved *that play* and, in my own way, loved James Barrie, as much as he did. So he just gave up and gave in."

"He gave them to you?"

"He was, as I think I indicated in my postcards, reluctant. No. He did not give them to me, in the sense of handing them to me. But one night I went to meet him in his study, and the phone rang, and he said it was business, and that he would have to go in another room to take the call. He closed the door behind him and I turned to look at his desk, and there, illuminated by the fire behind, were the letters. Tied with gold ribbon as you have seen them tonight, and glittering, as I'm sure you noticed, for they have a kind of energy all their own. Well, of course, I knew they were left for me. And I knew that I had to take them. And I knew that Mr. Llewelyn Davies, because of all his reserve, could never actually hand them over. What might I do with them? How might I interpret them? What secrets would be revealed? But he could, however, simply make them available for the taking, and I could, quite simply, take them. Which is exactly what I did. I slipped them into the pocket of my leather jacket. When the youngest and only living adopted son of James Barrie returned from his phone call, the letters were no longer on his desk. He didn't say a word."

"Did he look at the place where he had left them?"

"I don't believe he did."

"How do you know he knew they were gone?"

"Well, of course, he must have known. These are very precious letters."

"But maybe he thought he lost them."

"No, it was his way of giving them to me."

"How do you know that?"

"He wanted me to have them."

"Why would he?"

"I don't know. Perhaps he was afraid of them. Just as his older brother Peter was. You see, he would have had every reason to be."

Again, of course, I don't remember exactly what was said. I do remember that Leslie convinced me that these letters were dangerous, potent, almost magical in their power, and that somehow he — an aging, ugly, effeminate, minor homosexual scholar — had persuaded the guardian of Barrie's reputation to give him this tantalizing key to the great author's very private relationship with his adopted son.

| 41

On the other hand, it was also quite possible that Leslie had simply stolen the letters, and that criminal charges would most certainly be laid against him some time in the near future.

I was extremely frustrated that night, and remained frustrated for many long weeks. Leslie didn't show me the letters. Leslie never showed me the letters. So how did I get them?

I had to wait for Leslie to die.

Our relationship deteriorated somewhat after his return from London and the theft. The letters had set up a huge wall between us. I felt betrayed that he wouldn't show them to me. For all his perverse secretiveness, all his denials of sensitivity and emotion, I thought that I was his compatriot, and that he would wish to share his precious triumph with me. But no. Each time I asked him he said, "In due time, my boy, in due time." For Leslie, I suppose, it was just a game, but for me, it was terribly frustrating. My resentment mounted. I began to hate him. Soon I became discouraged with my Master's thesis. I was losing interest — partly because I dreaded my weekly meetings with Leslie.

I was beginning to realize that I loved my students at Robert Kennedy High School, and that I had no real desire to become a university professor. What I had thought were sincere aspirations to scholarship were, in actuality, a combination of emotions. I had been frustrated with my relationship with Ronnie. Well, Leslie had replaced Ronnie in my affections. I hardly ever saw my blond party-animal friend anymore. Which was fine. The old jealousy was gone. I was getting older, and my sexual desire was cooling. It seemed to me that my time with Leslie had been a transition period, a growing up. I had subconsciously wanted to be weaned of my sexual competitiveness and my adolescent romantic fantasies of love, which were in danger of turning into the usual pathetic boy chasing. Leslie had been a sort of safety valve, to help me through a difficult time. But I didn't need him anymore. I certainly didn't like him. Mother would just have to deal with my decision. I wasn't little Manny Masters anymore, slaving after that eponymous degree to prove he deserved his name. If my mother couldn't respect my efforts at teaching Black kids how to act, sing, and dance; if she couldn't see my little productions as valuable, if she couldn't love her teacher son and relinquish her dream of a professor son, then that was her problem and not mine.

I know that Leslie would have said that I was sounding like a Barry Manilow song again. But I didn't care. I didn't care anymore what Leslie thought about anything. As far as I was concerned, he was a very sad, sad case. The worse kind of homosexual, in fact; a lonely, selfish, solitary figure, lacking love, obsessed with sex.

I did not have the courage to withdraw from the Master's program, for this reason: when I informed my mother of my decision, she became hypochondriacal, and was consumed — as if under a strange spell. She can be a bewitching creature, who carries within her both the fragile heart of a wounded child and the indomitable will of an army drill sergeant. (I have no doubt that my affection for Barbara Streisand, Judy Garland, and all those other alternately swelling and collapsing divas has much to do with my intimate relationship with that intimidatingly stubborn, yet continually disintegrating, woman.)

When I told my mother that I intended to defect from academia, she accepted the news with equanimity. She almost never gets angry, for to express that unbridled emotion might expose her carefully concealed vulnerability. Instead, she began to develop bizarre physical symptoms, and demanded that I listen to her unusually detailed descriptions of them. (Unusually detailed, even for her.) I am embarrassed to reveal that she became obsessed with the notion that she had acquired a venereal disease. The notion that my dear eighty-year-old mother had contracted VD, was, of course, inherently ludicrous. First of all, she had long ago scorned the intimate company of men. Since the death of my father, in fact. And secondly, she had lost most of her female equipment during an extensive hysterectomy immediately following my birth. The doctors had, of course, not literally sewed her up. (It's embarrassing to have to relate these appalling details about one's mother, but believe me, her own endless ever spiralling worries about her vagina were much more grotesque and graphic than what has been related here.) But she had told me over and over that intercourse after the operation had caused her excessive pain. And yet she insisted on being tested and retested, and at a certain point began to develop the fantasy that she was losing her mind due to the advanced stages of syphilis! Thus we entered one of the most soul-destroying and heart-wrenching periods in our relationship. Now and then she would ask me, short of breath, fevered and pale, and claiming to be hallucinating in her hospital bed, whether I had considered, perhaps, finishing my Master's degree? Under emotional duress, and wishing to placate her, I indicated that I would return to my night classes at university, but that I had absolutely no intention of leaving my post at Robert Kennedy High for an academic career. Perhaps not so coincidentally, continued assurances of my commitment to complete this phase of my higher education precipitated a miraculous recovery, and the dreaded venereal horror was never heard of again.

I was awarded my Master's Degree and my mother attended the ceremonies. I don't think I've ever seen her so happy in my life. But I took this rather torturous climax to my academic career as a signal that I should stop seeing Leslie. By 1992 I was not seeing him at all. I was happily back at my job at Robert Kennedy, regretting that I had been forced to curtail my extracurricular activities with the drama club during the final year of my thesis. But thankfully I was back where I belonged, slaving away with the students on an all-consuming production: my own stage adaptation of the motion picture *Fame*.

Unsurprisingly, when I stopped calling Leslie, he made no effort to pursue our friendship. I knew he wouldn't. It wouldn't be acting like a top. I didn't think very much about the letters, or about Leslie. I had moved on.

Late in 2001, I received an unsettling phone call. It concerned the reading of the will of Leslie Sexton. Of course Leslie had died of AIDS.

I think you can understand that, under the circumstances, this is not a harsh thing to say. It was simply logical, considering his life. Leslie had spent his life pushing sexual boundaries, and had brashly ignored AIDS, even pretending that it did not exist. It only made sense that the disease would finally get him. I'm certain that he probably denied it (until it could no longer be denied), probably had sex parties in his hospital room, probably tried to seduce the orderlies and wore his leather harness to x-ray. In a way, I was glad not to have been around him near the end. I'm not ashamed to say that. He would not have been able to accept my love and support. It's a sentimental myth that those who are dying somehow undergo a deep psychological change. Those who are dying are merely themselves, only more so.

At any rate, Leslie was gone. I went to the reading of the will with little anticipation. I imagined that, taking into account Leslie's rather mean sense of humour, and his professorial ways, that he would leave me something he thought corrective, educational. A dildo or some anal beads.

To my complete shock, Leslie left me the letters.

At first, it didn't make sense. Why would he leave them to me, and not a museum, or return them to Barrie's literary estate? But of course, the fact of the matter was (and this took me a while to realize) no one really would have wanted them. Why? Because, first of all, if Nicholas Llewelyn Davies had wanted them, he wouldn't have left them for Leslie to steal. (Which he must have intended to do, since he never laid charges against Leslie for removing them.) No academic, except for Leslie, had ever set out in search of the letters. Why? Because no one was really interested in the intimate details of James Barrie's personal life, or his relationships with his adopted sons. Except for Leslie Sexton.

And except, of course, now, me.

Because I was interested. I was dreadfully interested. How could I not be? Had I not spent countless hours in Leslie's rooms arguing over the Barrie question, the Captain Hook question, taking sides this way and that over the famous writer's sexuality? I know that the literary world is often of two minds when it comes to the value of literary biography. On the one hand the homosexual details of a writer's life have traditionally been considered disgusting or irrelevant, and have often been politely ignored. On the other hand there is an ever-evolving new, so-called "queer" scholarship, which insists on turning over each detail of an author's biography in the quest for gay subtext. This was Leslie's preferred method of research. I detested it. The accusations he had made against Barrie were outrageous and, I suspected, unfounded. I had to find out the truth, if only to clear Barrie's name. Leslie claimed that these letters proved that Barrie was a homosexual pederast, in love with his adopted son. Could he have intentionally misinterpreted them?

Leslie left me only one message concerning these letters. There was no explanation, no analysis, no essay for posterity as to what effect these letters or their publication might have on literary scholarship. They were delivered to me in a rumpled brown paper bag. On the paper bag, in Leslie's characteristic hand, were scrawled these words:

"Dare you look into the mirror?"

At the time, of course, I was confounded. What mirror? Was this message written to me, and if so, why? Was Leslie suggesting that I had something in common with James Barrie? And if so, what? The only possible link between the two of us that I could possibly think of was the fact that Barry was reportedly celibate (that is, he never had sex with his wife). And so, of course, am I.

But otherwise, the cryptic message made no sense. I couldn't help thinking about something. Leslie had repeated one mantra about the letters, over and over again. Each time I had asked him if I could see them, and he had denied me access, each time he mentioned, almost casually —

"Why bother my boy? You only get out of these letters what you put into them. That's what makes them so dangerous."

Or something to that effect. I never understood that little mantra. But it might have had something to do with his challenge to me, scrawled on the paper bag.

I suppose I am a true student of Leslie Sexton, despite all my mixed feelings about him. Now you might understand why I have decided not to simply publish these letters, to drop them, as it were, in the lap of the world. Why I have surround them with background, comment, and interpretation. They are dangerous, they are a mirror, they reflect back what we offer up to them. So I will do my best to make this book my offering.

CHILDHOOD LETTERS

            I should state at the outset that I do not have in my possession two thousand letters. The letters which were passed to me are considerably fewer in number: fifty-six. I have no idea where the rest of the letters are. The ones which I have are enough.

We will begin at the beginning, which is in the letters passed between Michael Llewelyn Davies in his childhood and James Barrie. Since Michael was born in 1900, these letters would likely be dated between 1905 and 1907. I suggest that the dating end in 1907 because there is no mention of the death of Michael's father* in the letters, which would surely have been one of the subjects. Also,

---

* The death of Arthur Llewelyn Davies in 1907 is a particularly tragic story. Arthur was an exceptionally handsome and kind man, dearly loved by his children and all around him. He was only forty-three when the doctors diagnosed him with sarcoma of the jaw — a kind of cancer. There seemed to be a glimmer of hope for him when his jaw was removed and replaced with a prosthetic one. But the tumours came back and soon it was over. Throughout this torturous ordeal Arthur maintained a stoic altruism, for his own letters speak of nothing but his concern for his family. Could the little boy have known what was happening to his father? Certainly he would have known that Arthur was there, and then gone, and then gradually replaced by J.M. Barrie. But Michael was seven when his father died, and all of these childhood letters were written before that, and therefore present an idyllic, innocent, unspoiled picture of his young life.

these letters are evidently written to a very young child, one who could barely read or write. It is quite likely that some of these letters were read to the boy by Barrie himself, or by his mother Sylvia.

During the years when these letters were written, Barrie lived near the Llewelyn Davies family in London, by Kensington Gardens, and was a family friend — an adopted uncle. There was no real need for Barrie to write Michael letters; he saw him every day. These letters were written for the fun of receiving them and reading them. (The reader may notice that occasionally a word has been left out. This is because, in some cases, there was water damage to the paper. Nicholas Llewelyn Davies — oddly for a book collector — had a remarkably damp house. When the word is completely unreadable I have left a blank. When the word is almost visible or evident, I have filled in the complete word.)

Finally, I must say this about the letters. They are the purest, sweetest thing you may ever read. Leslie was prone to theorizing that all sorts of horrible things went on between the child Michael and the adult Sir James, but nothing of that kind can be found in these early letters. (The later letters are more complex, and require a more complex explanation.) But even a few of these early letters contain subject matter which may have made Leslie suspicious. In these cases, I take note of the controversial element more to highlight the idiocy of Leslie's theories than anything else. No, to read these letters as anything other than innocent documents of a beautiful and touching friendship does them, and ourselves, a disservice.

The earliest letters are less missives than poems. Some even take the form of word games. Barrie obviously enjoyed making poems out of Michael's name:

M is for the mist that lifts at dawn
I for me; I am your pawn
C is for the cut which soon will heal
H is for your hair; when I pull it, you squeal!
A is for "awry" a word you don't know
E is for eels which you won't find in the snow!
L is for love, which is what I feel for you
I'd better stop (unreadable), or I'll get in a stew! |51

It's obvious that at one point little Michael lost his sun hat. He sends a simple missive which expresses his concern.

Mr. James Barrie,

I lost my hat yestreday [sic]. What should I do?

Yours,
Michael

This was the occasion for a precious poem:

Dearest Beloved Michael,

So Little Michael has lost his hat!
How will he keep the sun away?
Did the fairies steal it, or the gnomes, or the elves of lore
Only Michael knows
— or did he leave it at the store?
or by the pond or on the bench or in big Jack's canoe?
The choices are many, the choices are few

For being lost is no fun
As any hat will say
But being found is like the sun
Time for dancing; time for play
Don't worry my beloved, we'll find it tomorrow,
of course we will!

Your Affectionate Uncle,
James Barrie

What follows is an exchange of letters concerning an incident where Michael cried when he shouldn't have, or cried when it seemed inappropriate. Barrie's answer to Michael's letter is the epitome of tact and parental concern. I am assuming that this exchange was later than the "hat" exchange, if for no other reason than that Michael has learned how to spell yesterday!

Dear Uncle James,

I'm sorry I cried yesterday. It was very bad of me.

Your loving frend [sic],
Michael

Beloved Michael,

You needn't apologize for crying. All little boys cry. Some of them don't show it. Some of them run home and bury their face in the pillow. Not Michael. Michael isn't afraid to let the other boys see his tears. Can't you see that makes him the very bravest little boy in the park? I read a story once that said that Sir Lancelot, one of the bravest nights of old, used to cry in front of the other knights. Sir Lancelot was the handsomest and the strongest of all his fellows. Michael, don't apologize for crying. The other boys just don't understand bravery. But we do, my boy, we do.

Your loving,
James Barrie

And the bug letters are some of my favourites.

Dear Uncle James:

When bugs die, where do they go?

Yours,
Michael Ll-D.

Master Michael Ll-D.,

When bugs die, they go to heaven of course. But it's a very special heaven. Only bugs go there. And they can crawl around to their heart's content. And they have bug dances, and bug picnics. Because unlike real life, they don't have to raid the picnics of humans like us. Instead you'll see ants and butterflies, ladybugs and bees enjoying wine and lemonade, mustard and pickles, chatting and buzzing around their red plaid tablecloths. Bugs are happiest when they're munching. And that's what heaven is for them.

Yours lovingly,
James Barrie

Now I have no doubt that the following letter must have caused some consternation for Leslie. The toad, as you may know, in dream theory is considered to be a sexual symbol. Of course, if we were to subject this innocent letter to sexual analysis, what would we do with the whole of *The Wind in the Willows*?

Dear Uncle James,

54 |

    I don't like toads. I think they're ugly and wrinkly and slimely [sic] and dirty. Jack showed me his toad and his slimey eel. I like fish, I think they're pretty, but not toads. If you catch a toad or an eel, will you promise never to shew them to me? I don't want to look at them. I never ever want to think that you had a toad and an eel. You don't have an ugly wrinkly toad, do you? You won't suddenly pull it out and scare me, will you?

                                  Yours truly,
                                  Michael Ll-D.

Master Michael Ll-D.,

    I have no toad, and I will never have one. I have no affection for toads or eels myself. They are nature's lost creatures. Just because Jack is so proud of his slimy pets doesn't mean you have to like them. Stick to your guns.

                                  Yours in love,
                                  James Barrie

I wish to make an example of these two letters. And I defend myself in advance from those who might suggest that I am setting up a straw man only to attack him. I don't think the hypersexuality of modern literary criticism is a straw man; it is very much the predominant aspect of our intellectual discourse. As I mentioned earlier, these days every other course at the university level seems to be aimed at teens who are gender confused. Thus it's possible that these particular letters might be interpreted as having a sexual meaning. This is the danger inherent to these letters (though I doubt it is what Leslie meant when he suggested they were a | 55 mirror). For those who read sex into everything, and who would assert that each mention of the word "wrinkly" means testes, and that eels can mean only one thing; or those obsessed with the sexual implications of every word or deed, I have one word of retort: innocence. There is such a thing as innocence — the innocence of childhood. And does anyone actually believe it probable that Barrie and the young Michael would have chosen to speak to each other (nay, to write to each other) about sexual games using code words like toad and eel? How likely is that? Enough said, I hope.

The following letters are charming and can only be interpreted innocently. They follow a private performance of *Peter Pan* which Barrie arranged for Michael when he was sick in bed. According to Birkin, the actors were carted over to the Llewelyn Davies household for a reading, so that the boy would not be denied his first viewing of the play. But if we are to believe what we read in the following letters (and why should we not?) we can see that Michael was upset (as apparently many six-year-olds were) by the performance. Michael was troubled by nightmares throughout his short life, and this the first documented instance. How ironic that they should have been brought on by seeing his first performance of *Peter Pan*!

Dear Uncle James,

Thank you for the play. Peter is a very nice boy. You say that I am as brave as him, but I don't think so.

There are two parts of the play that frighten me. What would happen if Peter weren't saved and he was drowned?

And what about if he had to walk the plank?

I dreamed about the plank and I was frightened.

Yours truly,
Michael Ll-D.

The letter is poignant, if only for the fact that Michael was capable of writing it when he was nearly seven. Of course Sylvia, his mother, was a charming teacher, and all the boys were precocious in one way or another. But Michael was the most precocious of all, called the "brilliant" one. But, as we can see from this letter, that brilliance didn't come without an alarming sensitivity. Barrie's answer is all a nascent tortured genius could ask for. He seems particularly adept at seeing things from a child's perspective.

My Dearest True Boy,

Let me say the most important thing first:

First of all, you are evermuch the bravest boy I have ever met, and just as brave as Peter. Not even Peter Pan has nightmares like yours, and if he did, I don't know if he would be as brave as you in enduring them. I want you to know a special secret. I'm going to write another Peter Pan, an extra special scene about Peter Pan coming to visit Wendy, and you'll never guess who I'm using for my inspiration. It's

*you! Peter is going to be just as brave as you are. That is very brave!
I'll tell you what inspiration means. It's what makes life worth living.
You inspire me, your mother inspires your father, and the birds with
their cheery songs inspire us to sing.*

*I have a simple answer for you about Peter and the Mermaid's
Lagoon. He did not drown. That's all. Because Peter would never be
drowned. Because Peter is the little boy who won't grow up. He will
live forever.*

*Michael darling, don't think about the plank. The best thing to do,
before you go to bed, is to have a cup of Mary's cocoa, and after she
tucks you in, to think about tomorrow. Think about the boat race we're
going to have in the park! Think about how funny Nico will look in
the new costume I made him for our play! Think about anything else!
They say the very last thing you think about is also the first thing you
dream about. I always think about tomorrow before I go to sleep.*

For tomorrow always comes.

*Yours in love,
J.M.B.*

Now is perhaps the time to address the thorny issue of language.
Here we have Barrie finishing a letter to a seven-year-old boy with
an epistolary farewell that may appear suspect ("Yours in love").
First of all, we must keep in mind that it is not likely the letter
would have been read by Michael himself; it is much more likely
that it was read *to* him, by his mother, his nurse Mary, or by Barrie.
One can imagine, in this instance, the venerable author giving
the tiny boy a chaste hug after reciting the last few lines. For the
language we utilize when speaking to children is necessarily very

different than the one we use for adults. Of course we would never tell an adult that we were "in love" with them, unless we meant it in a romantic way. But Barrie was not directing these words to an adult, but to a precious child. When we talk to babies we make fools of ourselves, talk gibberish, and make goofy, googly, cooing noises.[*]

---

[*] The letters between King James I and his court favourite George Villiers, Duke of Buckingham, have recently been the focus for a veritable mafia of homosexual scholars. These letters raise the formal issue of how to analyze affectionate language between men, especially members of a family (real or imagined) in an historical context. Unbelievably, David M. Bergeron has written a whole book, *King James and Letters of Homoerotic Desire*, which takes a hopeless stab at convincing us that affectionate letters between the two adult male seventeenth-century friends are private love notes written for erotic purposes. This specious argument can be easily discredited by noting that King James (a Christian scholar) was absolutely public about his love for his dear friend, telling the privy council that "Christ had His John (the Baptist) and I have my George." Why would this devout Christian monarch confess a homosexual love for his court favourite in 1617? The answer is, of course, that he could not, would not, and did not, love George carnally — they were simply friends. Paula Woods (in a review in *The Times Literary Supplement*) demolishes Bergeron's entire book (the poor queer man must be terribly depressed) by noting a fact that is quite related to our discussion of Barrie and Michael: "James had converted him [George Villiers] into a surrogate son. The King had virtually adopted the entire Villiers clan, turning them into an extension of his own family, and the articulate expressions of affection that we read in their letters are exactly that." Now Barrie, before he became Michael's adoptive father, was indeed called uncle by all the little boys, and was therefore a *bona fide* member of the Llewelyn Davies family. It is in the nature of familial intimacy for members to address each other more floridly than individuals who are unrelated.

It is not only this issue which we must address. We must propel ourselves, like a well-aimed croquet ball, towards the sticky wicket of historicism, in particular, the notion that a particular period is prone to excesses of language. In other words, though we may imagine, when reading certain terms of affection today, that they indicate desires of a romantic nature, in fact, the language of the period might simply be more baroque than our own. Barrie grew up in the Victorian period. Popular Victorian melodramas like *Black-Ey'd Susan* and *The Colleen Bawn* were written in a heightened pseudo-poetry which we would find laughable today. ("Oh what a giddy fool I've been. What would I give to recall this fatal act which bars my fortune?") One might argue that theatrical language, even then, was reserved only for the stage, and that people did not talk like that in real life. (For a fascinating analysis of the diction of Victorian melodrama, the dedicated reader is encouraged to turn to Robertson Davies' witty essay, "Oblivion's Balm," in *The Mirror of Nature*.)

There can be no doubt that modes of address during the Edwardian era were certainly more formal than our own. If Barrie were to sign his letter to his little adopted nephew "Yours in love," we should not find it any more strange or suspicious than we would if a Victorian mother addressed her dearest child in the same way.

This digression is lengthy because I don't want to miss this opportunity to confront a rank conspiracy on the part of increasing numbers of homosexual and lesbian academics, including Leslie Sexton, for what it is: a blatant attempt to further the political goals of so-called "gay liberationists," and nothing more. These wily, left-leaning intellectuals know intuitively that the more heroes of history they can claim as their own, the more legitimate their love will seem to the general public. Though I must (I suppose) be classed a homosexual man, I refuse to identify (even reluctantly) with something I consider to be a betrayal of art for selfish political ends. Quite frankly, it nauseates me. To quote Hal Jensen (again from that trusty old warhorse, *The Times Literary Supplement*), "the deluge of gendered readings of literature is doing more for the cause than it is for literary appreciation." Why, these crafty political opportunists would have us believe that Virginia Woolf, despite her long standing and dedicated marriage, was some sort of perverted Edwardian lesbian! Well I'm sorry, but militant Sapphic scholars will have to make do with *The Well of Loneliness* — as paltry and depressing a novel as it might be. I won't even mention the ridiculous desperation of those tired queer academics who attempt to claim the incomparable bard Shakespeare as some nelly queen. I am perfectly happy to concur with Edmund Malone, who, in 1790 set the record straight about the tasteless puns in Shakespeare's sonnets: "such addresses to men, however indelicate, were customary in our author's time, and neither imported criminality nor were esteemed indecorous." W.H. Auden (according to Richard P. Wheeler and C.L. Barber) was extremely skeptical of identifying Shakespeare's feelings for the beautiful young man of the sonnets as homosexual love; he, in fact, "mocked the eager claims of 'the Homintern' on the sonnets; he described the love for the young man as 'mystical' and observed that such passionate devotion, enthralled by a special type of mortal beauty, rarely survives physical union." In other words, Shakespeare's rapturous descriptions of his beautiful young patron in the sonnets could not possibly have been the result of a physical consummation with the boy, for grim reality necessarily destroys romantic illusion.

Finally, in these situations I sympathize with my own mother, who, soon after I revealed the truth about my sexuality (there have never been any lies between us) exhorted me (with fear in her eyes) thusly: "I DO hope you're not going to try and tell me that Cary Grant was a homosexual!" Mother has an alarming addiction to *People* magazine and the more lurid tabloids, and the gossip-mongers had done their damage. I assured her that I had no intention of telling her any such thing — no matter how much dirt certain small-minded, gossipy gay film critics had dug up about the man. In fact, I told her that the idea of a gay Cary Grant would disturb me as much as it would her.

"It was all I could do to handle Liberace!" she moaned.

Indeed, it was.

59

EARLY ETON LETTERS

In 1913, when he was thirteen years old, Michael was sent off to Eton, which his older brothers George and Peter had also attended between the ages of thirteen and eighteen. Eton was much more than what we today call a junior and/or senior high school. Boys lived in dormitories, and were instructed in the classics and religion; they were expected to participate wholeheartedly in games (which were taken very seriously). The younger boys (fags) were mercilessly harassed by the older boys (Pops) who had as part of their duties the disciplining of their younger charges.

Keep in mind that in the time that passed between the childhood letters and the Eton ones, Michael's mother had died. The death of his wistful, beautiful, mother was the second tragedy in young Michael's life. He was only ten years old at the time.[*]

Sylvia's will stated that Michael was to come under the care of

---

[*] After collapsing on the stairs of her home in 1909, Sylvia was diagnosed with cancer that was located (quite poetically) too close to the heart for an operation. The seriousness of her illness was kept from the children, and even from Sylvia for a while, but when the condition became clear, she, like her husband, bore her suffering with a brave face. Her illness was somewhat less dramatic than Arthur's; it was more of a pathetic fading away than an agonizing, sudden loss.

Barrie, and his childhood nurse, Mary. What were the effects of the death of both his mother and father (in a period of two years, no less) on an already sensitive child? Well, for one thing, Eton became a nightmare; Michael was very unhappy there, as the early letters suggest.

1st May, 1913

Uncle Jim,

I trust you won't think I'm being a little coward. I don't want to be a little coward, because I know it's the last thing you would expect of me. It's all right to be candid about my feelings, even if they don't seem appropriate, isn't it?

I can tell you this, because I trust you in everything: I don't like Eton! Just in case you think I'm being a silly blushing cowardly goose, I will tell you why.

Hugh seems fine and nice. Though the spectre of the ghost of my perfect brother George is sometimes too much to bear! We all love George and he was and is perfect in every way, but was there ever the possibility of finding George wandering the halls of Eton at night? Ever?

You really must understand what an embarrassment my affliction is. At home, if I were to walk about and worry a teddy bear, there was no one but you and Mary to notice. You endured my night terrors with monumental understanding. I knew that if I ever was to wake up, you would be there.

Would it be imposing on you awfully to speak to Hugh* and warn

---

*   Hugh Macnaghten, Michael's housemaster at Eton, was as captivated, it seems, with Michael, as Barrie himself. He said that Michael was "the most remarkable boy he had ever taught in all his years at Eton." (see Birkin) him about my sleepwalking? Imagine the embarrassment if I were to walk into some other boy's bed and wake him up! I could be accused of the most frightful things. As you know I'm nothing but a worthless fag, and those awful Pops can punish you just for looking the wrong way.

If you think I'm being a cowardly custard & I should just bite my lip then I will. The best solution would be to get me out of this dreadful place. When I say I am utterly miserable I am not exaggerating. Of course, if you tell me to have a stiff upper lip and act like a little soldier, I will.

The main thing is that I miss you. In the evenings, when we used to have our walks, I now walk by myself, and it's not the same. My hand is cold and dead; there is no friend to warm it. Of course I miss Mary too, of course I do.

I'm sorry to act like a blubbering baby. You have every excuse to give me the most brutal tongue lashing. I stand ready.

Your loving,
Michael

10th May, 1913
My Dearest True Boy,

Though it's almost impossible to resist imagining my handsome young man waiting obediently for his whipping, I must disappoint you.

No, my boy, I am not going to whip you, verbally or otherwise. I understand completely the agony which you endure. My feelings are equal to yours, and in some ways worse.

To imagine your hand, so much like a shivering bird, no longer clasped in mine, is a torture beyond belief. And you are lucky enough *to have a new environment, new duties, and the possibility of making new friends! I have my same dull rooms, the same charming view, made all the more lonely with only the indefatigable Nico battering about.*

For Nico is not you.

Sometimes I look at your favourite chair by the window, and I think to myself, I must turn it against the wall. But I can't bring myself to do that.

You are a special boy, not a cowardly custard. What makes you special is that you feel things more deeply than the other boys. Anything I can do, anything that must be said to Hugh, will be said. You can't help it if you find yourself where you oughtn't to be at night. The doctor said your night terrors might not go away — we hope they will, of course — but if they don't, it's most emphatically not your fault.

You know darling, that if I could remove you from Eton I would.

We both know that part of your specialness is your sensitivity and your talent. I expect great things of you someday, and so did your mother. Neither you nor I would want to disappoint her.

I will be by with this boy's favourite chocolate cakes very soon. Then I shall speak with Hugh.

> *With greatest affection — and not without some longing,*
> *J.M.B.*

I have not prepared the reader for these initial letters between the teenage Michael and the older Barrie (he was fifty-three). What is immediately noticeable is that Barrie calls Michael "darling," and speaks to the boy almost romantically of being abandoned and how Michael cannot be replaced by another little boy. The boy also talks about his "cold" hand, which Barrie refers to as a "shivering bird." This overly affectionate mode of address stands out even more than it does in the letters of Michael's early childhood.

These are sensitive individuals. I think it is fair to contend that Barrie, with his obsession with children and their inner lives, nurtured a kind of cult of childhood. That is, there is a part of him that would have had Michael (and each of his adopted sons) remain innocent forever. So, though we might not find it odd that an older man might cherish the tiny hand of a small boy — or call him darling — the reader might find it odd that a middle-aged man should have the same relationship with a thirteen-year-old. I submit that the reader shouldn't and mustn't disapprove. At least not in this particular case. As I have noted earlier, family members utilize a particular brand of affectionate hyperbole that may seem strange to an outsider. It's not amazing to me that the author of *Peter Pan* — the man who invented the notion of the boy who would not grow up — would want to freeze his relationship with one of his own sons in that particular idyllic phase of parent/child love. Though it would be tempting to assume that Barrie didn't encourage Michael to grow up, I think we will see as we read further that his feelings about Michael's impending adulthood were, at the very least, mixed. Barrie's mixed feelings are only natural, and typical of a parent.

As for the sexual connotations of these letters: again (as with the early toad letters) I think we must be wary (even ashamed) of reading things into them. For someone like Leslie, I have no doubt that Michael's request for a "whipping" and Barrie's rejoinder, "it's almost impossible to resist imagining my handsome young man, etc." would have been the cause for all sorts of weird sexual extrapolations. To read a sort of double entendre into these sentiments again displays more about the readers' repressed emotions and desires than anything else.*

The next three sets of letters I reveal with trepidation. I think it is here that we begin to see into the soul of this young man; we can't help but be afraid for him.

30th June, 1913
Uncle Jim,

Today I'm angry. Perhaps I shouldn't be. Perhaps I'm not being the good little soldier like my other teammates. Is that so very wrong? Of course you know that I adore cricket. I've always adored every sort of game when we've played it. I rather look forward to someday being an Allahakbarrie.†

I'm very angry. There's something about the way cricket is played here. There's something about the way they play at, well, anything, which is different than the way we played it at Black Lake.

---

* In this context, it is certainly not irrelevant to remember Charles Dodgson (a.k.a. Lewis Carroll) and his obsessive relationship with the real Alice who was to be the model for his immortal nonsense tales. Carroll, like Barrie, took photos of children sometimes dressed, sometimes undressed. Like Barrie, his work was dedicated to the child he loved. But no one has proved — or will ever prove — that Carroll had an inappropriate relationship with the real Alice. I think we need to seriously ask if perhaps we are looking back on these respectable Victorian (or in Barrie's case, Edwardian) gentleman with twenty-twenty hindsight, and with lecherous twentieth-century eyes, seriously influenced by Freud and Kinsey. Perhaps in Victorian times (despite the bloated rhetoric of the incomprehensible Monsieur Foucault) people were really innocent, after all.

† The Allahakbarries was the fanciful name for a cricket club founded by Barrie in 1893. (The title includes a mutilated translation of the Arabic phrase "God help us.") The group was a favourite of several literary figures. Famous Allahakbarries included

Of course these boys are not my brothers. Hugh Macnaghten, for all his sensitivity, is not you. He'll always be housemaster; that much is set in stone.

What's the difference?

I ask myself that. I think it might just be the talks that they give us about cricket. About the character building. I'm certain cricket is character building. If it is, though, why do they have to keep reminding us? Shouldn't they let it just build our characters?

I find it hard to say clearly because these words are so tragic to me, they seem to express an inexpressible sadness. Or have I gotten too poetic? I fancy the budding poet in me sometimes gets out of control.

They've made it so games are not fun anymore.

There, I've said it. I never thought I'd ever think that games weren't fun. If games are no longer fun, what is there? Tell me, honestly, Uncle Jim, must games be boring & competitive, & even frightening? Must one dread the playing field? Where is the laughter that should be an inextricable part of any game? Is that just all part of growing up?

I thought you would know.

Yours in confused affection,
Michael

Arthur Conan Doyle, A.A. Milne, and Will Meredith (son of George). Barrie contended that the fame of the literary cricketeer was in inverse proportion to the skill with which he played. On the surface at least, Barrie projected a lighthearted, almost adolescent attitude to sportsmanship. David Rayvern Allen's informative book on the Allahakbarries quotes Barrie: "I had to be guided by some principles in choosing the members of the club. The principles were these. With regard to the married men, it was because I liked their wives, and with regard to the single men, it was for the oddity of their personal appearance." The group often used to gather and play at Barrie's summer home at Black Lake. History has bequeathed us with a touching photo of young Michael (aged five) in a gigantic sun hat, surrounded by Allahakbarries.

10th July, 1913
My Dearest True Boy,

This letter is one of the the most difficult I have ever felt compelled to write.

The questions you have asked are terribly important ones, and I so much don't want you to be depressed at my answer. You know how much I love you, and how it pains me to see my little soldier — for I will call you that, even though you may not wish to hear those words — frustrated, sad, or lonely.

The truth is, I never, ever thought you would grow up. If you could have seen yourself, with your little sun hat — do you remember when you lost it? — and Jack shaking eels at you, and you running away and crying, but secretly laughing inside.

Yes, there is something about the games of childhood, and I feel it too.

I remember when I had to leave the bosom of my own family for school, with only my older brother for company. I felt an agonizing emptiness, a shocked longing.

I still have dreams, to this day, in which I am shouting and running with the other boys, and I can feel the shudder of twilight, as night comes, bringing a dreaded end to another never-ending summer's day. "It shan't be over!" we cry, and yet mother calls from the house, and it's time to put away our games, our bats & balls, our expectation of mystery & delight & surprise.

You must say that terrible good-bye, because you are a young man now, and you must put away childish things. Though it seems that housemasters, cricket masters, and the Pops are your enemies, they are doing their duty, helping you to grow into the man that you will someday be.

Oh how I dislike saying these most necessary words to you, my little man.

There is one consolation. It's a secret. A secret that you mustn't tell anyone. We have our art. What are the poems that you have shown me, if not the sacred dwelling place of childish things? Poetry is where the child takes up residence inside the man. You must protect that little poet child, soothe him, kiss his hot and fevered brow. The poet child is inside you and inside me; and no cricket game, however severe the rule of play, will ever kill him.*

| 69

I've tried here to talk about precious and difficult things; how to grow up completely and yet not at all. Don't tell Hugh or the other boys of this. They might not understand.

Yours with undying affection,
J.M.B.

---

*   This equation of creativity and childishness is not atypical of Barrie. It's important, I think, to mention something here of the great man's childhood. Most biographers confirm that Barrie's creative life found its troubled origins in the death of his older brother, David. Barrie was the youngest of eight children — five boys and three girls. His oldest brother, Alexander, was thirteen years older than Barrie. Barrie's father was a weaver, and they lived in a tiny "but and ben," in Kirriemuir, Scotland, a claustrophobic four-room hut that also housed a loom. Barrie's mother was very dear to him; in fact, he wrote a book about her childhood (*Margaret Ogilvy*). Barrie did not, however, begin life as his mother's favourite. Margaret first doted on the middle son, David — nurturing the hope that one day he would become a Doctor of Divinity. But David died in an ice-skating accident at the age of thirteen — when Barrie was only six. The death left a permanent mark on both Barrie and his mother. Margaret plunged into deep mourning, and was confined to her sickroom. The boy James found himself imitating his brother (down to his favourite whistle) in an attempt to revive her. Ultimately, Margaret was cheered through the simple routine of telling the story of her childhood to her youngest son. Barrie later isolated this ritual as the wellspring of his own creativity. In her moving biography of Barrie, Janet Dunbar quotes the author thusly: "The reason my books deal with the past instead of with the life I myself have known is simply this, that I soon grow tired of writing tales

20th July, 1913
Dear Uncle Jim,

I miss you terribly. I miss home. I even miss Mary.[†] *You know what I mean by that remark which might sound caustic & so I needn't explain!*

There are times when I feel like a mechanical man, or a dead person, walking around, looking but not seeing, going through the motions but feeling nothing.

Yet it is at night that I feel the most, when I should be getting my much needed rest for the duties of the day. Perhaps it is that my poet child comes out at night, and walks around the bed, and goes to the window, desperately searching for some escape.

Last night, I had the most terrifying dream.

I haven't remembered any of them for a while, and apparently my terrors haven't occurred too often (or the other boys, at least, have not been complaining of them), so I was lulled into imagining that the doctor's prediction would be true, and that my tortures might cease.

They have not.

Last night, I dreamed that I had grown up into my own father, and consequently I had his disease. The pain in my mouth was awful — when I woke up, I thought that I might have had a toothache — and the doctors told me that they would have to remove my lower jaw, so that I was only left with half a mouth. The pain was gone but there was a horrible emptiness — an emptiness that is hard to describe —

---

unless I can see a little girl, of whom my mother has told me, wandering confidently through the pages. Such a grip has her memory of her girlhood had upon me since I was a boy of six."

†   Mary was the family governess before and after Michael's mother's death. There was tension between Mary and Barrie.

where my mouth should have been. I could not open it, I could not speak, there was simply nothing.

That was merely the beginning. After that I was no longer my father; but I was myself, and suddenly my future was frighteningly clear. I can't tell you what it looked like. It was a feeling. A feeling of enormous certainty that there was nothing before me & it didn't stretch ahead like a road or anything; it was more like an abyss — but even that is too specific, it was just a harrowing emptiness. Looking back on it now, it was very much like the emptiness which had, earlier in my dream, hovered where my mouth should have been.

| 71

I tell you because I can't tell anyone else, and because I miss you, and our house, and our vacations at the lake, so terribly much. Sometimes I cry myself to sleep and I think it is that, above all things, that makes the other boys vilify me. They whisper that I cry, I know they do. But what can I do about it? Any day soon it will be vacation and we will see each other again.

Can I tell you what one of the other, horrible housemasters said to me the other day? It was so evil of him. I happened to mention to Hugh that I was looking forward to hols & to seeing you, because I imagined Hugh would understand. Then a rather disgusting man named William Throckmorton — I won't describe him expect to say that he is piggish in every way — quoted Dr. Arnold: "When one of the boys at Rugby told Dr. Arnold* that he was looking forward to holidays, Dr. Arnold mentioned that his own father one day preached

---

*   Dr. Thomas Arnold was the infamous Dean of Rugby from 1827 to 1842. From Michael McCrim's thorough book on Arnold, we learn that the school's reputation for severe discipline is somewhat unjust. Arnold must properly be remembered as the headmaster who introduced a uniquely Victorian attitude to teaching, i.e., that all Public School education should ultimately have as its purpose Christian moral instruction and "character building."

'Boast not thyself of tomorrow' and that a few weeks after preaching that, he was dead."

Well it all seemed to be apiece with my dream & the general hopelessness of dreaming or hoping for anything here. Too terribly appropriate and depressing. But I will see you soon and for a few sweet days, we will walk together again,

> Yours and still yet daring to hope for a tomorrow,
> Michael

1st August, 1913
My Dearest True Boy,

My heart aches for you.

I didn't mean to write you these words, because they are the flowered vulgarisms of popular fiction — in fact, I am ashamed to reveal that I read them in a particularly nauseating novel yesterday. You know that if I could, I would do anything to help you. The only thing that makes me truly unhappy is to know that you are in pain. If I could will myself, spirit myself [unreadable] myself to be by your bedside, you know that I would be there.

Isn't devotion strange? Why is it that I think that by obliterating myself, I will put you somehow at ease? Perhaps that is what is happening to you because you are separated from me? I sink down into my chair at night, and then I sink lower and lower into the cushioned fabric, thinking that if I were to disappear then your nightmares would somehow cease.

Now I am being self-centred. Your pain is not only due to being separated from me. It's from gazing into your own future. My strong-willed, angry boy who will not adjust; of course I am not blaming *you! For it is your anger that will save you! I remember how you used to stamp your little feet and stammer "I won't, I won't!" There is no adjustment to be made. You are a superior soul surrounded by mediocrity. That is why you have these painful visions. Your future is beyond Eton, to Oxford and then beyond, beyond.*

Can I tell you a secret? Let us set ourselves a task. We will endure the hours that we are apart, for one reason only. To be with each other again. If we can save something of the child poet for each other, then it will be worth all the agony the Gods may direct at us.

| 73

As for Dr. Arnold, he was a necessary evil, for without him we would be back before Tom Brown's Schooldays. Where boys lay quivering in their beds, fearing punishment & God knows what else. I can't imagine the horror!

And if your Pop beats you, you know it will mean more than summer for me to soothe you with my embrace.

It is only a week, and then we will be together.

> *With undying affection I am your only,*
> *J.M.B.*

Then, there is a break in time. Or that is, the next letters seem to deal with other subjects altogether. It's a good thing, perhaps, because one wonders how the boy's difficulties could be any greater, or how the old man's helplessness could be any more poignant. These letters seem, to some degree, like the letters of two lovers, rather than that of a devoted father and son. But, instead of setting us to any vain speculations perhaps they should make us wonder at how terribly similar different types of love may be, and how the naive *agapé* only differs by a hair's breadth from suffocating *eros*.

The next letters that are available to us concern a new topic in Michael's life. Obviously, he has somehow triumphed over his nightmares and begun to adjust to Eton. And he has a friend. And the friend is causing him some consternation.

4th October, 1913

74 |

Dear Uncle Jim,

I am afraid this has not been a very happy half for me, that is, so far. I fully expect Nitters will tell you everything, so I shall try and tell you first. It's messy and complicated and has become embarrassing, actually. Nitters is rather an alarmist about this whole tempest in a teapot. I'm certain you'll be more understanding. It's all about my friendship with a boy named Wright. He is two years younger than I am and in a lower form. Nitters claims that our hanging about together is not sensible for either of us. What harm could it possibly do? He uses the word sentimentality — which is utterly inappropriate, in my view! Wright's parents don't seem to mind. You simply must tell me if the whole situation upsets you. Neither Wright nor myself is a bad influence. How could we be? We may not be perfect Etonians but neither are we irresponsible little whelps either. Nitters says I am in love with Wright because he happens to be a handsome boy. Can you believe Nitters used that phrase? I'm surprised to hear such utter rot. The truth is I simply like Wright. The entire situation has put me into a sorry state. Can you, will you, help?

Loving,
Michael

10th October, 1913
My Dearest True Boy,

The most important thing, my dear boy, is that you don't worry about what I think or say about this matter. From the very fair and reasonable explanation that you have made to me of this affair it is clear it's nothing more than friendship. Though this boy, Wright, is younger than you, it sounds to me as if your relationship is one between equals. That's the way boys should be.

Do you have a photograph of your young friend you might send?

Yours lovingly,
J.M.B.

15th October, 1913
Dear Uncle Jim,

Your letter has taken a huge weight from my shoulders. I think the whole problem is Nitters. He is the most awful Tutor a boy could ever have. I know I shouldn't say that, but in this case it happens to be true. He is merciless with me, for some reason. He even brings up Peter Pan. I've told him over and over that I don't want to talk about that — not because I don't love the play, you know that, sweet Uncle — but because the boys will make fun. But nevertheless he finds it necessary to call me Mr. Pan now and then, which sends the boys off on another endless row of kidding.*

---

* All the five Llewelyn Davies boys were teased about their connection with Peter Pan. Who was the real inspiration? Well, George, the oldest, would have been closest to Peter Pan's age when Barrie actually wrote the famous play. It was probably Peter Llewelyn Davies who was hounded the most about his famous uncle, due simply to the unfortunate fact of his name. The image we have today of Peter Pan is most certainly based on Michael. Barrie sent several photos of Michael dressed in Peter

I can handle all of those things. What I cannot handle is having him nag me over and over again about sentimentality.

What do you think he means by it?

For instance, Wright and I went bathing the other day because it was very hot, and we were sitting by the pool and Nitters happened to walk by — when he should have been in class — and happened to see me towelling Wright's hair.

76 |

He made a big scene about it. I think it's piffle. Wright's hair is long and curly, and sometimes he can't quite get it completely dry. Besides, that day, he'd hurt his arm swimming and was having trouble stretching it. I just wanted to help. Is there something wrong with helping a friend get dry after bathing? I don't see any wrong in it at all, and I can't see what it all has to do with sentimentality.

Anyway, here's a picture of Wright. It's the school photo. He's the last one on the end. You can recognize him because of his naughty smile. Truth be told, Wright doesn't care what Nitters says about us. He even likes it! He's not at all bad, though. Just mischievous, in the same way mother used the word when Nico and I strayed too far when we were at Black Lake.[†]

I hope you like the photo.

Yours lovingly,
Michael

Pan garb to the artist who created the sculpture we all know and love in Kensington Gardens.

† Black Lake was the country retreat owned by James Barrie and his wife Mary. It was a favourite summer vacation spot for the five Llewelyn Davies boys, who often visited Barrie there. In 1901, Barrie first played pirate with the boys by the lake. He dressed up as "Captain Swarthy," a precursor of Captain Hook, and made the boys walk the plank in play. It was all great fun, and inspired Barrie to write a little book (ostensibly authored by the four-year-old Peter), which Barrie called *The Boy Castaways*. This creation served as the inspiration for *Peter Pan*, written two years later.

20th October, 1913
My Dearest True Boy,

How lovely of you to send a photo of your darling Mr. Wright. He is every inch the charming fellow. I don't think that his smile is naughty at all. It's just the type of smile a boy should have, in my humble opinion.

He looks as if he might be an athletic boy for his age, and he already seems to be growing out of his school uniform. I imagine he's quite a whiz at cricket.

As for sentimentality and Nitters, I would ignore them both. Towelling a chum's hair is not what I call being sentimental. It's what I call being a good friend. What's Nitters doing spying on you when he should be in class? You must tell me more about this Nitters. I have my suspicions about him.

There is one surefire way to tell if you are getting sentimental about a boy. I will tell you, because it sounds as if you need some ammunition in your talks with him. There was a boy at Dumfries* with whom I was very close. Like you and Wright, we did everything together. And he was a veritable whiz at cricket. But most of the time we would simply go for walks together and talk. He was an avid reader, as was I.

I went through a rather difficult period with John — that was his name — and I was forced to call on my older brother Alexander for help. Much in the way you are asking for help, now. You see, John and I were in the habit of making little excursions every evening at dusk, after prayers. In the summertime it was a still bright out, almost

---

*   Barrie spent his early teenage years in Dumfries, and attended the Dumfries Academy, in Scotland. He lived with his much older brother, Alexander (who, by all reports, was very kind to him). Alexander was the Inspector of Free Church Schools for the district of Dumfries.

glittering. I don't think I will ever forget the way the light danced on the leaves.

Every night, we walked and talked about the things dearest to our hearts, the way only boys can. There came a disturbing period when I found myself too dependent on young John. How did I know this? Well, the way I realized was that I began to get depressed when I wasn't with him. I started to look forward to our evening walks with inordinate eagerness. 78 | *In fact, John became more than just a friend. I lost myself in him. Quite literally, in fact. I began to think that John had stolen me from myself.*

It's a difficult idea. But if you come to understand it, then you will know what Nitters means about sentimentality. When we get sentimental about someone, we feel we are not really whole unless we are with them. Or, as in the case of John and I, we might feel that the other person is capable of stealing our personality away — almost the way Mrs. Darling steals Peter's shadow, without knowing what she's doing! The most precious thing we have is our own personality. We can't lend it away. We can't give it to a mischievous boy either. No matter how naughty his smile is.

But I don't think you have this problem with Wright. It seems to me that you are just chums, and that's the way it should be.

I hope this helps.

Yours lovingly,
J.M.B.

In these letters, we see Michael and Barrie at the height of their friendship. Michael is obviously so much better off, finally able to find a chum, and Barrie is every inch the loving father, encouraging him, even requesting photos of his son's newest friend. Barrie seems always to know exactly the right thing to say. He encourages Michael in his friendship while at the same time warning him of excesses that might prove psychologically unhealthy.

Thus ends the first set of Eton letters, those dated between 1913 and 1916. There is only one letter left from this first period, and it is an odd one, so I have left it for last. There is no extant entreaty from Michael, only this singular reply from Barrie. It's important to remember that the word fag, repeated over and over again in this letter, has nothing, of course, to do with homosexuality.

This letter, though undated (the damp smudged it), is probably from 1913, when Michael was enduring his first horrendous weeks. Obviously this queer letter was meant to cheer him up after some particularly unendurable fagging.

My Dearest True Boy,

So now you are a fag! I knew it would happen. In fact I was looking forward to it. A little torture — this time applied from outside, rather than from your own introspective little soul — is always good for you. Being a fag was very good for me, I must say!

Enjoy your fagdom, for it will last not long — though sometimes it seems like forever.

Do whatever your Pop says, no matter how degrading it may seem. Be proud of your heritage, be proud to be a fag!

Or else how will you learn to be cruel to your own fag someday?

With love and kisses from an older fag who has matured somewhat, but is not quite yet old enough to be a Pop,

J.M.B.

I have saved this letter for last because of the obvious possible misinterpretations. Again, it's very important to put all this in context. The term "fagging" was used as far back as 1835 by Dr. Arnold in his lectures at Rugby, and in 1854, George Melly published his adolescent memoirs under the title *The Experiences of a Fag at a Public School.* By the early twentieth century, when Michael was at Eton, the tradition of "Pops" and "fags" was firmly entrenched. Boys in the upper forms were expected to discipline their counterparts in the lower forms. This was considered to be a type of character building and a necessary preparation for the hierarchies the boys would encounter in the outside world. Some of the older boys would misuse that power, and ask the younger boys to do humiliating errands, and if they judged them truant, would sometimes treat them to brutal and humiliating punishments. The more benevolent masters, of course, made an effort to control the disciplinary tactics used, and thus the issue of "bullying" became central in the nineteenth-century Public Schools.

As for the homosexuality which seems to rear its ugly head in these Eton letters, again, the situation must be put in historical perspective. The novelist Robert Graves was a student at Charterhouse at the same time that Michael was at Eton, and went on to fight in, and somehow survive, the First World War. Graves grew up to be a confirmed heterosexual, and yet, in his memoirs, he frankly describes the romantic relationships between boys at Public School. He says that one headmaster even bragged: "My boys are amorous, but seldom erotic." Graves himself fell in love with a younger boy named Dick, but soon grew out of it. That did not mean, however, that he didn't write jealous and possessive letters home to the boy from the front. He says of Charterhouse that "the atmosphere was always heavy with romance of a conventional early Victorian type." So Michael's feelings for Wright, like those of Graves, were nothing more or less than a schoolboy crush.

I'm sure Leslie would have had a grand old time with the final Eton letter. But to imagine that it is about homosexuality makes just as much sense as imagining the same about childish discussions of eels and toads. As you forge ahead through these precious missives, you will perhaps feel as I do (to quote a Barbra Streisand movie) — that the mirror has two faces. Each time I read these letters, I am more convinced of Barrie's essential innocence. I think too, about love, and how often it is mistaken for something less dignified. Do I know what these letters truly mean? No, but Barrie's affection for his adopted son seem to me to be as innocent, and as easily misinterpreted, as the feelings I have had, from time to time, about various younger men that I have known. Sometimes youth and physical beauty spur a kind of love that requires no consummation.

LATER ETON LETTERS

The letters that date from 1916 are remarkably different in tone from the earlier Eton letters. Michael is obviously growing up, and forging new friendships. For the first time, these friendships do not always meet with Barrie's approval.

Michael's first letters, from early 1916, show the youth clearly exercising his independence from his adoptive father, and asserting his right to be himself. Indeed, the tragic rift that was to grow between this overly devoted father and son originates in the following letters.

12th December, 1916
Dear Uncle Jim,

I must make a request which is very indelicate and which, perhaps, I shouldn't ask you at all. You must understand & I'm sure you will, how uncomfortable it is for me to have to say this to you, but circumstance has forced my hand.

At any rate, to cut a long and far too complex little drama down to a one-act play, I would prefer if, when you come to visit next week, you take care to conceal the cake. Or, perhaps what would be infinitely preferable — not to me, but to the world at large, being the harsh world it is — would be if you didn't bring a cake at all. Of course I hate ever to miss one of your chocolate surprises, but Neil Grosshanks is absolutely merciless, calling me Mr. Chocolate, and asking me if he can see my sweet tooth. "How sweet is it?" he asks. In return I make fun of his receding chin — it seems to get smaller by the day, or is his forehead just getting larger? — but absolutely nothing discourages the endless barrage.

84 |

I know that these boys should just be ignored and now that I am nearly 17 years old they are irrelevant, really.

So we must put it down to my incredible sensitivity which will never leave me, I'm certain.

I found this letter very difficult to write, but I also knew that you would understand.

> *Yours lovingly,*
> *Michael*

20th December 1916
Master Michael Ll-D.,

I have to admit that I was taken aback by your most recent letter. Of course I will do anything you ask of me, your will has always been my command, but what you ask is very difficult.

Of course it isn't just about a chocolate cake, it is about much more than that. I understand that you are sensitive, and things will get all muddled if I am to be more sensitive than you, so I simply shall not be.

There will be no more cakes.

It is enough for me to know that you still long for cakes, as much as you once longed for mudpies.

And since you have started the proverbial ball rolling, perhaps you won't mind if I make a similar request of you. I think you have reached the age when it would be wise for us to use discretion in our epistolary addresses and farewells. As much as I would wish to sign my letters as I once did, now that you have reached the advanced age of seventeen — and seem to have outgrown your longing for chocolate cake, or at least the evidence of that longing — I will sign them simply, Yours, affec.

The abbreviation, though an inaccurate expression of my feelings for you, speaks, I hope, with a certain poignance about the situation which we have encountered: you are becoming a man.

You might wish to end your letters in the same way. Of course the way you address your letters may remain the same. I am in fact your "Dear Uncle Jim" and will continue to be so — young or old, dead or alive — and there are no two ways about that. But I can no longer address a young man who has outgrown the appearance of loving chocolate cake as My Dearest True Boy. So instead I will return to a form of address which I used even before you left for Eton — Master Michael Ll-D.

I shall console myself with the idea that a master is something less than a man — but still has the potential for mastery in him. (Let me say this: I will always think of you as My Dearest True Boy. The way you move your hands. The very incline of your vulnerable neck. As strong as your young neck grows, it will always be vulnerable to me!)

I'm certain that you will think that I am being melodramatic simply to punish you for chastising me over a cake.

So just to convince you of my sincerity I will change the subject.

What could show more presence of mind than that?

What follows is a rather mundane request which means this (unreadable) will finish enveloped in a cloud of impenetrable literary speculation, or more accurately, pure authorial ennui.

I have been busy scrawling a play inspired by Old Solomon Caw's jibe in Peter Pan, *which I'm sure you remember: "in this world there are no second chances." The play is about a group of older people — they are stumbling & crumbling & drooling; nearly my own age in fact — who are given a miraculous second chance to live their lives over again. Of course they make a mess of it, as we all would do, because that's the viciousness of living — we can never turn back to a prettier page.**

My question is this. Do you like the title Second Chance? *I don't, of course, or I wouldn't bother asking. Something from a quote, of course, would be much better. Something with poetry in it. I do hope it to be a poetic play.*

Perhaps this presents an impossible task, requesting a title for a play that you have not yet read, but then again perhaps not impossible for you, my brilliant, irascible boy.

Even if you lose your taste for candy next, I shall continue to call you brilliant.

Yours, affec.
J.M.B.

---

*   This play, which Barrie had started many years earlier, was inspired by the death of Michael's father.

1st January 1917
Dear Uncle Jim,

Let me assure you that I am not quite as clever as you assume. And not quite as clever as the delicious discovery which follows will make me out to be. I have found a title for your play!

You must call it Dear Brutus. *I'm certain this will cause you, and hopefully, your audience, to remember the justly famous quote from Julius Caesar: "The fault, Dear Brutus . . . etc." No, I did not spend the week since your last visit racking my brain for a title. Propitiously, we happened to be reading this hateful play — it is the most mundane of all Shakespeare's works, is it not? — with Hugh. Though the plot is somewhat predictable, and Brutus a frustratingly righteous character, it's got some of the juiciest quotes a fellow will ever find. If you don't use this title, I will be terribly hurt and it is I who will throw myself into the Thames.*

Of course I am only joking. If I'm a bit giddy you must forgive me, for I can't hold it in any longer. I've found a new chum!

I know what drove me to finally open myself to friendship. Hugh says I'm too solitary. All the snivelling boys — each little Grosshanks & Plather & Hobbledyhead & Piffle — they had a hand in it, I daresay. All right then, no boy is actually called Piffle — but many of them should be — there actually is a Nigel Hobbledyhead and he's needled constantly — tho' he deserves it much more than me. I think, if you must know the truth — and you will always have it unalloyed, from your most loving nephew, dear Uncle — tho' I cherish having my precocious little brother here at Eton, it is a trial that Hugh reports to you that, and I quote, "Nicholas is the heart and soul of the house." It's no good telling me that I'm the brilliant one and Nico has all the family charm. It still hurts.

Then again, I fancy nothing can really hurt me anymore, and it's because of Roger.

I must admit I get a special thrill just from writing his name!

I can't wait for you to meet him, Uncle. He's a little taller than me and he has a squidgy face. That's what I call it, squidgy. It's not handsome in the traditional way, more in a devilish way. The second thing is it's nice to have a chum that's taller than one, and at dusk one can lean one's head on his shoulder.

Where do I begin? Roger is certain the most jolly person I have ever met. Not counting you of course!

His full name is Roger Senhouse and he's just barely younger than I am & not quite as dedicated to his studies or bookish. Compared to him I am a prig. But he is enormously intelligent and dedicated to improving his mind. Just as an example, I gave him some A.E. Houseman* to look at and talked about George; I don't think Roger ever thought about poetry that way. And by that I mean, that poetry has an application to real life. He thought it was all Keats and Shelley — all dusty vases and sandy old Egyptian sculptures.

---

* It is no wonder that Houseman was Barrie's favourite poet. "A Shropshire Lad" (1896) contains a line about a soldier who dies that clearly echoes *Peter Pan* (1904): "And there with the rest are the lads that will never be old." One can easily see the danger in these poems, and how Michael and his new friend may have misinterpreted them, for Houseman's work is not merely concerned with death, but is clearly obsessed with suicide. Examine the following stanza, a defence of a suicidal young man. It is typical of Houseman's work:

> Shot? so quick, so clean an ending?
> Oh that was right, lad, that was brave:
> Yours was not an ill for mending,
> 'Twas best to take it to the grave.

We enjoy "To an Athlete Dying Young" immensely and read it to each other over and over. So you can see there's hope for him. He adores your favourite poet!

The next time you come and visit I will make certain Roger is in my rooms, and we shall have tea.

I want to tell you something else about him but I daren't. But of course I shall, because you are my Dear Uncle and I tell you everything. I think what I adore most about Roger, besides his squidgy little face, his large hands — they are inordinately large and heavy for a boy — and steel-blue eyes, are the games. Roger revels in games. In a way they are naughty but in a way they are not, or else we wouldn't play them. It usually goes like this. After studies and before lights out there is that exquisite time when no one is about and it's too early for sleep. Roger visits me and we dress up. He hauls over some old sheets in a canvas bag and we wind them around us in various ways. It's the ancient or Roman fantasies that are the most fun.

Eton manages to take all the fun out of games; after all the character building there is nothing left but perspiration and tension. But when Roger and I play we are careless and free, and somewhat silly, which is really the point of games, is it not?

I've trusted you with something that has cheered me so terribly much because I know you'd never forget your boyhood days, and that you will understand. Roger cheers me so much. Of course, I don't expect my night terrors to disappear — it's too late for that now. But I can endure them better with Roger around, and when Roger visits me before bedtime, it's as if my head is filled with chocolate cake, instead of worries about this or that.

I daresay this letter has been overlong, but for good reason. I shan't be able to sleep at all waiting for your reply.

You must like Roger I know that you will.*

And of course you may call me brilliant!

Yours, affec.
Michael

90 | *15th January, 1917*
Master Michael Ll-D.,

Brilliant is the word for you, my precious, precocious young man.

Dear Brutus *will be, without a doubt, the title of my next play. This means that if you do not attend the opening, I will be as hurt as an uncle can be — and we uncles can get very hurt, indeed. But I ask you not to dismiss* Julius Caesar; *indeed any playwright is wary when any compatriot's creation is dismissed. Shakespeare wrote large, small, quiet, sweet, violent, tragic, hilarious plays. Each is special and differ-ent. There's no advantage to be had in weighing them like peas and honey. I will agree that* Julius Caesar *is much less complex than* Antony and Cleopatra. *But complex is not necessarily better.*

The lesson is over now.

As for my new rooms they are most certainly larger; and there is a view. Yes, I can see each and every bridge on the River Thames. What

---

* Michael's new friend, Roger Senhouse, it must be noted, grew up to be an infamous homosexual. In later years he became the lover of the notorious Lytton Strachey, who is mentioned later in these letters. From all accounts Senhouse was rather manipulative, and — inevitably — also a very beautiful young man. He caused Lytton Strachey endless jealous anguish. One can only imagine the effect this charis-matic character had on Michael in his formative years. This information will perhaps put the severe letter from Barrie which follows in a less chilling light.

is most cozy and soul-nourishing is something I call my inglenook: nothing more than a large fireplace framed by two wooden settles to sit upon. I cherish it as much as I cherish your letters, because the ceiling is low enough that only I and small boys* are comfortable there. In fact, I think your new chum Roger would undoubtedly hit his head on the ceiling. I have treated myself only to the wooden settles with a few cushions because, first, I am a Calvinist at heart, and second, I can no longer indulge my depression by sinking into the cushions, forgetting myself, and thinking of you.

|91

This is good for the soul, in a Presbyterian way, as is what I am about to reveal to you.

There is a danger in this Roger business.

Please don't misunderstand me. I am overjoyed that you have found a companion, and of course ecstatic that another Etonian is discovering the joys of A.E. Houseman. What concerns me are these games, and that I think you might be getting too old to play them.

How shall I explain this? We have talked of games again and again. Of course I understand how painful it was for you to learn to play cricket in the Etonian manner. But you persevered. It may seem tiresome at first to think of games as a sort of preparation for life ahead, but that is their true purpose. When we are children, games are innocent and silly because what we are learning is how to walk and talk and play with others. As we grow, the games must be more carefully planned and watched. The wrong kinds of games, or games practised in the wrong manner, might hinder a youth's healthy development.

---

* James Barrie was only five feet tall.

Of course you love Roger, and he is a joy to be with. Of course you must have a chum. But is he the right chum for you? What was mischievous in childhood can become dangerous in adulthood. Believe me, I find this entire topic devilishly difficult to write about. Let's just say that I don't know if Roger's intentions are completely pure. Dressing up is quite all right when boys are organized together in groups and play-acting under the supervision of an adult or a tutor. But the kind of play-acting which Roger is initiating might have an unhealthy result, my dear boy.

What all this is coming to, and I'm almost certain this will be a terrible disappointment for you, is that I recommend that you don't see Roger anymore. This may seem a stern measure under the circumstances, but you must know I only have your best interests at heart. I can see that you are growing overly fond of him very quickly, and the longer you stay friends with him, the harder it shall be to break off.

In short, remember when you were a young Etonian whelp, and you were friends with Wright? Well, that was not dangerous because you did not invest any of your soul in him. With Roger it seems to me that you are beginning to imagine that he is [unreadable] & by that I mean your soul, that he is the bright and funny part of you. No, my dearest Michael, though you were always the moody one, you were always also capable of brighter laughter than any of my boys. The joy is in you, Michael! You don't need these silly dress-up games. Not at your age.

Trust a much older, much wiser Uncle in this. I know it will be terribly difficult to break it off with a new friend. But think of my inglenook here waiting for you. And of the view.

Adelphi Terrace's top floor won't seem like home until you've visited here. If I can wean myself off extra cushions in my wooden settle you should be able to wean yourself off Roger.

Yours, affec.
J.M.B.

22nd January, 1917
Dear Uncle Jim,

I must be honest with you and tell you that your last letter has precipitated not a few nightmares. Thankfully I can't remember them, but you know what a bad sign it is that I am knocking about again & doing things I shouldn't in the night. It means my spirit is unsettled.

I'm in a funk about your letter, and that's that. I won't pretend not to be! I can't believe that you would suggest that I break it off with Roger. How could you? After all I said about him and what he means to me?

I am particularly addled by your suggestions that there is something unhealthy or dangerous about our relationship. What in heaven's name does that mean? This is nothing other than love for a chum. This is the kind of love that develops between boys at any school, only up until now I haven't had the opportunity for that kind of affection because the boys have been universally loutish & brutish & devoid of any sensitivity whatsoever. Dare I say it? Surely this is the very sort of friendship that I shall have to call upon in Public Schools Camp. There, I'll be preparing myself for something which I know you would rather not talk about. All right, I will say it: I believe George was fighting for friendships like this when he died. There is a war on, as I'm sure you have not forgotten, and this is my own way of preparing.

I hope I haven't offended you, dearest Uncle, but your letter upset me terribly, as you can see.

I have made one concession to your concerns, however. I have suggested to Roger that we discontinue our games. I still insist that there is nothing unhealthy or dangerous about them. Roger was disappointed at first when I told him, but there are endless ways for us to have fun.

94 | 　*As you can see, I cannot bring myself to give up Roger, but I can make some compromises because I do not wish to upset my dear uncle at the same time.*

I hope this letter finds you well.

Yours, affec.
Michael

There is a short lapse of time after these letters have passed, before the next ones we have. One wants to pause and take a breath here, and allow it all to sink in.

What is more than evident from these letters is that Michael was experiencing his first pangs of homosexual desire, perhaps even love. But what is even more important is Barrie's response. It is calm and reasonable, certainly not the response of a lecherous old pederast goading his young compatriot into the hot loins of another steaming conquest. No, Barrie seems genuinely concerned, indeed full of a love which I find extremely touching, even kind. He shows proper parental concern over his son's burgeoning, impetuous puppy love. But is it merely the love of one puppy for another? For Michael was no longer an innocent fourteen-year-old who was infatuated with Mr. Wright. As Barrie himself so reluctantly recognizes, Michael was quickly becoming an adult.

One might question Barrie's wisdom in trying to break up the adolescent attraction. After all, from his point of view, wouldn't it have been better to let the affair play itself out, and then have it be just as soon forgotten? Certainly yes. But we musn't forget Michael's depressive and susceptible nature, something of which Barrie was inordinately aware. No, he recognized that his adopted |95 son was abnormally vulnerable, and that whatever joys he might find with his friend would likely cause inexpressible pain later on.

One must also put these events in historical perspective. The year was 1917, the First World War was not yet over. The eldest Llewelyn Davies boy, George, had died on the battlefields in 1915 (the same year as the Edwardian martyr poet Rupert Brooke). Weighing heavily on James and his adopted son was Michael's impending stint at Public Schools Camp, a military training camp for boys. As we can see from the following letters, Michael was not looking forward to his training, or his future as a soldier. Here we see the rift widening between the young man and his guardian. Interestingly, these letters do not mention Roger — either he no longer played a part in Michael's life, or Michael had wisely chosen not to bring up the contentious issue of his new friend.

20th March, 1917
Dear Uncle Jim,

> *I feel that of late I have been a very bad boy, complaining & whining & being Just Too Much Trouble. It's no surprise to me that you might want to ship me off to Public Schools Camp as quickly as possible.*

Not that you do.

I must say the prospect is a forbidding one. Can you imagine your clumsy little water rat — for I shall feel absolutely like a water rat in my wet uniform, because as you know, it always rains in Public Schools Camp — marching and training with the other little soldiers? What is especially frightening is I shan't know a soul there, and boys have never been very forgiving of my general ineptitude. Yes, it can only be called general, since I am not very good at anything other boys are good at, we both know that all too well.

Of course it's no use making an annoying fuss — and that is exactly what I'm doing — because it is every boy's duty. I understand that. I just can't help thinking how much more suitable for all of this George was, and Jack, and even poor Peter, for all his trials and tribulations.

Well I must grin and bear it I suppose. I'm sure it is worse for you than it is for me. What with George and all.

I wish sometimes that there could be some sort of dispensation for boys like me, who are less suited to this kind of work. Perhaps we could do our work behind the lines. I know it sounds like cowardice of me to say this, but how much help will I really be?

Of course I will do my best.

I'm beyond peckish right now, and the night terrors are almost constant. But the one blessing is I don't remember them.

Oh. I won't be able to make it down this Easter as I've promised Hugh that I'll correct some of his papers for him because his sister is ill. I suppose that's being too much of a Good Samaritan, but he's always been so supportive of me, and lately I've been just a heap of bones that cries and says, "Sorry, I'm off to my room," because I've just been so out of sorts. Hugh is very sensitive to these things.

We'll have to do without each other this Easter, I suppose. I miss you, of course.

Yours, affec.
Michael.

27th March, 1917
Master Michael Ll-D.,

Yes, you are being a very bad boy.

I read and reread your letter again and again. There is no disput-ing its meaning. I should prefer to think that I am reading between the lines, but your intent is clear. You would like me to find some sort of dispensation for you, some excuse to avoid Public Schools Camp.

You must know that this is impossible. Which is perhaps why you didn't come right out and ask. There is nothing I could do to get you to do work behind the lines, as you express it. In fact, I would not want to. It's every young man's duty to serve The Empire. When I think of your dear brother — well, you know I can barely [unreadable], and he was the soul of goodness, of graciousness, he was a saint in the body of a sweet young man.

Yes, it breaks my heart to have to send you there. Yes, you are the nearest and dearest thing to me, and if anything was ever to hurt you, I would most certainly find little reason left for living. That is why you must go to Public Schools Camp and prepare yourself for this awful war, and we can only hope and pray that you will not be one of the lads who will die in their glory and never be old.

I think you understand that I do not love this war. No one does. But I love this country, and if you must grow up — and you must — then you must grow up an English gentleman.

You can see why I find it so frightening that you would ask for special treatment. Michael, nothing would ever make me lose respect for you, but this is the first instance when such a possibility has crossed my mind.

So, if not Easter, perhaps another time? We must see each other before your camp.

Yours, affec.
J.M.B.

1st April, 1917
Dear Uncle Jim,

I'm sorry for my last letter. I can see that it upset you deeply and that's the last thing I would ever wish to do.

You have my promise that I will go to Public Schools Camp and be the best little soldier that there ever was. Or the best little soldier I am capable of being, at any rate.

Yes, we must find a time and it seems to me that end of term for a few days is the only answer. I'm sorry that I have to sign off so soon; it's exam time and I want to be as brilliant as you expect me to be.

Yours, affec.
Michael.

10th April, 1917
Master Michael Ll-D.,

I think I have a solution, my dear. We will take a few days and go to Scotland. Surely, you could fit this in? We shall go fishing & Jack will be there with his wife-to-be, Gerrie, whom we have heard so much about.*

Apparently Jack's new soulmate is completely delightful, though I don't know whether I shall be able to address a word to her, as her family hates me. Jack has not said as much — he never would — but the furtive melodrama is now abundantly clear. The Scotch — for they deserve the dreadful malapropist pun when they conduct themselves like this — are terribly jealous when one of their own makes good. And I have made it terribly good by Scotch standards. Jack has not confessed this abiding hatred on the part of his new in-laws in so many words. It was, however, evident from the malignant manner in which they went on and on about Gerald du Maurier when we met them for tea. Well, we all love your uncle Gerald — and didn't he make the most marvellous Captain Hook? — but he is not to be her new father-in-law, I am. I can't bear this deliberate pettiness and I daresay I won't address one syllable to this vile woman, delightful though she may be. Were you at dinner with your charm & your easy warm smile, I'm sure it would make the evening slide down like oysters. Also we could go fishing, you and I — and Jack; no women — which would be a tonic for all of our souls. Think of it as a fishing trip.

Please say yes. I know you will.

Yours, affec.
J.M.B.

---

* Jack was Michael's second-oldest brother. He was in the navy, and met the nineteen-year-old daughter of a Scots banker named Gerald Gibb on shore leave. They were married on September 4th, 1917.

17th April, 1917
Dear Uncle Jim,

Yes, I think your idea for a fishing vacation will certainly fit into my schedule. I will smile and use every ounce of the Llewelyn Davies charm I can muster for the occasion.

I must confess this whole let's-go-fishing-and-visit-Jack-who-is-to-be-married business has given me nightmares. If only I were not capable of remembering them.

I must tell you now that I can't ever imagine myself getting married. Not because I am in any way repulsed by women. I find them mostly funny and relaxing. Boys are more exciting, of course, but women I find calming. They seem to understand the manner in which my mind works. But I don't think I have the proper personality for married life. My mood swings are quite unbearable for most people. In fact, you are the only one who seems capable of putting up with them. I suspect that's all right, isn't it? I mean you never married again, and you seem to muddle along without a feminine influence.

I suppose I'm putting off telling you about the dream.

The dream is about an endless honeymoon.

My wife's face and her person are not very clear in the dream. But she's wearing a nightgown in a horrible shade of pink. What happens in the dream is that there is a forbidding marriage bed in a small, dark room. The room has sea-green curtains and it always rains outside (being Scotland) so they are often drawn. There is nothing in the room but a bed and she is lying in it. I am terribly afraid of her for a very odd reason. It seems to me that she must have some sort of disease, and if I am to pull open her nightgown I will see it, and perhaps catch it. So I make up excuses. I go fishing all the time and sleep out on the rocks where it's cold and damp. The alarming thing is that I am unable to catch any fish. Yet I trull and trull constantly, my line bobbing in the murky water. Finally I understand that it is my honeymoon, and I must go home after all and make love to my diseased wife. The room is dark and I can hardly see her, and when I begin to open the covers of the bed I discover it is filled with fish! They are jumping and flapping about in agony. The bed is a mess, and the woman, whoever she was, is gone.

| 101

At that point I usually wake up screaming.

If nothing else, the dream is a signal that I'm not cut out for marriage. Do you think every boy is?

> *Yours, affec.*
> *Michael*

25th April, 1917
Master Michael Ll-D.,

We have never talked deeply of my marriage to Mary, and perhaps now is the time to do so.*

You have seen her on stage, so you are acquainted with her charm, wit, and beauty. I'm certain you can see why I would have been

---

* Barrie married Mary Ansell in 1894. She later divorced him and became Mary Canaan. The marriage lasted until 1909, when Mary admitted her adulterous relationship with Gilbert Canaan, a prominent barrister. Birkin suggests that Mary confessed at the divorce proceedings that she and Barrie had been effectively separated since 1902. Birkin also repeats some nasty gossip to the effect that Mary accepted Barrie's proposal when he appeared, for all intents and purposes, to be dying; he was ill and staying with his mother when he popped the question. It was rumoured that Barrie miraculously recovered immediately after Mary accepted his deathbed proposal. Thus she was saddled with him for fifteen long years.

infatuated with her. It was more than a treat to be able to marry the woman who was the marvellous star of so many delightful plays, a woman who was obviously in love with me, and we were certainly happy for as long as it was meant to be.

I must confess — and this topic must only be traversed between you and me — it was the physical side of our relationship that baffled me. I simply didn't understand it, and ultimately I wanted no part of it. My feelings for Mary were always warm and affectionate, and, yes, she understood me and my work. I very much enjoyed talking to her, and she was eternally sympathetic. When it came to the intimate side of things — in truth, the opportunity just never came up. It was not a dilemma of Faustian proportions from my point of view. I could see that Mary wished for much more than a passionate friendship. This hurt me at the time, but there was nothing I could do about it. When I started to notice that Mary was flirting, understandably, I suppose, with other men, I knew that the marriage could not continue. It's a shame, because we really were such good friends.

I tell you all this to assure you that certain people are just not designed for marriage. It may have something to do with the very nature of artists, their innate sensitivity. Or with being moody, as we both are. At any rate, I don't think you should trouble yourself with the idea of marriage yet. You are far too young and have much more important issues with which to concern yourself.

Maybe when you are actually catching fish, those nightmares of your unsuccessful trolling will disappear.

Yours, affec.
J.M.B.

There is another gap; the letters from 1917 have come to an end. They resume again after Public School Camp. There certainly must have been a number of letters from camp: what happened to them? Or was Michael's depression at camp so intense that he could not write? Or were the letters merely mundane greetings? We may never know. Anyway, when the letters resume, Michael has somehow survived his preparation for war. Barrie's letter below, in fact, seems to suggest that Michael has become a successful Etonian, and that the dark dreams of Roger, empty futures, and beds of fish, have vanished into thin air. Keep in mind that by the winter of 1918 Michael had nearly reached the age of enlistment and the war had not yet ended. Yet Barrie's letter contains nary a whiff of worry.

8th October, 1918
Master Michael Ll-D.,

   I am quite overjoyed to see my very favourite nephew has become such a powerful force in The Chronicle.* *I opened up my latest copy — with no warning from you, I might add. Such a heart-stopping surprise. To see that you are represented not only as a poet, but as editor, made this uncle terribly proud. I cuddled deep into my inglenook, as much as anyone might cuddle into that rocky, wooden enclosure, and read your work with feverish glee.*

   To say that I am intimidated by your talent is an understatement, my dear boy. Of course I have always respected your opinion in

---

* *The Chronicle* was the Eton school paper.

everything, and taken your advice whenever it was right, which is
always. Yet still, no matter how much effort I expend, even my darkest
dramas prove to have a sunny side, and my most serious thoughts are
too often dismissed by critics as sentimental claptrap. Perhaps it comes
from being a child at heart, but as the saying goes, one is always
remembered for what one dreads the most. And as much as I adore dear
Peter and his antics, it would be a cheerful surprise not to have every
104 | *new project of mine compared to it. You, on the other hand, have*
distilled your dark moods into poetry, & a poetry that chills the soul.
This is the reward for all your nights of terror, dear! For you have
made something of the fear that at times drove you nearly mad.
Inevitably, that is the artist's job. I suppose my brain will be forever
filled to the brim with perambulating pixies, and shall always dance
into fairyland, however serious my intentions. But you have the gift of
*exploring the deeper recesses of the human heart.**

---

* Michael's only surviving sonnet (written a year later, when he was nineteen) shows that, indeed, Barrie's analysis of his strengths as a poet was not exaggerated. Neither was Barrie's characterization of his adopted son's work as dark:

> *Throned on a cliff serene Man saw the sun*
> *Hold a red torch above the farthest seas*
> *And the fierce island pinnacles put on*
> *In his defence their sombre panopolies;*
> *Foremost the white mists eddied, trailed, and spun*
> *Like seekers, emulous to clasp his knees,*
> *Till all the beauty of the scene seemed one,*
> *Led by the secret whispers of the breeze.*
> *The sun's torch suddenly flashed upon his face*
> *And died; and he sat content in subject night,*
> *And dreamed of an old dead foe that had sought and found him*
> *A beast stirred boldly in his resting place*
> *And the cold came; Man rose to his master-height,*
> *Shivered and turned away; but the mists were round him.*

The photograph of you "in Pop" is too excruciating for words! This cannot be my Michael! You look positively imperious! I imagine countless young fags are wincing at this very moment. You don't look as if you would countenance the slightest infraction; I daresay you don't! But surely this cannot be the same sunhatted child who dug in the sand and ran screaming from eels? Doubtless you have been replaced by a ghost, the walking, talking, spanking image of a dignified and perilously handsome young man.

Your room at Adelphi is still here of course; it will not go away. Your reasons for not staying here on your last leave were more than exemplary; however, next holiday I will brook no argument. For what did I spend countless afternoon's searching Keitmans and Dwars for the perfect dresser? There it sits, a deserted bride, drawers open, embarrassingly hungry, always ready to receive whatever intimate apparel you may chose to store there.

If you don't visit me soon I will be heartbroken. That is typical, of course, of Old Uncles, to look out their windows at the Thames and be eternally heartbroken. I have laboured all my life not to be typical. Have all my efforts been for naught?

At any rate, I miss my handsome young man, whom I will resist calling beautiful because he is far to old to be addressed in such a manner. Oh willows & cranberries! Watermelons & bees! I shan't resist. And if some pimply undergraduate opens this letter you need only punish him roundly, which can only be fun.

If you do not visit this leave I will be inconsolable, my beautiful young man.

Yours, affec.
J.M.B.

What's interesting about Michael's answer is the distance that has grown between the two. How the tables have turned. Here Barrie has become the gushing schoolboy, and Michael the cold and heartless Public School tutor doling out brutal realities by the shovelful.

15th October, 1918
Dear Uncle Jim,

    I don't quite know what to say. I suppose I should have warned you about my impending editorship at The Chronicle, *but surely I am only a co-editor & that is not as melodramatic an event as you indicate.*

    I'm terribly pleased that you like my poetry; to compare it to your own work is silly. You were the one who once warned me that literature is not a bag of groceries, and that every artist's work must be considered separate even from their own extant creations. Of course I am complimented. To have the world's greatest living playwright, who also happens to be one's own uncle, go on at length about one's work, is very flattering.

    And I am flattered.

    As for Adelphi, Christmas is the time. I shall be there of course. How could I not?

    I must say that I am partly if not completely amazed by your singular ability to skip by one very important impending fact: I shall be called up soon. I only mention it because as much as I am prepared and resigned to my fate, it has been haranguing me; the dark moods are back. I wish I could think, as you do, that my poetry is a repository for all that madness. Unfortunately, there is no such neat solution. My dreams are more persistent than ever, and seem to be conspiring to convince me that I have not grown up at all, that I am still a terribly young, vulnerable, frightened boy.

You told me once that my dreams were sacred and that my child poet was wrapped up with them. You told me that if ever I was in terror you would listen. Please remember that I can't help the content of my dreams; of course one cannot censor one's nightmares. It is not for me to wonder what they mean, but in the telling I receive some release, and sometimes they seem to lose a bit of their power. Dear Uncle, it is important to me that someone knows about them, in that horrible instance that my dreams, or the remembering of them, drive me to some terrible distracted deed.

Please remember, when I recount this nightmare, that I am fully prepared to do my duty, and that George and his sacrifice are foremost in my thoughts. Also remember that I have seen little of Roger. It pains me greatly to say that when I did see him after Public Schools Camp, he informed me that he was having a great deal of fun playing his demented games with someone else. I know it shouldn't have hurt me at all to hear this, but I must honestly say it did. I will always be honest with you, Dear Uncle. Nevertheless I have rarely seen Roger and hardly ever talked to him, and yet he crops up in my dreams still. I wish I could say it was someone else, but the unmistakable squidgy face & steel-blue eyes are most certainly his.

So here it is.

In my nightmare, we are waiting in the trenches. It is the endless, dreary wait of the kind they told us to expect. They tell you about everything, so that you will be prepared, but the soldiers I have talked to say that the horror of it all is not quite what one expects. It is raining and very muddy. The landscape is sparse and almost unreal. The sky is very dark except for what seems an eternal sunset; something that cuts the bleak gray clouds in two, and hangs there like a crimson wound. We know that the waiting will be broken at any moment by guns and shouts and hot running blood, that we must be on the alert always. Roger, who is beside me, keeps nodding off, and I am terribly worried about him. Then, when we least expect it, comes the attack. All is hazy and shrouded in a fierce mist, but here and there is the face of a crazed Hun. Some of the faces resemble my enemies among schoolboys and tutors, among them Nitters and Grosshanks. This is not the horror. This is just a vague terror. Then I realize that I have lost Roger. I am running about the field, distracted and unbuttoned, like Lear on the heath, until I find him, like my Desdemona, lying gracefully supine on the ground. I am in horror of course & I run to him & he seems to be dead. But his wound? Where is it? I can see nothing for his skin is clear and soft & then I look at his mouth and where his jaw should be there is nothing. I am suddenly in the dream from before and when I reach down to touch my own mouth there is nothing and then I fall on him, completely, and my jaw, which is now just air, falls against empty space — it's as if I want to kiss him or give him resuscitation or both. Then the horror is over & I wake up in the midst of this kiss where there are no mouths.

I'm sorry to have written this, for the account somehow seems vile or obscene. That is a new aspect of my dreams, and of their ability to plague me. I am more ashamed of them than I ever was, and I can't seem to stop thinking about them. There is nothing you can do but *read. It's likely I'll have another dream to tell you about when I visit you in your inglenook and I'm certain you will listen, and not hate me for these demons I cannot control.*

See you at Christmas.

Yours, affec.
Michael

Nothing remains of Barrie's response, however one can only assume the sensitive playwright was deeply disquieted by his adopted son's disturbing dreams. But on November 11, 1918, the root of Michael's worries had been spirited away. The war was over. In fact, the final German surrender occurred precisely one day before he was scheduled to be called up. Considering the torture of anticipation that Michael endured, it's hard to imagine that he survived the whole ordeal unscathed. However, the joyous news was the occasion for a loving letter from Barrie. It seems that at last the two are emotionally joined again; their only argument is over how Michael should celebrate his good fortune.

15th November, 1918
Master Michael Ll-D.,

My blessed boy I am so happy for you! Darling, it will all be said now; everything. Of course I was terrifically frightened & and in agony to see you go. But how could I tell you that? How could I reveal that: to me, you will always be a little boy running from terrors both real and imagined, with a tender and all too responsive soul that must at all costs be guarded from adversity? Oh, how I wished to quote Sylvia's letter where she prompts me to protect you always, her very favourite & beautiful & most fragile child, from the slings and arrows of all that fortune unfortunately allows. If I had told you all this before your being called up, it would have made your fearful duty much more difficult. But now with this tremendous release, you can be the artist you were meant to be, and pursue the career you were destined for. There are no accidents, dear boy & God has saved you for one thing and one thing only: to change the world.

How marvellous to be able to say all this to you at last. We must celebrate after the opening. Please, please, let's have a big reunion this year at Christmas; promise me yes. Wish me luck with Mary Rose; *I think, in fact it's my very best play, truly, since* Peter. *As you said, I do that kind of thing very well.*

Yours, affec.
J.M.B.

25th November, 1918
Dear Uncle Jim,

I am ecstatic like you, of course. In another way I'm very calm though, because unlike you, I never really imagined myself going to war. Or instead I should say, I had imagined myself shot dead in the first few minutes or so.

We shall skip past your startling revelations about mother, though of course it does make some sort of sense I suppose & it is good for me to hear of her concern. Let's just say that — well, never mind. It hurts me sometimes to think of how much she worried over me, and

I actually don't know if I am up to the task of hearing it ever again.

Enough of that. I've made a decision. As you mentioned, I must celebrate & now I will tell you about a dream I've had for the last six months. I haven't revealed anything about it before. What would have been the use? No, I don't mean dream in the horrible sense of nightmares, no. It's the kind of dream other people have — and I'd never until this moment thought I'd had a right to wish or want or desire — but with this astonishing news there seems no reason not to. |111

What I would love more than anything, dear Uncle, is to travel to Paris and study there, the way Great Uncle George did. You know that it was there he studied drawing, and he was — as I am — a writer. The stories Uncle Gerald told me about his father's bohemian life inspire me greatly. Is it possible to feel that you know a place, even though you've never been there? I feel as if I know Paris, and can smell the flowers and the Seine, and taste the wine and just feel the very freedom of it all. I was thinking perhaps I could take a trip around the world and then alight in Paris for my studies. That would be my dream, dearest Uncle. It would be absolutely the most perfect present! Please let me hope that I am, like ordinary people, entitled to the kind of dream that isn't a terror in some way.*

I've never really begged for anything, but I hope your joy, intertwined with mine, can bring you to consider this.

Yours, affec.
Michael

---

*   George du Maurier, the Victorian novelist and cartoonist (who caricatured Wilde in his cartoons) based his best-selling novel *Trilby*, which features the classic archvillain Svengali, on his experiences in Paris.

25th November, 1918
Master Michael Ll-D.,

It's important for me to begin by telling you yet again how much I love you, because your letter touched me deeply. You will be pained by my answer.

Darling, of course you have the absolute right to dream, as anyone else does. You must have all sorts of fancies & delights — indulge yourself in them! What boy, young or grown, does not? But the idea of going to live in Paris is just that, a fancy. It bears so little relation to reality. How would I see you? How could you keep contact with your dear brothers? What about the fact that two of your brothers have been to Oxford, and your tutor expects you to go to Oxford, and, in fact, everyone is looking forward to you attending? What about the brilliant scholarly studies you've been making of modern poets, of A.E. Houseman and Rupert Brooke? Rupert Brooke was quite the star at Oxford, as you know, all they do is talk about him there. I'm sure that after you've been there for a very short time, they will be talking about you. A trip to Paris is always possible. Why at this particular time? A trip around the world will be a perfect present upon your graduation from Oxford. My boy, the most spectacular present we both have is that you are still alive, and will continue to be with us now, for many years to come.

Just so you won't pout and deny us the pleasure of your charm, I have something I know will excite you even more, dear boy. I have decided to buy you a motorcar. And so that you'll have something to do besides drive around in circles, I'm buying you a cottage in the country. Something small; no mansion. A quiet place which can be an escape during holidays and where you may write sonnets to your

*heart's content. I will come to visit, of course. Imagine you wearing
one of those spiffy little caps — all the young men have them — and
raising the dust! Why you shall have all the young women flirting
with you — a terrifying thought for both of us! — but it's quite
inevitable & we must resign ourselves to it all the same.*

*I'm so sorry I can't grant your wish, but I hope you will be content
with a house and a car. It may not be Paris, but it's better, as they say,
than losing at cricket.*

|113

*Congratulations again on your future. I can't wait until we can
start gossiping about Oxford.*

*Yours, affec.
J.M.B.*

*3rd December, 1918
Dear Uncle Jim,*

Oh, Uncle Jim, I'm in a horrible state!

*Of course I will love you & you are the dearest Uncle a boy could
ever have, and a house and a motorcar is more than lovely.*

*But I am also a selfish little poet child, and I did want terribly —
so much that I ache! — to travel to Paris and study. I know I should
be looking forward to Oxford. But it's terribly difficult looking forward
to something when you know that you should. Just the prospect of not
knowing a soul once again & you know how pathetic I am at making
friends.*

*I'm not going to say no to the house or the car, but I can't help
revealing that I'm disappointed.*

I'm not sleeping well again. I actually went to Hugh's door the

other night, completely asleep, and started banging on it and yelling
incoherently about Oxford.

We both know that when the terrors come, there is nothing to be
done, is there?

Let's not go to Scotland this Christmas, but I'm certain we shall
find something to do, even if it's simply lolling about Adelphi Terrace.

I hope this letter finds you well, and I'm sorry I'm not more
cheerful.

Yours, affec.
Michael

114|

One may wonder about the origins of Michael's fascination with Paris. Most likely it was born, as most adolescent fantasies are, from an overactive imagination. Wherever Michael's obsessions originated, he was not to forget them soon. Both Paris and Roger were at the forefront of his imaginings at this time. As it turns out, Michael was to meet Roger again at Oxford. In 1919, Roger invited Michael to a dinner party at Ottoline Morrel's house. Lady Morrel was the quintessential bohemian hostess, and a standard-bearer for the revolutionary bisexuality that characterized what has since become known as the Bloomsbury group. Michael's experience at Lady Ottoline Morrel's house party was the occasion for an intense epistolary disagreement with his Dear Uncle Jim. There seems to be less bile spilled here than in the previous letter of disappointment over living in Paris. In the following letters Michael and Barrie come as close as they ever would to sparring over ideas as adults and equals. It is the most stirring of dialogues: a debate between a younger man and an older one who love each other deeply, and still dare to differ.

9th May, 1919
Dear Uncle Jim,

I have so much to tell you. First of all, I must say that you were right, as of course you almost always are, because Oxford is not quite as horrible as I had imagined. Let's just say that the society is more welcoming than I had expected. I am not twelve years old anymore and that's a fact!

The first stupendous achievement is meeting up with Roger again. There was some rumour of him going to Cambridge, but who should I meet in my Plato seminar but the young man himself? Don't worry — as I know you will — I have calmed down about him and we have no plans for any games. Roger is always mischievous — he's trying to coax one of the old dons into playing his nasty dress-ups with him. Just to make the pompous old bookworm look ridiculous! He is very naughty, but of course it's impossible for me to be angry. Now, I know you don't approve of Roger, but certainly there's nothing wrong with me chatting with him in seminar; I daresay I shan't catch a microbe from just talking. I know that you will be pleased I'm not all alone here, and am going about in society.

Roger is friends with the several flamboyant Cambridge types — you may or may not have heard of them — and he insisted that we go to a house party at Lady Ottoline Morrel's home on the weekend. I was shy, but also thrilled to be invited. I had heard of Lytton Strachey obviously — he and his brother are now and then down at Oxford. But I had never heard of Lady Ottoline or Dora Carrington.*

---

* Ottoline Morrel was an overeducated society lady who enjoyed holding gossipy parties in her home at 44 Bedford Square. At these gatherings, the Bloomsbury crowd held court, flirted, and planned their assignations. The Apostles were a rather

Lady Ottoline's house is very strange, though welcoming and utterly comfortable. It's filled to the brim with flowers and there are paintings on the walls — some of them by Dora. Can you imagine anyone painting directly on a wall? There's something about a frame, isn't there, which gives one a sort of assurance. Well, Dora paints her own frames, which seems somehow deliciously sinful.

They're a very bizarre lot, but also stimulating. They frighten me somewhat. The men all act a bit womanish, and the women exactly like men. Lady Ottoline, for instance, is frighteningly aggressive. She pounds about like a disgruntled gardener. She's also enormously fun. I've never met a woman like her. Dora (she likes to be called Carrington) is boyish too, but much more refined. She and Lytton Strachey are husband and wife; they make a very odd combination. When we arrived Lady Ottoline marched directly over to us and took Roger & me by the arms and propelled us into the sunroom, where all & sundry were chatting, & announced in booming tones: "Here they are, two adorable Oxford Embryos!" Everyone laughed. At first I thought they were making fun of us, which they were, in a way. But it turns out that Lytton calls all the young university sort embryos — you know, not yet fully formed? At any rate, the laughter made every-one — oddly — comfortable and people were talking to us right, left

---

radical and somewhat mysterious group, ostensibly a debating society at Cambridge. Lytton Strachey (b. 1880), one of the leaders of this nefarious clan, was a notorious pederast and close friend to Virginia Woolf. Strachey's claim to fame is a rather thin volume entitled *Eminent Victorians*, which caused a scandal in Edwardian England. A somewhat nasty man and an early self-styled gay liberationist, he married the equally sexually ambiguous Dora Carrington, who apparently out of misguided love for him put up with his intergenerational carryings-on. Strachey's reputation has become exaggerated lately, due to a bloated biography written by Michael Holroyd, yet another academic who shamelessly promotes the gay agenda.

& centre. I felt very popular. Quite the man-about-town. You would have been proud of me. You know how I usually am at parties. I'm certainly capable of being charming but it's always a trial.

Lytton took quite a shine to me. I know he did because Roger told me afterwards that he thought me charming and intelligent, what Lytton calls a rare combination. I daresay I can't see a thing wrong in being flattered. He seems a very nice gentleman. Terribly tall — almost a giant — he pots about in very unflattering hats, rather like the sunhat you're always going on about, the one that I wore as a child. His manner of speaking is alarming at first. Quiet and almost like a girl's really & and he has a very sarcastic drawl. At first one thinks, why listen to him? Then you do, & soon he has you in fits of laughter & you're not certain exactly why. Somehow it doesn't matter.

This letter has gone on for ages so I'll stop now. We shall be visiting them again next weekend, and I can't wait. I'm sure there'll be more scandalous gossip to report.

To think that there are such fascinating, outrageous people in the world! I'm sure you meet them every day in the theatre, but for me it's quite a fresh experience.

This society is perhaps a pale replacement for Plato, which I know I should be perusing, but it seems ever so much more important right now.

Please don't chastise me, dearest uncle, for neglecting my studies. I'm getting about and having fun, which, as you know is most alien to my nature!

I promise to write you again after the next weekend.

Yours, affec.
Michael

20th May, 1919
Master Michael Ll-D.,

I daresay this letter won't reach you in time; most likely you'll receive it after your second weekend with the avant-garde.

Certainly you are old enough to make your own decisions and spend your spare time as you wish, but I can't think of a more disagreeable group of people with whom to spend a weekend.

Doubtless you will think my disapproval of Mr. Strachey is due to his review of What Every Woman Knows *from twelve years ago. But contrary to popular opinion, playwrights do survive even the most mean-spirited critics. Strachey was then — and is still occasionally now — writing for that spiteful* Spectator,* *which is simply crawling with Stracheys. There are hundreds of them. I find Stracheys all rather repellant. It's not just their unsettling visages, but the drafty old house that they have owned for so many years. It is most certainly haunted. I suppose one can't hold a man responsible for his surroundings, but it often says something about a person to glance up at at his ceiling. Does it perhaps need a bit of painting — always excusable — or is it a sort of crumbling black hole like the ceilings at the Strachey digs? At any rate they are a dire group, in need of better grooming (rumour has it they are Jews, not that this matters).*

I'm sure Mr. Strachey is very proud & fancies he has vanquished me in public. I only remember his critique because it was so ill-informed it made me laugh. He called me the "master of theatrical bluffing" which was, I suppose, written tongue firmly planted in cheek. What he

---

* *The* Spectator *was a political weekly, edited by Lytton Strachey's cousin, St. Loe Strachey. It was an extremely popular magazine, but rather frowned upon by some, because of its pompous, arch tone. Strachey was a regular, but far from devoted, contributor.*

meant to say, I imagine, was that my plays are flimsy artifices, light-weight sugary confections. Something, had he bothered to write a review, Mr. Shaw could have said rather better.* What Mr. Strachey ignores is that theatre is all bluff. Anyone who is not aware of that shouldn't waste our time by calling himself a theatre critic. But I suppose when one's great-uncle owns the magazine, one can call oneself quite anything one wishes.

The only reason I mention this silly detail is so you'll know that I | 119 have accepted Strachey's barbs over the years with equanimity. It bears no relation to my animosity to him — in fact I have no animosity, I just think he is a thorough reprobate & undesirable character. It's no surprise that Roger has introduced you to him; Strachey is the sort to whom a silly boy like Roger would be drawn.

You may visit anyone you like; I'm certainly not about to try and stop you. I know I'm too late to discourage your from your second weekend. Let me see if I can wean you from a third.

Mr. Strachey is an unhealthy influence. He is the sort of person who has become notorious, especially after the well-known trials of Mr. Wilde. I'm certain, in fact, that he fancies himself a Wilde-like character and models himself after that disgraced man. You're too young to ponder what any of this means. Wilde and Strachey are, quite simply, a malignant influence on the minds and morals of boys. Their ideas and practices lead to the pollution of body and soul, rest assured of that.

I can't see how you can avoid Roger, and if it gives you pleasure to see a familiar face then certainly chat away. These decadent house parties where pictures are painted directly on the walls — I think

---

* Shaw's disdain for *Peter Pan* was infamous. He claimed it was "foisted on children by the grown-ups."

you're absolutely right to be suspicious of the lack of frames — and people act contrary to nature are not the place for a proper English gentleman. Your soul is naturally pure, no matter the nightmares that torture you. Surely you can find other friends your own age with whom you will have more in common and who will not manipulate you for their own base ends.

Hoping this finds you well, and breathlessly awaiting your reply, I am always,

Yours, affec.
J.M.B.

These two letters crossed in the mail, for Michael's letter betrays no recognition of his guardian's admonitions.

22nd May, 1919
Dear Uncle Jim,

Well I must say the second house party quite outdid the first, if such a thing might be imagined. Upon arrival, Roger and I were immediately cornered by Mr. Strachey, and herded on to the sunporch. Though I can't say I minded. He's certainly a pleasure to converse with, despite his bizarre nature.

The ideas that man has! I was struck dumb at some points, and I'm sure I sounded a perfect prat. When one encounters a monologist who is so brilliant and even slightly obscene — in the most tasteful way, he never utters a nasty word — it makes you feel a bit like a babbling idiot. I know he's still terribly impressed with me, I can tell.

First of all, he has this marvellous way of dismissing people, which is rather cruel — but then again he's not really dismissing them at

*all. You can quite see people before you when he describes them. I must
read his* Eminent Victorians. *I know it has everyone talking.
Painting pictures, he calls it. "I'll paint you a picture of him," he says.
For instance, at one point when Lady Ottoline was being particularly
aggressive with us all — she put on a gramophone record of some
Arabian chant & demanded everyone dance about like harem girls
whilst holding hands — Lytton whispered to me, "She reminds me of
a crimson tea-cozy trimmed with hedgehogs," which I know sounds
nonsensical but absolutely captures her essence if you'd only met her.
Then he launched into a monologue about Maynard Keynes, whom he
seems to despise for some reason. Well, he made me blush. He called
Keynes "a safety bicycle with genitals," which just sent us all giggling.
I hardly know what he meant by it but it was very embarrassing &
terrifically funny. Then one of the Stephen sisters complained of a
stain on her dress & Lytton said something which is absolutely
unrepeatable, but made us all laugh ourselves silly again, hiding our
faces in our hands — like the schoolgirls in* The Mikado!

    *He can be serious too, which is the other half of his charm. He says
I would make a marvellous Apostle — I don't know if you've heard of
that society — which I took as quite a compliment. Apparently it's a
secret Cambridge organization where gentleman, and some women too,
gather to recite poetry and talk. It all has to do with George Moore,*
whom Lytton absolutely idolizes and whom I absolutely must *read.
Contemplation of beauty and [unreadable], very Platonic.*

    *The things Lytton said about Rupert Brooke! Something quite
unrepeatable about Mr. Brooke's naked swims, and the state in which
the handsome young man would always arise from the water. For some*

---

*   George Moore was a philosopher at Cambridge and contemporary of Wittgenstein.

reason Lytton despises Mr. Brooke! Can you imagine anything more odd? To criticize the most celebrated of our war poets? I was scandalized of course, but I couldn't stop listening. He said that Mr. Brooke was a dreadful flirt and a puritan, which he called absolutely the worst combination. Then he suggested Mr. Brooke didn't die a hero in battle but was bitten by a diseased fly! This I couldn't believe, but Vanessa and Virginia confirmed it was true, and they seem very sweet. He also mentioned something about Mr. Brooke and choirboys which was simply so dreadful that, well, I couldn't believe it. How it made Roger and me laugh!

Shall I tell you what I've been thinking about my terrors, about my dreams & sleepwalking & obsessions? Could it simply be a case of being bored? I shan't paint myself as overly intelligent, but I am bright enough to need quite a bit of intellectual stimulation. I wonder if, when I don't get it, I turn inward. What impressed me most of all was the sheer gaiety of the occasion. I wasn't bored for one minute and I slept like a baby after.

I feel a bit guilty after lolling about with these very witty, idle people. Especially Lytton. I remember once you telling me that when a young man feels guilty about something then the young man is probably guilty and should stop.

Or am I just growing up?

We always knew this growing up business would be a frightening thing!

Yours, affec.
Michael

1st June, 1919
Master Michael Ll-D.,

Well, I had a feeling this might happen, dear boy.

At one point you might truly fall in with the wrong crowd and it would be up to your dear Doddering Old Uncle to rescue you. In a way, I'm not sorry that our last letters crossed in the mail. It just proves that you are a decent chap who has quite outgrown his Uncle's advice. Your letter shows me that know very clearly the difference between right and wrong, and I must give myself some of the credit for your discernment.

I won't waste a lot of time denouncing Mr. Strachey, and repeat my last letter. You indict him quite well in your own missive. I am returning your letter with this post suggesting that you read it again.

Of course you know that Mr. Strachey is an evil, obscene, and petty individual. The tidbits of wit he tossed your way were nothing more than gossip of the vilest variety, lies laced with the arsenic of bitterness. You said that you felt that you were doing evil by spending time with such a layabout. I couldn't have said it better.

I haven't read his book, I don't intend to, and I don't think you should either. It's nothing more than mean-spirited hearsay about upright and virtuous individuals. Of course no one imagines our predecessors were perfect — who is? — but his book, which I daresay I would not finish anyway, throws dirty bathwater on a whole era, which is foolhardy, to say the least.

The one thing I will waste time in decrying, in no uncertain terms, is Mr. Strachey's attitude to Rupert Brooke. * Nothing more neatly*

---

* Barrie's proprietary tone concerning the matter of the poet Rupert Brooke, is prophetic. Brooke was the author of several much loved odes to the young men who encapsulates Strachey's disgusting, ill-informed opinions. It is self-evident to any right-thinking person that Rupert Brooke is our nation's hero. I forbid you ever to say another word against him. To speak against Rupert Brooke is to speak against your country, and yes, against your brother George. I suppose if Rupert Brooke was bitten by a mosquito then so was George? When of course we know they both died heroes doing their duty & serving king and country. Such absolute sacrilege. This is what Strachey is all about: dragging young men from their duty, from serious thoughts. Don't mention that man and contemplation in the same sentence. It is difficult, in fact, for me to believe that he has ever contemplated anything.

I'm severe because this kind of claptrap deserves severity. If you need stimulation I'm sure you can get it from a good game of cricket, or a good pull at fishing or, I daresay, from a mountain hike with myself or Peter or Jack. Conversation is for the good-natured dissemination of ideas & opinions, not for the purpose of spreading lies and maliciousness that tears at the very fabric of our culture, manliness & godliness.

Enough of all that.

No, you will not have anything to do with the Apostles. I forbid it. There's no point in you even thinking about them as they won't have

---

died in The War To End All Wars. One, of course, famously begins — "If I should die, think only this of me: that there's some corner of a foreign field/That is forever England." Unfortunately, Strachey was right and Barrie was wrong about one ultimately minor detail. Brooke was felled by a fatal mosquito bite and died in bed, not, as legend would have it, on the field. This, however, does not make him any less the patriot. Nevertheless, contemporary historians, including Paul Delaney in his book *The Neo-Pagans*, have seen fit to drag Brooke's reputation through the mud by suggesting he was a repressed homosexual. Delaney actually sees fit to quote in full a very tawdry letter in which Brooke unabashedly confesses losing his virginity to another boy.

anyone from Oxford anyway. Suffice it to say that they are a depraved society led by the immoral Mr. Strachey. Read George Moore if you like, though I think he's highly overrated by that bizarre crowd.

That's all for now. I apologize for my severity, but then I don't. For you have already been severe with yourself, as you most certainly should have been.

Yours, affec.

J.M.B.

17th June, 1919
Dear Uncle Jim,

I am duly chastised by both your letters & feel quite embarrassed that I sent two letters without hearing from you. I'm such a silly ninny sometimes! I hope you can forgive me.

There are no more weekends with Lady Ottoline Morrel at any rate; she has cancelled them due to sickness. I daresay you're right and they're all sick anyway. How can I argue with your articulate critique of that wayward crowd? I suppose I am bitter about it all, but right now I'm quite simply so tired I don't know what I feel.

It's amazing how quickly these depressions come upon me for no discernible reason. I find I can barely right [sic] this letter, much less play cricket or even go for a walk or [unreadable]. Roger depresses me these days, too, and unless one of my tutors begins to inspire me, I will once more begin to wonder why I'm here.

I know it's all about my duty, so I won't talk about that.

I tried to write a sonnet the other day but I couldn't move my pen.

Sometimes I think I'm a bit withered by all your reasonableness, dear Uncle, but I suppose that's why I love you.

It's all very depressing. So there's no point in my writing a letter really. I'm certain I'll be down on the holidays, and we can talk more then.

Yours, affec.
Michael

Nearly a month passed. Behind the good-natured sparring of equals that we see in these letters there was a fundamental problem. Michael and his adoptive father were growing apart, and it must have been terrifying to both of them. Michael was at the age when he might act without his Uncle's permission. This is exactly what happened in 1919 when Michael and Roger Senhouse disappeared for what we might presume was a pretty wild weekend in Paris. It wasn't so much the incident that angered Barrie, it was the renewal of Michael's demands to be able to live in the city of love. Michael's dependence on Barrie is evident even in these final letters. And as the fragile and tender trust that connected them was gradually broken, Michael experienced a loneliness that may very well have led to his friendship with Buxton, and ultimately to his death. The following two letters are crucial in that process, and mark the end of what I call the Later Eton Letters.

10th July, 1919
Dear Uncle Jim,

So by now you know, because Nico has spilled the beans. Yes, we're off! Senhouse, Boothby, Burt, and me — we're the four musketeers!
Uncle darling, we had the most ripping time! You can't imagine

what it was like. Well, of course you can. You were young and visited Paris once, didn't you? What they say about Paris being a sinful place is just rot. It's terrifically fun, that's all, and chock full of adventure. Everything was made so much easier by my fluent French. I was so happy to discover that I can actually survive. I'm certain that they knew I was English, but no one spit at me, the way they spit at Anglos with offensive accents, and we were served all our meals and absinthe with nary a rude incident.

Boothby is a bit of a prig when it comes to travelling, but I suppose someone must be sensible. Roger, of course, wants always to run off and cause trouble, and Burt tends to be sullen, which means that I'm comfortable around him when I'm moody.

We wanted to see the Peace Procession of course; in fact, it was our excuse for going there. As we had imagined, the crowds were enormous & a bit frightening; we couldn't actually see a thing, so Roger bounded up into a tree & ultimately we realized this was the only way we would actually see the parade. It was quite fun because the soldiers looked so handsome and people were acting terribly French, kissing each other and dancing about.

When it came to evening we had to find a place to stay so I suggested the Hotel Meurice, because you had recommended it. Well the sleepy man is still behind the counter but there was not a room to be had, because of the celebrations, I suppose, and it was a very cool fall night and I certainly didn't fancy sitting out in the park. Roger was game for anything. The sleepy concierge recommended a Turkish bath which he assured us was always open & usually had vacancies.

I daresay a Turkish bath is the most decadent thing in the world. Everything is tiled with several rather exotic mosaic designs. There's a

*gigantic pool of lukewarm water and places where people tap them-
selves with birches — I don't quite know why, I suppose it's to
stimulate the skin — and there's steam everywhere. The room was very
small & only two could sleep there comfortably but it was the last
room left. So what Roger decided to do was very naughty! He had
heard that the boy prostitutes sleep four to a room: two sleeping at one
time while the other two roam the streets. So we took turns sleeping. It
really was quite an adventure. All my feelings of affection for Roger
have gone away — he seems a bit of a Svengali to me now. I couldn't
help noticing, as we took our steam and then slept, that he's built
quite differently from me! I remember when we used to go swimming
naked & I would be shy, mother would say, "Don't worry dear all little
boys look the same," but of course they don't. Roger is a very large boy.
I tried not to feel inadequate. When it was our turn to wander we saw
the strangest sights. There were boys on the streets wearing lipstick and
women even more masculine than Lady Ottoline Morel! One woman
was even wearing a man's tie and tails!*

*This outing has fired my imagination about Paris and what it
would be like to live there. I know I shouldn't mention it, Dear Uncle,
but I must! I have such a longing to live there. I'm terribly unhappy
at Oxford. It's not the place where I was meant to be. I wish I could
explain why, exactly. I think it's because — and surely you must
identify — everyone is so grown-up and serious here, and no one
laughs or plays jokes. They all seem to think that's what being grown-
up means — that is, being boring. Staying in Oxford any longer will
drive me mad. I'm not a scholar, I'm a poet and an artist. My soul
needs to wander. Please Uncle, please, let me go to Paris. Simply
think how pleasant it would be to be rid of my ceaseless nagging*

about the topic!

The frightening thing is that even though I'm not plagued by nightmares at the present time (and I had none in Paris, which is a good sign, I slept soundly on Roger's massive warm chest) something dreadful is happening to me. There's a vacantness, a deadness about my life that reminds me of my first days at Eton. There's no use in saying it will go away. I think part of the problem is that when I have a taste of freedom I suddenly see what I'm missing. I feel that if I stay in Oxford I'll be moving through a grey cloud all the time. It's almost as if Oxford is the trenches, the dreaded trenches that I thought I had been saved from by the Armistice.

| 129

Please say yes, Uncle.

I'll not bother you any more with my pleadings, but you know how important this request is to me.

Yours, affec.
Michael

19th July, 1919
Master Michael Ll-D.,

I am very angry with you. I suppose we shall have to talk about it when you come down. This letter will be brief and to the point.

I don't mind that you absconded to Paris for the weekend, it's the kind of mess that undergraduates get themselves into, and all your adventures sound typical. But your persistent requests for a life in Paris — to call them childish and irritating would be an understatement. I shall not give you permission to leave Oxford and if you leave I will consider you have betrayed your mother, George's memory, and me.

I can't play nursemaid anymore. The truth is you must take your medicine.

Yours, affec.
J.M.B.

12th August, 1919
Dear Uncle Jim,

I'm writing you even though I feel too listless to hold a pen.

I will do whatever you say, but I feel that a voice which I long to preserve is dying inside me, and that is the difficult part. There is an aspect that won't let that part of me die and that is somehow dangerous.

Sometimes even during the day I feel like I'm missing part of my face again.

It's my mouth.

Maybe I simply don't see the use of talking anymore.

I can't drag this pen across the paper another time. Not in a proper way.

I won't leave Oxford, my duty is here.

Yours,
Michael

The significance of this exchange cannot be underestimated, especially in light of the final set of letters. It's also important to note that this is the only surviving letter from Michael to Barrie in which he signs it simply "Yours" with no adjective of affection. Now, admittedly, the term "Affectionately yours" had already been abbreviated in a business-like way to "Yours, affec." But since "affec." was an important part of his official epistolary goodbye to his adopted father, it seems particularly poignant to view the naked "Yours" here. That Michael was sinking into a depression is abundantly clear. Barrie was not completely oblivious to his nephew's symptoms, as the later letters indicate.

LAST LETTERS

The following letters were all mailed during the summer and fall of 1920, except for the final letter which was mailed in late March, 1921. These are letters of farewell, though not self-consciously so. The writers are quite simply and tragically speaking at cross purposes (or in code) or not to each other at all. It is through these letters that we see how difficult and ultimately irrelevant it is to classify the affection this man and boy had for each other. To call their mutual feeling familial love seems inadequate, to call it erotic passion would be to assign to it a physicality which is nowhere in evidence. But it is unbearably poignant (for me, at least) to witness the gradual disintegration of this unique relationship. From this point on Michael and Barrie desperately strain to reach each other, while at the same time they might as well be addressing the air. Reading Michael's attempts to tell Barrie about his new obsession (young Rupert Buxton) is heart-rending. It is not simply that Barrie doesn't listen. He is afraid to hear. In a very real way (at least when it comes to discussing the important issues in his life) Michael has, in effect, lost his mouth.

25th April, 1920
Master Michael Ll-D.,

I have been disturbed by the unhappy tone of your recent letters. It certainly seems to me that you could use some perking up. I'm going to suggest this summer that instead of coming to Adelphi — not that I don't wish to have you, of course — that you take a rest cure with Dr. Maurice Craig.

You will be impressed, I'm sure, to know that he worked with Rupert Brooke before that famed young man marched off and became our nation's hero. Dr. Craig is very well respected, though his methods do sound a bit bizarre to the uninitiated. He's had surprising results. Brooke was in a funk, not unlike yours & in no time he was doing his duty and saving The Empire.

The treatment is called the fill-up cure by those who have taken it, and apparently it works like a charm. You begin by filling yourself up with food. You eat practically all the time, and lie around idly. This is apparently the cure for any seriously introspective condition. One becomes energized by all the calories and immensely cheered up. It's important to mention that the doctor, unlike the fashionable psycho-analysts that are so much the rage these days, doesn't allow you to confess your worries and concerns. He encourages you to keep them bottled up. I suppose it's all part of the filling process. Finally, you are injected with a drug that represses the baser instincts. We all know those urges can be troubling at times, and are best gotten rid of permanently, I should think.

I won't force you to take a cure if you do not want to. This doctor seems the best of the bunch, and has had smashing luck with some of England's finest young poets in the past.

Tell me if you'd like me to make an appointment for you.
I am still,

> *Yours, affec.*
> *J.M.B.*

1st May, 1920
Dearest Uncle,

It's very kind of you to be so concerned about me. I don't know if I shall be able to take a rest cure this summer, as I'm going to be very busy. That is to say, I'm significantly behind in my studies. So I would be a very bad sort if I didn't stay here and work, wouldn't I? So of course that is what I shall do.

It's interesting that you should mention Rupert Brooke. First of all, because I've met another undergraduate named Rupert, who seems to be a nice person. Or perhaps I should say he is a quiet person. Someone more of my nature than Roger. Rupert Buxton is his name. But I won't go on about him until I've got to know him better, for that has most certainly backfired in the past.

Oddly enough, I've been thinking a lot about Rupert and of course, the person who was our own Rupert Brooke, my dear brother George. I've been plagued by the idea that they died for us & because of us & here I was all the time being a nasty little Etonian whelp & what did I know of his sacrifice? It doesn't seem to me that it's right that I should be able to live on and he, not. Why should that be? You may say he died so I could live, but if this is true, then what am I? How could I ever live up to him? I haven't, obviously. My life seems pretty worthless right now.

Then I look around me at the other esteemed undergrads and they look rather dead. A bit like walking corpses actually. They go to seminars & cricket matches & God knows what else. I can't imagine what they see in their future. I've seen some of them flirting shamelessly with waitresses and barmaids which I simply can't see myself doing.

Then it seems to me that perhaps it was not just George and Rupert Brooke and all the rest who died, but a part of all of us.

I hope this doesn't sound like utter rot. If it does, please ignore it.

My theory is that the human species is of one mind. It's a kind of Darwinian idea that one portion of humanity can't be killed off and endure the tortures of the damned without the others somehow enduring it too. Could it be possible that our whole generation died in the war, not just the ones who died a physical death?

At any rate, it feels sometimes as if everyone is dead here. It would certainly explain the warmth of my tutor's smile (i.e. non-existent).

Wish me luck as I bury myself in my books.

Yours, affec.
Michael

10th May, 1920
Master Michael Ll-D.,

All right my dear, sweet boy. I am going to have to be very firm with you. I've been talking to friends about you, and, believe it or not, to Mary, and her advice is always true.

I've been indulging you, it seems, but only been out of love.

It is because our natures are so incredibly similar that we have grown into such close friends. It's one thing to sympathize and *encourage a chum, quite another to lead him into bad habits. I fear that I have been far too lenient about letting you wallow in your depressive tendencies. This behaviour is not at all good for you and must stop this instant!*

I read your last letter all about feeling sad about dear George. Of course we are all deeply wounded by his death, and will forever be so. However, George has been dead for five years. For myself, it was visiting his grave — remember when all and sundry du Maurier relatives thought me such a melancholy & melodramatic uncle? I knew that if I visited George's grave I would be finished with any morbidness once and for all.

You must finish with it too, darling. These are morbid thoughts. Instead of sitting by the fire sulking, and not studying — your Uncle knows everything; I was once an undergraduate too you know — you might consider taking a leave.

I've taken the liberty of renting an island. Yes, an island. But it's not quite as grand as it sounds and it's only for a week. It's off the Scottish coast — where else — and perfectly beautiful and quiet. It's called Eileen Shona, and we can fish there to our heart's content. We must go, with Nico, his two friends Audrey* and Evan, & if you wish, Roger. I've momentarily tossed aside all my prejudices against him, because he is your friend, and decided to have him along too. Warn him that I shall be contrary, just in case I can't bring myself to address a word to him. I will have him along. You know what that means.

You need to rise up out of this terrible emotional malaise that's

---

*   Audrey Lucas was the daughter of Barrie's close friend, author E.V. Lucas. She was two years older than Michael.

eating away at you. I absolutely refuse to indulge it anymore.

Please don't accuse me of being heartless for loving you desperately and renting you an island.

So what do you think?

Yours, affec.
J.M.B.

21st May, 1920
Dear Uncle Jim,

Now I'm in a state. I'm finding it very difficult to make a decision.

I shan't lie to you uncle, even if that means admitting to my depressive moments now and then, so I must tell you that Rupert has invited me to go hiking this summer.

It's a dilemma certainly, because I know that, for him, it's an important invitation.

Yes, I suppose I've fallen for him, but not in the way I fell for Roger at Eton. I'm much more grown up now and my affections are more intellectual. You see, Rupert is terribly intelligent, in fact more intelligent than me. With Roger, I was constantly pushing him to read, but now it's Rupert who pushes me.

I must warn you that Boothby and one of my tutors dislike him. They think he's a depressive character. That's not true at all. He just thinks about things. I daresay it's his dark hair and eyes, and the way he slouches about. He's very tall and slender, and just as different from Roger as night is from day. His face isn't squidgy, but his lashes are dangerously long.

He's introduced me to Massenet. Have you heard of him? I think

the only French opera composer I have ever listened to besides
Offenbach is Messager — is Bizet Spanish? — I always forget.
Everyone in Paris was singing and humming his "Philomel Waltz" from
Monsieur Beaucaire, *an opera based on an American novel.*
Apparently Massenet lived a very long time and was terribly popular
before the war, though now apparently he's fallen out of fashion. We've
been listening to Werther *late at night when the lights are low and*
it's absolutely heart-wrenching. I'm quite flabbergasted that Rupert | 139
feels exactly the same way about music as I do. It seems to me that I
can travel inside a piece of music and almost never come out, as if the
music consumes me; it's like taking a drug, I would imagine. At any
rate this aria is called "Pourquoi me reveiller," which quite literally
translates as "Why Awaken Me?" & of course Werther is talking about
being awakened by love — a love which must remain unrequited. I
must say this has a corollary in my own life; feeling awakened and
aroused by joy, but which so often leads to decadence or to unhealthy
associations. I must admit that I too sometimes wonder why love, or
joy, or beauty bothers to awaken me, since it all seems so hopeless.
When we listen to this music we cry, Rupert & I, for hours. It's not
at all like Young Werther, *that stuffy novel by Goethe. Or maybe I*
just had a bad tutor — it was Nitters! It's immediate and we sort of
dissolve together. At times we listen to the music and it's as if we're
hypnotized & can't remember what happened at all.

I'm certain that you'll side with my tutor, as usual, and tell me
this is all very unhealthy, but Rupert's all there is for me now and I
won't give him up! I won't! I'm stamping my feet! Rupert Buxton is
different from any other boy I've ever met, but you needn't like him,
of course, and that's perfectly all right too.

But since he wants to go hiking this summer I have to consider his wishes too, because he is my new friend.

Yours, affec.
Michael

4th June, 1920
Master Michael Ll-D.,

Don't imagine you can predict my reaction, young man. I might surprise you.

I'm not going to tell you that you mustn't see this Rupert Buxton character. I will say that at this time, it seems that the two of you are encouraging each other's more morbid impulses by listening to Massenet. This cannot be healthy for either of you. Just remember that Massenet is a very decadent composer, which is why he has fallen out of fashion. Shaw said a very funny thing about Werther, calling him a lovelorn tenor whose only dramatic moment came when he shot himself. The rest of the opera, apparently, is all morbid depressiveness.

Despite operatic differences, I daresay I would invite Rupert with us to Eileen Shona but I hardly know him & as I've already asked Roger, and he's accepted, it would be terrifically awkward without you. He's asked if he can bring his dog & since generally I love dogs I said yes.

Now that Roger has confirmed, as have Nico & friends, and we have a hound to help us fish, I don't see how you can say no.

We shall find sun at Eileen Shona. I paid good money for that island, and I was guaranteed sunshine.

We'll pick you up a week from Friday in your own motorcar — which, playing my part as Dear Uncle, I am obligated to remind you *that you never use! — and if you're not packed and ready for our week-long trip, Nico and I shall take out guns and shoot ourselves, which, I'm sure, will be of dramatic interest, if not to Shaw, then to your fellow undergrads at Oxford.*

Yours, affec.
J.M.B.

Michael went on the vacation that summer. We know this, because there are pictures of him and Barrie sunning themselves and catching fish. But that the week was somewhat of a bust is evident, if we read between the lines of Barrie's next letter to Michael.

20th July, 1920
Dear Michael,

It's finally over. You have got a fine sonnet out of it too! It moves me greatly to watch the way you can turn a rainy week into a misty poem!

I certainly learned quite a lot about dog keeping. The fact that you and Roger adore fishing in the rain much more than I do meant that I also learned a lot about clock-golf.* I am incapable of winning! All I have to say about the portraits you made of me is that I could not possibly look like that. I shall always insist that I am a sweet little boy, or a dangerous young man, but certainly not the wizened old Scotch monument which you portray — oh so accurately, I fear — in your portraits.

---

* I have done my best to research clock-golf. From what I can discover, it is a putting game that can be played alone.

Roger seems the type who needs prodding in everything. But there is obviously a grain or two of affection left between the two of you. Why not pursue it?

It seemed that you spent more time with Audrey than with Roger. At least that's what a handsome young spy named Nico tells me. What were you and Audrey whispering about? You are perfectly within your rights not to tell me, of course. I'm only your old Uncle.

Yours, affec.
J.M.B.

5th August, 1920
Dear Uncle Jim,

We were talking about Paris.

So that you don't start worrying again, I must tell you that Audrey is a sensible girl — it seems to me that all girls are, or all the nice ones at least — and she quite talked me out of any and all fairy tales that were still dancing in my head about that place.

The holiday was the sweetest effort on your part to cheer me up and set me right & and of course it worked. You need have no fears about me uncle. I daresay you expend an incredible amount of energy these days worrying about my state of mind. This became absolutely clear to me during our fateful weekend. It's most certainly my fault for upsetting you with my dreams — both the nightmare and the hopeful variety. As Audrey pointed out, it's perhaps my dreams of Paris that fuel my nightmares. It's really all a matter of calming myself down and leading a more adult life. I can't imagine that Mr. Rupert Buxton helps with that, so I shall probably drop him too.

I can't bear to see you worry about me any more. It brings up *memories of mother, about whom I vowed I wouldn't obsess ever again. So stop.*

Yours, affec.
Michael

7th September, 1920
Master Michael Ll-D.,

I knew that I could ferret that bit of information out of you. Audrey is a lovely girl, and you're right, sensible too. Women are, as a whole, a sensible lot. That's why we associate with them. Men are boys really and we can get in a muddle over the most trivial matters.

I knew the day would come when you would stop talking to me of nightmares, and start talking of nice sensible girls. It's terrifying, of course, but nonetheless to be expected.

Then next thing you know you'll be driving around in the motor-car with her or some other beauty.

Yours, affec.
J.M.B.

These letters seem, on the surface, to betray little of the turmoil raging inside the young Michael. Whether he was lying to his uncle, or actually deluding himself, he did not in fact forget Rupert Buxton. For he died, clasped in his arms, in Sandford Pool in May of 1921, eight months after this letter was sent.

What happened during those eight months? We may never know. And even if more letters passed between the two them than the ones that have survived, they may have been of little interest.

After all, Michael had promised to stop worrying Barrie with either his nightmares or his fantasies of Paris. And the hopelessness of discussing Rupert Buxton with his uncle must have been apparent to him. What, in fact, was there left for them to talk about? Michael was obviously still apathetic about his life at Oxford, but Barrie had made it clear that he would not allow the boy to leave. Barrie, for all his mixed feelings, was happy to encourage Michael in his friendship and possibly flirtation with Audrey Lucas. But was Michael actually flirting with the girl, or just pretending?

The final letters between Barrie and Michael are difficult to put into context. Michael's letters are strange. The strangeness may perhaps be indicative of the complete lack of communication between the two men, or simply of the increasing distance Michael seemed to be putting between himself and the world. For though these letters are obviously intended to communicate *something*, the writers rarely acknowledge the correspondent's concerns to any significant degree. For instance, the next letter seems to take up the possibility of Michael's adventures as a young man about town, but the tone and content are very peculiar. All of Michael's letters, in fact, seem to be written in a sort of code. It is a code that Barrie, try as he might, was obviously unable to decipher.

In a first, very uncharacteristic letter, Michael tells of meeting a new girl.

1st October, 1920
Dear Uncle Jim,

Women are the most complex and frustrating creatures. I have met a girl. I shan't tell you her name. I hope you won't think me too mysterious. It is she who makes me so.

The essential thing to tell you about her is that she is dark. A very dark girl. With dark hair and eyes. She is trying to tempt me. Women have a way of doing that, don't they? What's a fellow to do? I know that one musn't trust them, and one musn't believe everything they say, but how are you to tell if a girl is very very nice or truly awful? I suppose I should tell you that she is in the habit of painting her face. Is this a bad thing? I wouldn't be surprised if she smoked and was a suffragette. | 145

What is most bewitching about her is the blackness of her eyes. They are like pools which seem to beckon one. You have warned me so often that I would someday fall under the spell of a woman, and now it seems to have happened. What does all this mean?

Yours, affec.
Michael

Who was this woman? And why does she figure nowhere else in Michael's letters? Well Barrie's response to this strange letter is correspondingly bizarre, with a very long (it is one of the longest letters) description of his own marital relations.

13th October, 1920
Master Michael Ll-D.,

I must say I find your last letter quite upsetting, although I refuse to be frightened by you ever again.

The first question which comes to mind is where did you meet this young lady? Is she a student at St. Hilda's? A friend of the family? She doesn't sound like anyone I have ever met. You tell me absolutely nothing about her, only that she is dark and has dark eyes. Could you be more specific? Do you mean dark in complexion? Surely she is not of the dusky race? Since Audrey is not dark, I cannot imagine you are speaking of her. Who in heaven's name is this woman?

Though I don't know any more details, I can still respond to the essence of your letter. It brings up some terribly important questions. So in fine Allahakbarrie tradition, here's my best try at batting around some solutions.

146 |

You have reached that dangerous age when women will start to hang about and moon over you, this is what I have to say about them. The fact is that women set a kind of trap for men, and thus your dream about fishes so many years ago — do you remember it? — was somewhat prophetic. We are the fishes and we have to be aware of the nets — which are their eyes.

I have never really talked very much with you about Mary Ansell — beyond mentioning that our marriage failed because her interests were ultimately different than mine — but since you have sent me this rather unsettling letter, perhaps now is the time.

What I have written is a little intellectual diagram of what actually happens when a young man becomes involved with a woman and ends up marrying her.

At first the girl may seem quite merry, and very pretty, and just the perfect person with whom to pass some time. She may charm you, possessing every bit of the wit that a man does — and all wrapped up in a package which is neat and soft and cheery. But Nature is crafty. The charms women set before us are a kind of trap. You must understand that women and men are very different creatures, and this is something which Mr. George Bernard Shaw, callow critic though he is, has aptly described in the best of his rather preachy plays. There is something, which I will tactfully call the biological necessity — your old Uncle is nothing if not always tactful. Now, this biological necessity affects women very potently. And men not at all.

Let me put it this way. The human race is determined to go on and on, and settle even the most inaccessible corners of the globe, and will continue to concern itself with industry and business, and all those other things which we sometimes forget about, for you and I are nothing but airy poets and weavers of dreams. In order for the world we know to continue — and in order simply for the race not to die out — there must be babies. Children are the most precious thing in the world — as you once were, and sometimes, I think, still are — and we are duty bound to protect and nurture them as best we can. It is the actual making of the children that is the problem. It's something which I would be surprised to learn that anyone actually enjoys, but it must be done, and someone must do it.

Now what mischievous Dame Nature has done — God knows why she's arranged things this way, He and only He alone knows — is to make the possibility of children dependent upon the union of man and woman as husband and wife. However, He has also played a nasty trick. Though man and woman are both needed for the mixture to come to a boil, it is only the woman who feels the desire and need to produce children. Men are gleefully unaware that there is such a responsibility, and would rather not be involved. We all know that most men are happiest when in each other's company, or when smoking their pipes, playing their games, or planning their careers.

But cunning Nature has designed it so that women are incapable of ignoring their biological imperative. Thus women pursue men ceaselessly and mercilessly. Now, what happened between Mary Ansell and me, was that I had no idea, though my dear mother had warned me,

*that the charms of women could be a lethal snare. When I met Mary,
as I have told you before, being in her company was like taking a ride
on a fairy carpet, or dancing in a glade filled with morning dew. We
had the theatre in common, and so much to talk about. She, I daresay,
flattered me, and I flattered her back. But then our relationship
changed. I explained this to you when you were an Etonian whelp by
saying that something was missing in my relationship with her. That is*

148 |

*because you were too young to understand the wider implications. But
when people characterize my time with Mary as devoid of intimacy
— and I know they do, I am not completely deaf to idle gossip —
they betray an immense misunderstanding of male–female interac-
tions. What happened to Mary — and I pity her for this infirmity,
because it is the handicap of even the best of all women — was that
she was compelled by Mother Nature to crave children, and to demand
I assist her in producing them. It may very well have been an unconscious urge. I'm almost certain there was no little voice in her head
saying, "Mary Ansell, it is your responsibility to populate the world
and advance the human race." No. But the pressure was there, and she
could not resist it. She put pressure on me. A pressure that was all the
more oppressive because it was never put into words.*

*Of course, as a typical male, nothing really could have been
further from my mind than the future of the human race. (You see
women are the guardians of humanity. Men will always be humanity's
wayward children.) What finally put an end to our relationship was
a perilous, remarkable, evanescent discovery — the discovery of you
and your charming brothers! From the very first day that I saw little
George setting out sailboats on Kensington Pond with his mother, I
knew that my life would have one focus and one focus alone. I had
fallen deeply and hopelessly in love with the Llewelyn Davies clan and*

there was no antidote except to dote on the intrepid little group as much as possible, which is what I have done ever since. I think this is what finally pushed Mary and me apart.

Please do not think that I blame you or your brothers in any way for this. I was fulfilling my own destiny, and furthering the human race in my own very male, but very cramped and quaint little Scottish way.

So that is the story, that is what happens. The important thing for you to remember is that the black limpid pools of this girl's eyes — did you use the word limpid, or did I just imagine it? — though they seem as powerful as sin itself, are merely one of the lures that Mother Nature has set in our path to achieve her end.

| 149

These lures can lead to snares, traps, and a lifetime of frustration and unhappiness. Before you fall into such a beckoning pool, do an old fellow a favour and check with your Uncle first. Uncles always know best, or think they do!

Yours,
J.M.B.

One cannot of course help noticing that Barrie talks of falling into a limpid pool of a woman's eye — an irony when you consider what later happened to Michael. As we will discover soon, there was an irony in these last letters, one I think Michael was completely aware of, one which is evident when we read between the lines.

The next letter we have from Michael seems like one final attempt at a more personal and honest communication with his uncle, but one which Michael seems to know is doomed to failure.

One can imagine Barrie's surprise upon reading it, and his confusion over his adopted son's motives. The writer that Michael refers to, George Moore, was the official philosopher of the Apostles at Cambridge. It's poignant that Michael would have insisted on sending this letter, which could obviously have done nothing at this point but upset his uncle. Poignant, and interesting. Was it, in its own way, a last cry for help? (It's important to note that the opening quote is from one of Shakespeare's sonnets.)

20th October, 1920
Dear Uncle Jim,

> *My mistress' eyes are nothing like the sun;*
> *Coral is far more red than her lips' red;*
> *If snow be white, why then her breasts are dun;*
> *If hairs be wires, black wires grow on her head.*

I have made an enormous discovery, dear Uncle, and it was while reading this poem, which means so much to me. How can we ever communicate with each other except through the deepest resources of art? Sometimes it seems to me that we should abandon ordinary human speech altogether and speak to each other through the language of poetry. After all it is more beautiful, more pleasing to the ear.

I am going to quote someone now who you warned me was a bit of a prat, but let me present it as a quote with which you may take issue. For I am so happy today, and it is so rare that I am happy these days! It seems that I only receive my inspiration from art, and from enjoying art with others, and perhaps from reading a certain philosopher whose name I won't mention because I know you don't approve of him. Here follows a quote from his works which has so charmed me, and you must tell me your objections. Perhaps I shouldn't have mailed this letter at all, but I just couldn't help it. I'm bubbling full of joy today, and I had to share it with my favorite uncle! The quote is this: "No one, who has asked himself the question, has ever doubted that personal affection and the appreciation of what is beautiful in Art and Nature are good in themselves."

I chose this quotation because it seems, to me, to be so inarguable, *and such a self-evident truth, so simply and, indeed, beautifully stated, that no one could possibly disagree with it. My first thought was to fool you and pretend that it was someone else's idea but I realized that I could never fool my wise old uncle. It would be nasty of me to try.*

Surely there is nothing more beautiful than friendship? Surely that is what you taught us as boys, when you befriended us & rescued us from all our perils & extended a kind hand during our times of need? If there's anyone who taught me the true meaning of friendship, it's you.

And then there are the matters of Art and Nature, two things which, it seems to me, are indescribably beautiful, especially on a day like today, when one is tempted to take a walk or go swimming and ignore the pangs of guilt that inevitably come when ignoring study.

If I am wrong, please tell me so. But how can you argue with a placid lake on a sunny day? Or with a sonnet by Shakespeare? Isn't it pointless to try? Shouldn't one just give in to the pleasure of aesthetic appreciation? Isn't that one of the finest joys of life?

I'm certain that you will tell me that I am wrong, but I'm in the sort of mood today where I just had to attempt to convince you.

Yours, affec.,
Michael

30th October, 1920
Master Michael Ll-D.,

    I will answer your letter in the spirit in which it was sent; this
means that I will dispute you, point for point, like the debaters of old.
For, admittedly, you bring up some important notions, but ones with
which I most certainly disagree.

152 | *We will deal with the subject of friendship first, since it is a touchy*
one, and also, I hope, not the largest issue. The most important point is
that one cannot speak of friendship in a general sense; there are many
kinds of friendship. There is the friendship between an older man and
a boy, or a father and his adopted son, and that constitutes our friend-
ship, something which is forever pure. Then there are the associations
that one makes with fellows older than oneself. One always has to be
aware that older fellows can be corrupt and lead one into temptation.
Then there are the friendships that one has with boys who are one's
own age. The danger here, which we have discussed many times, is a
kind of sentimentality that leads one to question one's own sanity. This
must be avoided at all costs.

    Of course I cannot discuss the quotation you present without
acknowledging its author, and in this case that authorship is par-
ticularly relevant — G.E. Moore, a favourite of the Apostles at
Cambridge. My first concern, is that you are reading this claptrap at
all. I will explain why it is claptrap, in detail, below. My second con-
cern is that you have come into contact yet again with these so-called
Apostles. Perhaps your new friend Rupert is friends with one of them?
I cannot add anything to what I have said before. Perhaps it will help,
since you talk so much of language and poetry in your letter, to use
more potent verbiage. Let me tell you then, once and for all, that what

the Apostles and Strachey and their ilk have been up to at Cambridge, is none other than a kind of programmatic Freemasonry — at least that is what some have accused them of. I shouldn't be surprised if it was all connected with some sort of depraved magic, and if the rituals of their secret society didn't involve the slaughtering of some poor, dumb, helpless, four-legged animal. Word has it that their initiation includes voluntarily taking the name of Our Lord in vain! Need I say more? It is a sick brotherhood, and can bring nothing but misery to those who become entangled in it.

| 153

If the friendship you are talking about has anything to do with those people and their obscenities, then I would suggest you stay away from it for your own safety, if nothing else.

Let us move on to a more rewarding topic, that of Art and Nature. I have not read this particular passage by G.E. Moore, but it is typical of his thinking. And also typical that he capitalizes those two words, and treats them as equals.

They most certainly are not.

If there is any crumb of knowledge I had hoped to impart to you through the years it is this: art and nature — we can do without the capitals — are, in actual fact, opposites. They were meant to quarrel, and will always hate each other. The essence of Moore's mistake, and I am not at all convinced that it is an innocent one, is to imagine that the two are somehow connected. Nothing could be further from the truth. Peter Pan, to pick an example at random, is a boy who refuses to grow up. He is fleeing, in fact, from reality. Now, this is a children's play. And we adults all know that we cannot flee from reality, that we avoid it at our peril. You and I know this to be so, and I have always urged you, as any loving parent would, to meet your responsibilities head on, no matter what misery it may cause us for you to do so. You know that I would have proudly watched you march off to war, no matter how bitter that pill would have been for both of us to swallow. But ever so fortunately, you were not called up.

But here is the very important point. All art is a flight from nature, all fancy is the dance of a fairy on the head of a pin. That the fairy should fall and get her pretty feet dirtied by the muck and the slime of daily living is unimaginable, and anyone who advocates some sort of affinity between art and nature should contemplate the truth of one dictum: fairies are not of this world. That is why we trust them and need them to carry us away. We know in our hearts that they know better, and that they can free us from this noxious burden we call life. The web of art has nothing to do with the machinations of a spider or the grotesque and heartless world of insects. It is as light, airy, and ineffable as the stuff of dreams. Art is what we aspire to. It is who and what we can never be.

I hope my explanation doesn't upset you too much. I think that Moore's motives are suspect. Though some say he is a kind man and has been misinterpreted by the Apostle crowd, I find that hard to believe. His work is fundamentally flawed, as I hope I have made clear. Anyone who advocates a marriage between art and nature is urging a kind of scientism that was a hopeless failure in the morbid naturalism of Zola and came to sad fruition in Poel's depraved little Parisian theatre. I satirized some of this naturalistic hogwash in my play Ibsen's Ghost. You might return to it, if you are looking for a lighter view of these issues.

We musn't get bogged down in this quagmire of seriousness. You are young and handsome and full of life — and it seems, full of joy too — so I urge you to put aside your books for an afternoon if need be, and take that swim, though this warmest of Autumns seems to have

*taken a turn for the worse. Remember that you must always come back
to the books. That is as close as art and nature will ever be — as close
together as swimming and studying.*

> *As always, I am your loving uncle,*
> *J.M.B.*

There is only one more letter, sent in February 1921, from Michael
to Barrie. We have no response. Michael's last letter to Barrie is
perhaps the strangest one he ever sent to his adoptive uncle. It's
surely the most moving. At first glance, it seems like a straightforward, if overly sentimental, thank-you note. Closer examination
reveals that the letter is a coded message. A message that reveals
that Michael Llewelyn Davies had decided to kill himself.

27th February, 1921
Dearest Uncle,

*Last night it was unseasonably warm, and I took the liberty of
leaving my books for a few moments. I suspect they didn't miss me.*

*I know that it's been eons since we've corresponded — before
Christmas, in fact. Of course you know that it isn't that I don't love
you, dear uncle & in fact, that's mainly what I wish to say.*

*For this warm night reminded me of another night, many years
ago, when five little boys — I will not reveal their names — went for
an extended vacation at a Lake which they used to call Black. But
their favourite Uncle had resisted their invitation to accompany them.
The reason? Why, his work, of course. Uncle was busy preparing
another revision of his most famous play. And tho' he always made a
special effort to accompany the boys on their rollicking jaunts, a*

rigorous deadline made him unavailable. Well, mother and father decided to take the rambunctious fivesome to Black Lake, alas without the dear Uncle who so often tagged along. This saddened the boys. Secretly, they tried to manufacture joy, if only not to disappoint their well-meaning parents. But, after all, father was incapable of playing Captain Hook, or of participating in any of the rough-and-tumble which obsessed the boys on their lakeside adventures. And tho' mother was a dear, she was always busy sewing new clothes for her tiny ruffians.

156

Without Uncle, it was a lonely jaunt. And tho' the sun was hot, and the sand grated beneath their toes, tho' the eels were just as frightening and the fish just as elusive, it was with joy that the boys greeted their father's revelation that he had been called back to London. For yes, he had received a telegram! Father's services were required immediately, in court! Mother might have stayed on at Black Lake with the obstreperous fivesome, but there was only one day left of their vacation. So the whole obstreperous gang of miniature thieves and pirates was trundled on the train lickety-split, and, before you knew it, the ten pairs of perspiring hands and ten pairs of grubby knees were back at Kensington Gardens, and almost nearly safe at home.

But before they reached their house, the treacherous five took a vote — in truth, it was somewhat more disorderly than that — and begged their mother that they might visit their dear Uncle Jim.

You see, on their trip (while adventuring) they had missed him, missed him so.

Mother said that the esteemed writer would be busy, and the boys should not disturb him. She was right of course, but that didn't stop our cagey little crew. They knew that mothers were often malleable on such occasions, and that after much whining, pleading, and skirt-pulling she might give in. (Perhaps this is why children have nurses!) And so the intrepid little gang dragged her across the park, in the gathering dusk. As the five tiny soldiers stood outside the house in question, they could see for themselves that the light burned brightly in their Favourite Uncle's study, for his charcoal silhouette was painted on the white curtains, revealing him bent over his little desk.

"Oh we mustn't bother him," Mother said, for she was always | 157 well-informed about everything. "He's busy writing another play."

But the boys all stamped their feet at once. So, as usual, she gave in. Mother knocked on the door. There was no answer. But because the boys loved their Uncle — and had missed him so terribly much while they were out adventuring — they let themselves into his house.

What must it have been like for the esteemed author to have five screaming boys invade his study unannounced, placing a punishing period on his feverish work?

In case you haven't guessed, dear Uncle, you were that esteemed author. And I was but one of those five little boys.

I have often wondered, since then, at your generosity and good spirits that night. I remember that as we burst through the door, all clatter and sandy sunburnt arms — didn't Peter drop a wet clam on your study floor? — you rose wearily from your chair. I remember the smile on your face, and I remember your loving arms opening and enveloping us in a warm embrace.

Indeed, you reacted not with the irritation of an Uncle, but with the generosity of a father.

When I look back on those five boys now, I ask myself, how is it that a father acts, when a child returns unexpectedly from a long and challenging journey? Does the father turn the child away? Why no.

The definition of a loving father is one who hugs his child, even if he or she returns unexpectedly, and disturbs his most peaceful thoughts with shouts and tintinnabulum.

Though we might not live up to expectation, though we might not do our duty, or eat our peas, a loving father is always waiting, arms open to love his sometimes errant son.

It seems to me that this is not only the definition of a good father, but of God.

158 |

I have been remiss, dearest Uncle, in never thanking you enough for being the best father a boy could ever have.

And so I know you will understand.

> *Yours, with love returned,*
> *Michael*

What's amazing about this letter is that, first of all, it echoes remarkably Barrie's own writing; the loving introduction to *Peter Pan*, for instance. Michael perfectly captures the sweet tone of Barrie's reminiscences of his vacations with the five boys. In other words, not only the content, but the style of the letter seems to be part of his homage to his dearest uncle.

Why did he write such a letter three months before he died? Well, on one level, it's obvious that he was saying farewell. But a closer reading of the letter reveals a buried metaphor.

This particular letter obsessed me, if only because — sitting there all alone, like a solitary rock on a perilous shore — it seemed to point nowhere. Of course, I could only guess at who might have chosen the letters that I inherited, or whether or not they had been chosen at all. Had Leslie saved what he considered to be the most important ones? Had Nicholas only given Leslie his favourites? Or were these letters the only ones to be saved from the water damage in Nicholas's wet study? We shall never know. I imagine that, by fate or by design, this letter must somehow hold a clue to the reason for Michael's premature demise.

In my desperation I went to all the works Michael cites in his letters. I scoured Strachey's *Eminent Victorians*, and even tackled the philosophy of George Moore. In Massenet's *Werther* I hit the jackpot. This letter is a paraphrase, in fact, of Werther's moral justification for suicide. In Goethe's novel, Werther says, "When the child returns unexpectedly soon from a journey, far from harbouring any resentment against him, at the mere sound of his footsteps the whole household flutters and the father, full of joy, clasps him in a long embrace." And most importantly, he continues, "*Oh God, who hast created me, woulds't thou be less merciful?*" Werther is literally asserting that God will not reject him for committing suicide, that on the contrary, He will embrace him. This passage is the subject of the famous aria in Massenet's *Werther*: "*Lorsque l'enfant revient d'un voyage.*" | 159

Michael and Rupert were obsessed with Massenet's *Werther*, and, it appears, with suicide. It is likely that Michael might have turned back to that "stuffy novel" by Goethe, which had been brought to such vivid life for him by Massenet's music. This final letter, therefore, serves a dual purpose. It is not only a gracious and moving thank you to his beloved uncle for two decades of love and care, but a coded suicide note. Michael was telling his adoptive father that he would be returning to God — but not to worry, because God would be welcoming him back home.

That Michael was a homosexual, I think, is perfectly clear.

From his early obsession with Mr. Wright, to his loving descriptions of Roger Senhouse, and finally to his obsession with Rupert Buxton, it is clear that the feelings that he had for his closest companions were more than just friendship. Indeed, his chums are almost exclusively described in terms of physical beauty, and with the exuberance and romance of infatuation. Whether or not he physically consummated relationships with these boys is ultimately irrelevant. The fact is that he was in love with them.

What is the answer to the mystery of his suicide? For I think we can say now that Michael's death was, in fact, a suicide. If we search the letters carefully, we can see that there are many possible roots for this extreme act. Was his own depressive nature a significant factor? What of his desperation to escape his nightmares of the war? Did he feel guilty for having survived that "War To End All Wars" ? Had he devised a suicide pact with Rupert Buxton so they might realize their impossible love beyond death? Or had Barrie's negations of his Paris fantasies driven him to an emotional impasse?

It could be many or all of these reasons. What makes these letters dangerous? And as Leslie would assert, are they a "mirror"? I think the danger lies elsewhere. These letters epitomize a polarization of two very different ways of life. A bitter conflict between two diametrically opposed philosophies do battle in their tender pages.

In order to examine more closely the ideas in these letters, to release their power, and reveal their danger, I must tell you another story. This story is about a boy who appeared magically in my life, and, just as magically, disappeared into thin air again. A boy who came to be very close to me, but who now is lost. (Like so many others.) That's why I call this section:

ANOTHER LOST BOY

First, let us deal with Leslie Sexton's assertions. That old perverted professor would have had us believe that these letters were pederastical, and that James Barrie harboured sexual desire for his adopted son.

I think (as I have attempted to prove in notes to the early letters) that Barrie did not molest his little boy. There is certainly no proof of that in the letters (unless one reads sexual innuendo into every nook and cranny). A modern abuse-obsessed psychoanalyst could infer that Michael's nightmares originated from childhood molestation. Not every person with a sleep disorder, however, was molested in childhood. Ironically, the letters suggest to us that Michael's earliest nightmares might well have been brought on by the combustible mixture of a sensitive nature and an early in-house performance of *Peter Pan*.

Though I challenge the reader to find any documentable proof of a sexual relationship between James Barrie and his adopted son, I think there is ample proof here that James Barrie was inordinately devoted to Michael, and that his adopted son may have been the pre-eminent love interest in his life. Barrie repeats over and over in these letters that he found his wife's sexual demands dismaying. Both he and Michael seem to treat women distantly. The exception is the strange letter in which Michael claims to have met a mysterious dark-eyed woman. Michael is as obsessed with his various Eton and Oxford boyfriends as Barrie is with Michael. In fact, it seems clear from the letters that Barrie was jealous of Michael's infatuations. But is this the jealousy of a lover, or of an old, repressed, Victorian Scot with little opportunity for passionate emotional release?

162 |

For me, the primary question that arises upon reading these letters is moral, not sexual. (I'm not much interested in sexual perversions, including pederasty.) If we examine the letters closely, we see a recurring pattern. Michael, starting with the earliest letters at Eton, writes to his uncle joyously, or from a state of passionate teenage befuddlement. His uncle often plays the role of calming rationalist, even to the point of dousing the unruly fires of adolescent passion. Barrie, the very opposite of the homosexual libertine, seems to be playing the role of the strict Victorian/ Edwardian father. Now, whether he was somehow morbidly interested in his adopted son has little relevance. What does have relevance are his actions. And though Barrie may have championed the cause of the "boy who would not grow up" in *Peter Pan*, he does everything he can to make sure that his adopted son does grow up. In order to ensure that it happens, he was forced to oppose Michael's most extreme personal and emotional impulses.

Without judging Michael, I think it is clear that he was caught up in a spiral of sex and death. That his dreams were morbid is beyond question. That he began to wallow in those dreams is perhaps Barrie's fault, for Barrie was not only open to hearing about these nightmares but led Michael to believe that they were somehow connected with artistry and poetry. If Michael was to follow the romantic suicidal impulses of Rupert Brooke and A.E. Houseman would he not merely be following a pre-ordained pattern? Indeed, Michael, as frightened as he is of his military service, seems almost to regret that he has not been called to an early death. It certainly would have neatly ended both his night terrors and his romantic confusions about Roger Senhouse. | 163

If we look at these letters closely, we can see that there is a never-ending dialogue around issues of sex and death. Or, rather, Michael is fixated on these issues — these inexorable twins — and Barrie is torn between his early impulse to indulge his adopted son's whims and his reasoned decision later to press Michael resolutely towards motorcars, Oxford, and a healthy flirtation with Audrey Lucas.

Of course one could look at these letters in another way. And this is where they become dangerous. We need not view Barrie as a civilizing influence, or as the voice of reason. We might see him as a frustrated homosexual (with the impulses of a pederast) whose repressed sexual desire for his adopted son caused him, in turn, to repress the boy's blossoming homosexuality. According to this theory (which comes from a position of so-called "sexual liberation") Michael would have been, in effect, a "happy homosexual" had Barrie encouraged his flirtations. I suppose an extremist gay view might be this: if Barrie had been healthy, too — if he had been a gay man who expressed his sexuality with like-minded adults — he might have encouraged the same impulses in Michael and not frustrated them.

According to this theory, which I have no doubt must have been Leslie Sexton's, Barrie was his adopted son's murderer. Michael's nightmares are the articulation of his repressed desires. As a sensitive child, his night-terrors might have passed away or become less of an obsession for him had he been encouraged to express his sexuality. As it was, Barrie, the archetypal "evil" Victorian father, crushed every positive sexual impulse towards life and fruition. What if Michael had been encouraged to have an affair with Roger Senhouse, instead of being warned that it was "unhealthy"? What if he had been able to discuss his attractions to young men openly with his parent, would he then have been so ineluctably drawn to suicide? Wasn't his suicide with Rupert Buxton the only possibility for him? Could his love for another boy, in those post-war days, only be expressed in death? Like Werther, did they prefer to die than live, deprived of the opportunity to express their love openly? What was this lolling about and listening to romantic music and crying, other than a frustrated, very Victorian substitute for the orgasm which they were cruelly denied?

According to this theory, James Barrie is something of a monster. Even in the context of his era, it seems heartless of him to oppress consistently his adopted son, whose only sin was, in fact, that he was so much like his uncle. Are these letters not a classic example of the Victorian repression which weighs down upon homosexuals and stops them from gaining complete social acceptance, even today?*

So which is it? Is Barrie a compassionate, earnest, well-

---

* For what it's worth, D.H. Lawrence's remarks concerning Michael's death have been duly documented: "No, I hadn't heard of the boy's drowning. What was he doing to get drowned? J.M. has a fatal touch for those he loves. They die." What could be the

meaning (if somewhat sexually confused) uncle, trying his best to steer his adopted son away from what he believed to be sexual perversion and what seems to be a concomitant death wish? Or is he a jealous monster whose own closed-minded insensitivity inevitably steered his favourite boy to commit suicide?

This, I submit, is the dangerous and very important question these letters pose. We must not be afraid to answer. My sympathies, as it may or may not be clear, are with James Barrie. I think | 165 he was a kind man who not only meant well, but did the best he could — and what every father must do — for his child. This may seem a paradoxical position for a homosexual, like myself, to take. But let me insist that I am not a typical promiscuous (or even sexually active) gay man. I did not come easily to this point in my life. My sympathy for Barrie's Victorian sensibilities and celibate state, came not only from reading these letters, but from events in my personal history. Events involving someone who was, for a time, terribly important to me.

And so I come to Another Lost Boy.

If I am to tell you the story of Alan Peche — and I am — then I must begin again in rather seedy surroundings, in a bar where I found myself, quite inexplicably and, I'm ashamed to say, quite recently.

You see, after Leslie's death I was, to all intents and purposes,

---

origin of this excessively nasty remark? Lawrence and Barrie were certainly not close friends. Indeed their work could not be more different; it's hard to imagine the hardnosed sexual libertarian having any sympathy with Barrie's twee bittersweetness. Lawrence knew Mary Canaan, Barrie's ex-wife, and also would have known of the deaths in the du Maurier family — Arthur, Sylvia, and Michael's brother George. Incidentally, the drownings at the Crich water party in *Women in Love* bear a marked similarity to Michael and Rupert's case. But that book was written five years before the tragedy explored here.

friendless. I had removed Ronnie Connaught unceremoniously from my life. (The aging blond bimbo was still living the high life, even with his HIV-positive status.) My obsession with my post-graduate work left me little time for him. And I felt for a while that I had outgrown the relationship. In fact, I had. But after Leslie died and my ambitions for scholarship were achieved, there was a huge empty space in my affections. It was an emotional hole that demanded filling. Neither my mother, nor my hugely successful award-winning productions at school were quite enough. Ronnie and I have so much teacherly business in common. So for a while, I reverted to being his ugly stepsister. I had not yet reached my present state of celibacy, but had certainly stopped putting much effort into cruising. I had given up the search for love. And of course, as they say, that's when it usually hits you in the head, like a falling rock, an errant football, or a poised dagger. It was on one of the nights when I had foolishly followed Ronnie to one of his low-life haunts, that I received the nearly fatal concussion.

The Works is an upscale bar in mid-Manhattan which has its downscale side. The imagery for the bar is particularly revealing. It's a dripping water tap. We all know what that particular object might represent. But the logo, unlike those of The Anvil, or The Eagle, is not obscene. In fact, you could wear your Works T-shirt to your sister's wedding (or at least to the reception). Basically, the name of the bar was a dirty pun. But it worked in that nauseating way that so many camp puns do: only those sexually inclined would get it. Others might assume the leaky piece of plumbing pictured was simply a draft tap overabundant with frothy suds.

The bar itself was not decorated according to any particular theme. It boasted huge windows that gazed out on Central Park. It was a clean and modern space, with the requisite exposed brick, trendy lighting fixtures and black television monitors that displayed (no, not porn, but) replays of recent gay television obsessions: *Friends*, *Ellen*, or *Will and Grace*. There was nothing to offend anyone's mother about the bar itself. It was a place any homosexual could take his heterosexual office girlfriend to. Later she might have occasion to boast to her friends: "Oh it's just like a straight bar, really. Except that there's men with men, you know. But nice men. They were all dressed very well. In fact you wouldn't even know they were gay."

| 167

But behind this crafty, bland facade, were the all-important bathrooms. They were located at the very back of the bar, veiled by an imposing bank of television monitors high above a dimly lit brick wall.

Since the women's powder room was at the front of the bar, these bathrooms were most decidedly men's territory. They were vast, sparse, and clean, and decorated in the modish Italian style. The sinks were smooth shallow black ovals and the taps were lean, glinting, polished brass spouts shaped like the graceful necks of golden swans. There were no urinals, but instead a sleek and intimidating trough of painted black metal dominated the center of the room. Above the trough were lights, strategically placed so that, coincidentally, they tended to illuminate the genital area — if one was actually brave enough to relieve oneself there. Not surprisingly, most gentleman preferred to wait in line for one of the six cubicles which were in a darker area around a corner. Each cubicle could be locked, and these elegant stalls quickly became famous for the sexual activity that occurred behind their reflective black doors.

I know about all of this only because Ronnie was kind enough to describe, in glorious detail, of course, each of the fabulous sexual encounters he had enjoyed there. I rarely ventured to the cubicles, preferring to run to a discreetly placed trash bin outside to evacuate my bladder, rather than set foot in that rather tastelessly posh den of iniquity.

When Ronnie wasn't pleasuring himself and others in the stalls, he preferred to hang about in front and below the nearby television screens. Since there was always a large crowd of conversationally challenged men staring blankly, almost glumly, at the videos, one could, if one stood beneath them, at least fantasize that one was being cruised. And since the screens were up high, the area below them was dark, and felt vaguely dangerous.

It was here that Ronnie and I had parked ourselves on that fatal night. I must point out that I had to be persuaded to come to the bar at all. I only did so because Ronnie was late for dinner, and I hadn't had the chance to fill him in on the day's school gossip over the appetizer (soup) that he chugged down rashly in order, as he put it, "Not to kill my stone."

Stoned he was, weaving slightly to and fro, as I sipped my mineral water and chattered in his ear. Ronnie soon left me for someone he claimed was cruising him, and they disappeared into the ominous bathrooms. I was left alone until the young man beside me staggered — completely, utterly, and fatefully — into my arms.

The staggerer was Alan Peche.

I begin my description of Alan Peche by stating, as I have before, and will again and again, that he was, quite simply, an angel. If I have unflatteringly revealed myself, Lear-like, as a somewhat foolish, fond old man, I must be forgiven. But that is the function of those whose personalities are beautiful. They touch us in an an almost religious way; their souls are apostles of a tender gospel.

Alan was nineteen years old when I met him, small and slender, with hair that was stunningly, alarmingly, and quite naturally blond (almost white). He wore a pair of khaki slacks (Dockers), | 169 brown penny loafers, and a tasteful bluish-white pinstripe shirt with a button-down collar. His style had a simple dignity, a return to old-fashioned preppie elegance that I immediately respected. His clothing seemed to me, at the time, to show respect for traditional values. So many young men go in for punk or trendy flash. The clubs are full of men in tight T-shirts and body-hugging apparel of sleek and moist spandex or other equally exotic synthetic blends. As you perhaps can tell, I have always been suspicious of the theatrical tendencies of gay fashion. Leave theatrics to the stage where they belong! Here was a young man who looked as if he had just walked off a small-town university campus, or was on his way home from the bank or church. I found the naive innocence of his simple, modest garb absolutely bewitching, and I was almost ashamed to find myself obsessed with what lay beneath.

But I have not dwelt on the singular miracle of Alan's face.

His skin was pale and his cheeks only slightly rosy, reddening the way a boy's cheeks may when he is excited or upset. His lower jaw had the fuzzy smoothness of a ripe peach. Though Alan assured me later that he did shave, this would always be hard for me to believe. And then there was that petulant shock of blond hair that fell teasingly over his forehead, gently grazing an eyebrow; a shock of hair that Alan was occasionally required to brush away. I don't know if you happened to see the famous cover of the art magazine *General Idea* during the late eighties. It featured a boy who looked exactly like a Nazi storm trooper, dressed in a smart and sexy little SS uniform. The boy sported a shock of blond hair identical to Alan's, which fell over one side of his brow. He was sipping milk from a glass and had given himself a milk moustache. The model stared directly at the viewer with the quizzical innocence of a cat who has unwittingly just acquired a canary. It was a very attractive photo, but the political implications were alarming, as one found oneself lusting after a Nazi youth.

I still feel that I have not told you enough about Alan's face. It's very important to me that you form a precise mental picture of him and that you see him, living and breathing, before you.

When I saw him for the first time, he reminded me very much of Peter Stone. I have not told you about Peter before, because the story is a sordid one. I will quickly summarize it here.

When I was in the habit of cruising with Ronnie so many years before, I happened on Peter. Our association lasted only for a couple of months, we saw each other rarely and in irregular circumstances that I won't delve into here. He was a sweet young lad, of the punk-rock variety, who, for some reason, found himself besotted with me. I found him charming and very, very beautiful. His facial features had the same cumulative effect as Alan's. His face could only be described as noble. His nose, like Alan's, was long and straight, his eyebrows strong, and his eyes dulcet and soft. His straight lips were perpetually parted in expectation. Peter and I had nothing in common, other than sexual matters (which ultimately become dull) so we drifted apart. Years later I learned through Leslie that he had died from AIDS. Though our relationship was brief and relatively uneventful, the image of Peter would often haunt my dreams. Sometimes I would imagine, when viewing another young and singular face, that I had encountered Peter again, that he had somehow risen from the dead. This was the feeling that I had when I looked at Alan for the first time.

I had no idea, when I first saw Alan Peche, that our meeting would have enormous personal and literary implications. What I could perceive, with my trusty emotional radar, were the vibrations of an earnest soul.

When he fell into me he apologized. I was touched. Both physically and emotionally.

It was only a momentary glitch. Holding onto my arms, Alan was able to right himself quickly. He was definitely drunk, but except for his stumble, not visibly so, the booze just made him more voluble. Because, as I would soon learn, when Alan wasn't drunk he tended to be quiet, almost serene. When tipsy, the placid pond that was his usual temperament was pleasantly troubled by an alcoholic breeze.

I noticed immediately that he was an effortlessly sweet human being. By effortlessly I mean that the sweetness of so many boys and young women is overripe. It seems forced. Alan had an honestly shy and self-deprecating way about him, to which I responded on the spot.

Under my gentle questioning, he revealed that he had been in New York City for only a couple of weeks. He was planning to stay for the summer. He was residing with his sister in a very small, and what was proving increasingly hot and cramped, 7th Avenue apartment.

Alan had been born and raised in Plattsburgh, a town small enough to have nary a gay bar, and certainly no bathhouses or any of the other amenities of a gay scene. He was nineteen years old, and had just finished high school. During the final term he had written an article for his high-school newspaper about another student — the only other "out" gay boy in his year at school. The boy had made a valiant attempt to take his boyfriend (who was older and a student) to his school prom. The article concerned the trials and tribulations of growing up as an openly gay youth in a small town. Staring up at me with his trusting eyes, Alan told me, very seriously, that now that he was in New York he wanted other people to know about his classmate's struggle, and that his sister had suggested he approach the *Village Voice*.

Coming from anyone else such a query would have seemed either ridiculously impractical or embarrassingly ambitious. Coming from Alan it was simply a naive and earnest suggestion. He seemed quite honestly to want to help people through his work. "Wouldn't the *Village Voice* be the only magazine interested in a story like that?" he asked. Then he turned away, without a trace of self pity. "Well maybe there's no point in it now, I mean the guy broke up with his boyfriend after the prom . . ." I could tell immediately that Alan was revealing merely the tip of the iceberg. His feelings about this article obviously ran very deep. Luckily, my many years of experience with high-school students had left me abundantly tactful in these matters. So I carefully probed, attempting to discover the real reason Alan had come to New York

172|

City — which I thought I had correctly surmised — though he refused to reveal it. I craftily asked him if he had been to any of the usual tourist sites: the Empire State Building or the Statue of Liberty. "No, but I went to this bar, opposite Columbia, where the Beats used to hang out. It's just a deli now." I knew the place of which he was speaking; I had been there many times for lunch. "And I spent all day today looking for this bar where Dorothy Parker and her *New Yorker* pals used to go to. But I don't think it's there anymore." He looked at me appealingly, the way a little boy might query his father. "That's kind of a waste of time, isn't it?" When Alan looked up at you (which he was invariably required to do, since he was only five-foot-six) he had an appealingly rabbit-like quality — all quite irresistible.

Well, my heart opened up. I can honestly say that, gazing down on him, I saw myself at his age. For I, too, had once been an aspiring writer.

I have not mentioned this before because it is not an aspect of my character I thought was relevant to this discussion or the Barrie–Llewellyn letters. But my relationship with Alan is very relevant, and so you must know.

As a youth I aspired to a career as a playwright. I laboured for nearly two years over a play called *Do the Duty*, which was, as you might guess, the tale of a young man who resists the draft in order to evade participation in the Vietnam War. The play was written in collaboration with my high-school drama teacher, a sweet, pot-bellied old fussbudget named Mr. Chalmers, who — though he'd never been able to make a career of his own — offered opportunities for young people to write and direct their own plays in his innovative drama program. (This was back in the sixties when this type of pedagogical innovation was popular. Today these activities unfortunately take the form of much-vaunted, and underfunded, extracurricular activities. Most of my best work at Robert Kennedy High School, unfortunately, now falls into this category.) I have no doubt that Chalmers, who was a kind and selfless man, became the model for the kind of drama teacher that I would one day become.

174 |

At any rate, the production, which I directed and my drama teacher produced, was entered into the local high-school drama festival. It made quite a hit. I was proud of the tragic irony that constitutes the climax of the play, for the young man ends up being conscripted and then killed in battle. At the funeral, the boy's domineering mother and his girlfriend (the only one who understood his conscientious objections and supported his protest) fight over the coffin. The young girl is clearly the heroine, and the mother the selfish and evil villain. Looking back I can see the play was over-written and hopelessly jejune. But at the time I had all my hopes wrapped up in it. When I left high school I began submitting the play (and another I was working on) to alternative theaters in Greenwich Village. My lack of success was almost startling, and the letters of rejection I received were more than discouraging. I found I didn't have the heart to continue in the professional theater, so I enrolled in teacher's college and my fate was sealed.

Looking down at Alan, I could see all the symptoms of the aspiring young writer (and many similarities with my own history): the article that was such a hit in the high-school paper, the trip to New York, the dedicated visits to the haunts of his favourite writers. When I thought I had diagnosed his affliction correctly, it was time to start the cure. The cure could only come from an honest discussion about his aspirations. So I asked him if he wanted to be a writer.

There was a fear in his eyes as he looked up at me. This was a good sign. This meant that writing was a real dream, something he really wanted.

"Well I guess I . . . it's something I imagined I might be . . . maybe, some day."

Knowing youthful prevarication like the back of my own hand — and all it stood for — I recognized this stammer as the closest Alan might come to expressing his heart's desire. I knew that in situations like this forthrightness was required, or an artistic soul might be lost to self-deprecation and lack of self-esteem. I plunged right in.

"Well it's all about what you want to be. If you want to be a writer, and you believe in yourself, and you have the talent, and you do the work, that's what you'll be."

"But do I have the talent? That's the question." He gazed down at the polished Italian floor tiles. "I don't know."

"I'm an English teacher. "

"Where?"

"Here, in New York City. At Robert Kennedy High School just down the street. If you can get me a copy of your article, I'll give you my opinion on it."

"Well I . . . " He looked down again, sheepishly. "I have a copy here."

Then he did a very touching thing. He pulled a rumpled piece of paper out of the back pocket of his pants. The article was only a page or two long, and appeared to have been typed, double spaced, on a typewriter. (I didn't know people still used that antique machine.) The fact that Alan had brought his article with him, ready to show it to anyone at anytime, was a detail so real and at the same time so sad, that I almost hugged him on the spot. I wisely resisted the impulse, and instead, invited him back to my apartment.

I can honestly say that my intentions with Alan at that time — and really up until this very day — were innocent.

I wanted to help the boy. That is all. To help a young person in need.

Alan seemed undecided. "Well . . . it's late."

"It's not too late to read your article."

"You don't live far from here?"

"Right down the street."

"Well, okay. You can lead the way, I guess . . ."

I didn't want to lead the way, but I did. Our conversation on the way to my apartment was rather halting, mainly due to Alan's excitement that someone was finally going to read his article. I remember thinking that though I had for so many years owned a large apartment smack in the middle of town, here was the first instance when my lucky rental situation would be used to full advantage. Here I was, walking home, not with some trick (oh my God, the fruitless, unhappy years of doing that) but with a mar- vellous young lad, a writer, a boy with potential.

For just as my intuition had told me that Alan was, indeed, an aspiring writer, it had also told me that he must have talent. Of course, at the time, I had no proof of that, beyond the honesty of his manner, his obvious dedication, and the intelligence flashing in his eyes.

When we reached my apartment, I felt that Alan had always been meant to be there.

This evaluation was actually a selfish one. Of course Alan looked very right to me, but he was obviously uncomfortable. I made him a cup of herbal tea, and we moved from the kitchen to the living room, and sat down by the fireplace, which — though it wasn't working at the time — has always had an appealing feel. Alan looked around at a room filled with books and paintings. A room that was overloaded, in fact, with culture. I had a suspicion that his family's house in Plattsburgh was quite a different place. I wanted to ask him about that — indeed, I wanted to know everything about him — but clearly he was enormously nervous about having me read his piece, and wanted to get on with it.

I sat down in the old leather chair by the window which looks out over Eighth Avenue, turned on the light, and settled down to read.

I must say that I was not inordinately impressed by what I read. But neither was I appalled.

That is the criterion I apply when reading any student's effort. I don't expect to be carried away by adolescent scribblings, to be inspired the way that one might be by Shakespeare, Tolstoy, or Dostoevsky. On the other hand, I *do* expect to be appalled: by spelling, grammar, and a general lack of sense and care. So what Alan gave me, though perhaps not inspiring, was certainly not dull. In fact, there was nothing extraneous: it was simple, direct, and to the point. It was journalism in the truest sense, a straightforward iteration of the facts, with no frippery or philosophizing — nothing of that irrelevant and irritating verbiage, the filler, which, in fact, masks a lack of real content in most student writers. I can honestly say that the piece showed true potential; for the talent here was not yet formed — it only needed a teacher, mentor — another ear, another eye, an older, understanding friend, to shape it from the clay. And it seemed to me that I was the perfect person to do so.

I rose from my leather recliner and took my place in front of Alan on one of the twin couches in front of my fireplace. My first impulse was to put him out of his misery.

178|

"It's good." I said.

"You think so?" he said. He looked at me almost skeptically. There was eagerness in his voice, but also what I perceived (even then) to be a touch of dangerous lassitude, a torpid taste of self-deprecation.

On the one hand, I could tell that his self-esteem was shaky. On the other, I saw no point in coddling him, for that would have done neither of us any good.

"I didn't say brilliant." It was sometimes kind to be cruel. "I simply think that it has potential, and that you should pursue your writing."

"Well, I *want* to," he said, tentatively.

I asked him in what direction he would like to continue.

"Well, I don't know, you're going to think I'm being stupid. I probably am. It's probably a stupid idea."

"No, tell me." I loved drawing him out.

"Well, I know I'm too young and everything, and I haven't had enough experience, and I haven't read enough, to even suggest this, but I think I'd like to write a novel."

Ahh. A novel.

The experience of dragging this confession out of him was, I will have to admit, almost a sexual one. It was as during the act of lovemaking, when it is possible to derive from one's partner a confession of their deepest desires or most cherished fetishes. "What is it you like to do best?"

I asked him who his favourite novelists were, and he told me that he had always loved J.D. Salinger's *Catcher in the Rye.* (I expected this typical teenage favourite.) He also mentioned Jack Kerouac's *On the Road.* I explained to him carefully, and without condescension, that J.D. Salinger's reputation had been pretty effectively demolished by most modern critics, and that the fifties' wunder-kind was no longer the great Jewish hope (Philip Roth had taken up that mantle), but instead was viewed as a somewhat facile, even overly commercial scribbler. I also mentioned Truman Capote's criticism of *On the Road* ("typing, not writing") and suggested that he take a look at Capote's first novel, *Other Voices, Other Rooms,* and compare it with *On the Road* to understand the difference between the two styles. I did everything short of requiring him to write an essay — which I realized would have hardly been appropriate.

| 179

I could tell that he was a bit daunted, as students often are, by my suggestions. Most young people find their dreams ignored by those who are older (and often considered wiser) than they. I think it was shocking for him that I not only took his dreams seriously and encouraged him, but was willing to offer him practical ways to pursue his goals.

Our discussion continued for another hour or so. I discovered that he had not read wisely nor too well. I directed him towards a better understanding of the classics, pointing out that it was important not to simply read what was "fun" but that which requires work, too. When our discussion drew to its close it was nearly one in the morning, and Alan apologized for taking so much of my time, explaining that he had to be off.

I asked him if, like Cinderella, he turned into a pumpkin after twelve.

He told me it was only that his sister had to leave for work early in the morning, and since her apartment was small, she was liable to wake him up early. As he dragged himself to his feet, obviously not enjoying the prospect of the tramp downtown to a hot little apartment, I suggested what seemed to me merely a practical notion. Why bother to march all the way down to Fourteenth Street when he could easily sleep here? I told him that I had a large double bed and air conditioning, and that he would be very welcome to stay. Also, not wanting to put him under any sort of obligation, I made it clear he might sleep over as a "friend."

Alan's acceptance of my offer was mixed with such shyness and obvious relief that I couldn't help but feel sorry for him.

I went into the bathroom to do my late-night business, and told him that if he had to use the toilet he could follow me in there and then into bed.

I always sleep naked, and I saw no need to change my usual habit. I was wide awake, of course, when he climbed under the sheets.

I think what astonished me most about his body (for I kept one eye cocked, and there was a night light shining in my room) was how much like a little boy's it was. I won't go into detail, but suffice it to say that his limbs were thin and pale, like those of a youngster rather than a boy in his late teens. I remember watching, with amusement, a slight moment of indecision as he worried whether or not to remove his underwear, glancing at my naked body on the bed. He finally decided to let his underpants fall to the floor. I don't so much remember what was revealed by their removal, as I do the image of the discarded garment resting on my bedroom carpet.

They were the underthings of a child.

I took his nakedness as permission, after he lay down beside me, to hold him in my arms. We went to sleep like that (spoon fashion) with not the slightest attempt at any sort of carnal connection on either of our parts. One of my hands was gently wrapped around his tender stomach, and the other lay on his little chest. The feeling of his rib cage gently moving in and out from breathing made me feel that I was holding in my hand the heart of a bird. I couldn't help thinking of Michael Llewelyn Davies and Rupert Buxton clasping each other's frail bodies in Sandford Pool, so many years ago. |181

To say that, for me, the evening was auspicious, would be a gross understatement. I did not sleep very much that night, and I knew that in the space of a few hours, I had fallen in love.

I know this might seem bizarre to you. You may think it was just an infatuation, or a superficial lust. I assure it was not. In order for you to understand my feelings for Alan, I think you must put them into the context of my entire emotional and even political situation.

Here I was, a homosexual man approaching his fifties, one who had become largely alienated from his so-called community, one who had been used and then discarded by countless superficial homosexuals in search of Mr. Right. One whose perfectly adequate body, face, and personality had not managed to satisfy the requirements of those who demand perfection in the area of romance. One whose only joy was to be found (outside of periodic visits with his mother) in the company of students who were less than half his age. One who had a distaste for everything which calls itself "gay."

Indeed, I had become, I suppose, what must be called an apolitical homosexual. That is, I never marched, never protested, and never really saw myself as part of a visible or invisible minority. In fact, I'm quite sure that my Jewishness makes much more of a difference to people than my homosexuality. I am evidently a Jew, and even in New York City, in this day and age, that precipitates innumerable prejudices and assumptions, however minor they may be. But the idea that I am a part of a separate — queer — nation (oh, how I hate that word, queer!) makes no sense to me. I have very little in common with other gay men. I am not particularly effeminate or promiscuous. I don't understand the allure of leather or drag. And most of all, I feel more at home with straight people than gay ones. Except for my friend Ronnie, all my acquaintances — for mostly the rest are acquaintances — are heterosexuals. Never have I experienced anything remotely like prejudice in respect to my sexual inclinations. Most people are not interested in what images I might happen to call up to induce orgasm during my masturbatory fantasies. I honestly see no reason to acquaint them with the nauseating details.

What attracted me so much to Alan Peche — and perhaps caused me to fall in love — was the purity of his commitment to his ideals, which seemed to have no conscious or unconscious attachment to the so-called gay movement. Alan was angry because a school friend of his was not allowed by the powers that be to bring another boy to the prom. He smelled injustice, and felt compelled to speak out against it. He was not, in my opinion, advancing a gay cause, he was merely speaking his mind on a subject that he felt was overwhelmingly important. He was a young idealist, pure and simple.

I must admit that the fact that Alan didn't look, act, or talk anything like most homosexuals, appealed to me too. Of course there is something about the chatty bitterness of someone like Ronnie or (of a more academic variety) Leslie, which can be diverting on occasion. It's the kind of humour overeducated academics like Susan Sontag enjoy pointing to with pride and labeling as *camp*. Well don't believe it! *Camp* isn't fun, or in any way profoundly funny. *Camp* is nothing more or less than a nasty, bitter, dirty, witless sneer, marked by an inability to take anything seriously. Contrary to the unwritten philosophy of the *camp* sensibility, there are certain ideas which must never, under any circumstances, be mocked. Ideas such sincerity, integrity, and truth, for instance. I noticed immediately that Alan was plain-spoken, and not the least bit ironic. I could never have imagined him being sarcastic. He was, from the first moment I met him, extremely straightforward. I never had to worry that he would make fun of me. I think those of us who move in homosexual circles forget the extent to which the "gay" world can truly pervert us, draw us away from the (I hope much more natural) impulse that lies in all of us to require honesty in our personal relations, rather than to risk constant ridicule and humiliation at the hands of brutal, sad, and bitter queens.

In short, Alan was a breath of fresh air.

As for my expectations of him, they were no more complicated than the expectations I have of my students. I neither wanted nor expected to have a sexual relationship with him. That didn't stop me from feeling that I was in love with him. I don't know how I can defend myself from the accusation that my feelings were inappropriate. What I felt for Alan was a very deep emotion, the kind of feeling that James Barrie himself described, when he wrote in *The Boy David* of the love the biblical David had for his friend Jonathon: "It surpasses the love of women." And though this notion might seem antiquated or even laughable to many, it is neither of those things to me. You will forgive me if I quote the immortal Oscar Wilde in this context. This, from his speech on the witness stand when he was asked to defend the "love that dare not speak its name," may help to illuminate my feelings: "It is intellectual, and it repeatedly exists between an elder and a younger man, when the elder has intellect, and the younger man has all the joy, hope, and glamour of life before him. That it should be so, the world does not understand." When Wilde made this statement in court he received a standing ovation. I doubt I would receive the equivalent response today. Has gay liberation, in its mad messianic mission to free the libido, somehow transformed a pure and luminous sexless passion between an older and a younger man into a heinous crime? Sexual liberation has caused every tug of the heartstrings to be sexualized. I, and I'm sure many others, long for the days before Freud turned every longing glance into an erotic invitation.

But please understand. I am not saying that I felt absolutely no physical urgings towards this tender nineteen-year-old. Of course I did. How could one not? Beauty is beauty, and the appreciation of it can span all gender, age, and cultural divides. The point is, however, that I did not act on these urgings, and would never have imagined doing so. Or perhaps I should say, I could have imagined anything, except doing the act. Why? This I cannot explain. I put it down to the mystery of a very special kind of love, which I hope will be further illuminated by this modest volume.

The only urge I did have, on that first night with Alan, and on the many nights after that when we slept together, was to perform an act that can barely be called sexual, one which was apparently a common practice in ancient Greece. This is the exercise of inter-crural lovemaking. (For those of you with weak stomachs, you might want to obscure the next sentence with a finger.) In this practice, the older man places his penis between the thighs of the boy, and rubs it between the boy's legs, to orgasm. (The fact that Alan and I often slept spoon fashion, caused this particular expression of affection to cross my mind.) Now, I considered this act, but I never actually carried it out. The only reason I bother to mention this potentially distressing detail at all is because it calls to mind the man/boy love of the ancient Greeks. Although these relationships were at times sexual, the emphasis was, in fact, on learning. The man was, quite properly, the teacher, and the boy the student. This was the model that Oscar Wilde had in mind when he talked of the intellect of the older man and the joy of the younger. Indeed, that was precisely the relationship that soon developed between Alan and myself. What I lacked in joy, I could offer in experience. With Alan, the opposite was true.

The day after Alan slept over for the first time I took him to breakfast at the deli across the street. It was there that I proposed my plan. It seemed more than simple and obvious to me. Why, when I had a huge one-bedroom apartment (more like two bedrooms with the den) should he be confined to a hot little room with his sister? If he stayed with me he could continue his writing and forgo the necessity of working at a mundane day job. And, I could help him with his novel; I was, after all, an English teacher, and more than perfectly suited to the job. Gazing across the table at his youthful, charming face, it seemed much less like a duty than a pleasure.

186 | Alan was hesitant about everything, because that was his way. The last thing he would have wanted would have been to impose on me. Even after all that has passed between us, I still cannot bring myself to believe that there was any guile in him, any trace of a master plan. Alan had no idea, when he literally fell into me at the bar, that I was going to invite him to stay with me or that I would offer to serve as his mentor. On the contrary, my felicitous idea made so much sense to both of us, that there was obviously no point in him refusing.

"But I don't know you very well," he said, munching on a bagel and cream cheese. "What if we get on each other's nerves? What if we get into fights?"

This was a rather bald, almost childlike statement of the discomfiting facts. Obviously Alan was no stranger to life's travails, and perfectly aware that any happy scheme could have its drawbacks, and was pragmatic enough to clear the air before setting forth on the grand plan. Though startled by his forthrightness, I respected his concerns. I explained to him that he would have his own room to work in, but that it only made sense for him to sleep in my bed. After all, I already had a double bed, so why go out and buy another? (And where, after all, would I put it? My apartment was large, but certainly not cavernous.) I reminded him that I would be teaching all day and that he could use that time to work in solitude. I would buy food for the both of us. I couldn't imagine that an animal as small and pale as Alan would require very extensive or even frequent feedings. The only stipulation would be that he worked during the day, and have chapters of the novel to show me when I came home from school. I was clear from the outset that what I was offering was not charity. (What charity would it be, after all, since I had to pay rent and buy food | 187 anyway?) It was patronage.

"But what if I don't have the right number of pages finished? Will you get mad at me? Will you let me have supper?"

This rather naive question made me wonder about the upbringing of the poor boy. I assured him that whatever might have been the custom in his home in Plattsburgh, things would be very different here. There would be no need to produce pages daily, and no punishments for inactivity. Though on those happy days when he did produce writing, I would be glad for him. No, it would be necessary merely for him to discuss with me, each night, the process he was going through as a writer, and the ideas that he was struggling with. I would be there to help. I also suggested that I would be available to read to him from the great novels of the past, during our evening talks. I suggested that we start with Dickens, which I was not at all surprised to learn he had not read. (This, our very greatest novelist, is sometimes ignored in our schools!) Dickens is a master plotter, and the very king of character delineation. His detailed portraits of all people, high and low, are consummate models of humanity and charitable observation. One need not even mention the writer's noble ideals which, it almost goes without saying, illuminate his prose with the purest passion of a loving human heart.

Alan looked at me very sweetly over his eggs and the remains of his bagel. "It sounds like a good idea to me," he said, "as long as you're sure I won't be putting you out."

I felt it might be forward of me to tell him that the truth, in fact, would be quite the opposite.

He went back to his sister's apartment that morning to retrieve his things. Later that afternoon when I returned from school I waited for him on the steps of my apartment. My building (as I mentioned earlier) sits directly across from the Café Lalo. This café is the essence of charm itself. Little yellow Christmas lights dot the trees all year round and give the place a magical, other-worldly quality. It was late October; one of those windy, swirly late afternoons when the gathering dark reminds one of the not unwelcome approach of winter. As Alan marched up from 9th Avenue, the glittering lights of the café framed his frail angelic body. He was dragging a rather large laundry bag full of clothes and an oversized airline carry-on bag which — I discovered soon — touchingly, contained his typewriter. I ran to help him, and felt (for that moment at least) that all was right with the world.

The first thing I did was to put his typewriter in my closet and shut the door. I explained to him that he would be free to use my computer during the day. As quaint and romantic as a typewriter might be, it was the least efficient technology for getting the job done. Alan looked at me like a little boy lost. "But I like my type-writer!" he said.

"A real writer can write on anything," I said. "He writes because he must, and because his soul demands it."

"Okay, if you say so. But I'll miss it."

I dismissed this quibble with good humour, but I remember that the comment irked me a little. Alan had a tendency to stubbornness. To me, it seemed patently obvious that any young, modern writer would need a computer. How was he to revise his work? Of course, I didn't want to go into the details of why a computer would be necessary for him. I expected that, in this matter, as in so many others, Alan might simply understand that there was some wisdom in the advice coming from someone so much older. | 189 I didn't see anything ominous in the conversation at the time. But I look back on this discussion as a very early warning signal. I had imagined that Alan might be the perfect student. Even at the moment when he moved in, I realized (perhaps subconsciously) that he might not be perfect; that there might be a problem. Indeed, as you shall soon see, Alan did not follow all of my advice to the letter, to his own detriment, and to the detriment of our relationship.

I don't pretend that I am a novelist myself. I don't even pretend to be a writer. As I intimated in the introduction, the importance of this book comes not from what I have to say, but from the Barrie–Llewelyn Davies letters, and the effect they ultimately had on my life. But the old adage "those who can't, teach" is more apt and perhaps less damning than one might think. It wasn't necessary for me to be a consummate writer myself (though I fancy myself as somewhat of a skilled amateur) to appreciate good writing or to nurture it in others.

I recommended to Alan only two textbooks to aid him in the study of his craft. These (in addition to the Dickens read in the evenings) were the only formal pattern that his education with me would take. You may be surprised to know the two books I picked.

One was a little-known writing textbook, *Write What You Know* by Thelma Truewhistle Morton, and the other was equally obscure: J.R. Ackerley's memoir, *My Dog Tulip*.

I know these two books may seem like odd and even insufficient choices.

Let me explain.

The history of great writing tells us that those who made their mark wrote only of the things that they were familiar with. Chekhov wrote of the dwindling aristocracy who were his neighbours. The reason these portraits are so effective is because the formidable Russian was painting verbal portraits of his friends and acquaintances. Evelyn Waugh's novels are concerned with the trials and tribulations of, again, the aristocratic world to which he was connected for his long and productive life. Truman Capote wrote about his society friends. When Capote did not (as in *In Cold Blood*) he travelled to the country and researched a tragic family and their savage murderers. Capote, in fact, was incapable of finishing his documentary novel until the murderers were actually executed. Surely there is no more poignant example of a writer whose work had literally to be wrenched loose from the reality to which it was so intimately connected, for Capote and the murderers had become close friends. The one significant outstanding exception to this rule is the great and hallowed Shakespeare. As we all know (except for Leslie, who went to his grave still imagining that Shakespeare was not Shakespeare), the profound plays of the bard of Stratford-upon-Avon chronicled, in the main, the tragic tales of kings and queens, but were nonetheless written by a businessman farmer who — outside of his experience as a bit player — had no experience at all with royalty or at court. But in the case of Shakespeare, the exception proves the rule. As Thelma Truewhistle Morton tells us in her not very widely read but nevertheless engrossing textbook on creative writing, Shakespeare was able to write about what he did not know, and that is what made him a genius, a once-in-a-millennium quirk of fate. How he was able to conjure the hopes and dreams, the loves lost and won, the tragic flaws and ecstatic epiphanies of the ruling classes when he was merely a super-numerary of the lowest order is certainly one of the greatest aesthetic mysteries of all time. But, Thelma wisely tells us, it is not for us to reason why. It is for us to put our shoulders to the wheel, and understand that none of us is Shakespeare.

Thelma makes it clear in her invaluable volume, that one need not live a fascinating, exciting, or crowded life in order to be supplied with the subject matter for a great novel. Some of the greatest writers led very simple lives, indeed never left their houses. Proust spent most of his life in bed, and Eliot worked every day in a bank. But Thelma goes to great pains to explain how these geniuses — who, however, were not on a par with Shakespeare — still managed to cull the from the to and fro, the sometimes grim reality, the mundane pitter and patter of ordinary existence, the details of their art. In the last chapter of *Write What You Know*, the author undertakes an invaluable exercise. Mrs. Morton lived alone in a very small town in Ohio during the thirties (her husband was killed in The Great War) and her daily duty, once she retired from teaching, was to water the flowers. The last chapter is thus a careful and loving description of her modest garden. Aptly titled "My Garden," it offers little in the way of thrills, or passionate eroticism, but it is nevertheless a charming piece of writing. There is truth — there is beauty to be found — even through the eyes of a little old spinster gazing out of her kitchen windows, watching the petunias grow.

In a similar vein — but less a writing manual than a practical example of Morton's principles — is Ackerley's charming memoir. J.R. Ackerley is a little-known homosexual writer, who was born late in the nineteenth century but lived well into the twentieth. He has written an entertaining travel memoir (mostly, Ackerley wrote memoirs) as well as an account of his strained relationship with his father. But what I find most interesting of all are the two books which describe his intimate, almost romantic relationship with his dog.

Yes, his dog.

In *We Think the World of You*, Ackerley describes the fictional story of a lonely man who befriends an abused dog named Evie. In *My Dog Tulip*, Ackerley tells the true story of himself and his own pet. Ackerley is frank about his own homosexuality, his effeminacy, and even his rather unpleasant sexual problem (he was, I believe, what is technically termed a "premature ejaculator") which severely limited his romantic connections. So instead of turning to human beings for love, Ackerley instead cast his eye on the animal world. It may sound hard to believe, but Ackerley actually convinces the reader that the love between a human being and an animal can be emotionally satisfying, even ennobling. Here again is a story from someone whose life has not been crowded with incident, the details of which might seem at first glance to be incredibly sad, or perhaps even in poor taste. But as Ackerley writes with poignant love of his "beautiful bitch," one can't help but fall in love with her too. Dogs, as many gay men and elderly women have discovered, can sometimes make better life partners than people.

Alan, I think, understood my literary advice and took it to heart, almost alarmingly so, as I was to discover later. He took to my plans for educating him like a duck takes to water. We began work immediately. For a couple of weeks after he moved in, I would come home late in the afternoon, according to my schedule. After dinner we would discuss the reading he had done during the day. Then we would sit on the couch and read Dickens late into the night. | 193

I resisted the urge to put my arm around him when we shared these moments. Why was I so shy? Well, I don't see it as shyness. Since (as I have made clear) it was not my intention to have a sexual relationship with the boy, I felt there was no sense in moving in that direction. It's true that at times, I could not resist giving him a hug, for Alan was a quick study and immediately repaid my confidence in him. When I did hug him — or occasionally let my feelings of affection overflow into a kiss on the forehead — Alan would accept my blandishments with quiet, almost passive goodwill. At least I imagined it was goodwill. At any rate, he didn't direct any negative energy my way. At these moments it was actually quite impossible for me to discern the exact nature of Alan's feelings towards me. Alan had a startlingly even temperament. If he experienced emotional highs and lows he almost never made them evident to me. Some days, certainly, he seemed more cheerful than others. But if he ever felt the urge to return my modest signs of physical affection, he certainly kept his inclinations well hidden. Ultimately, I came to think of him as one of the boys described in K.J. Dover's groundbreaking and thorough study, *Greek Homosexuality*. Greek boys were students, and were thus destined to be only the objects of love, never the initiators. The love object himself had no actual desires. He was too busy learning. It was his lot only to *be* desired.

This model fit my relationship with Alan perfectly. Most of the time he would listen quietly to my lectures, but I could tell from his pointed questions that he was listening attentively. After nearly a month of reading and discussion, it came time for him to begin his novel. I was pleasantly surprised to have Alan come to me one evening and say: "Well, I've decided. It's going to be about my home town. It's going to be about Plattsburgh."

I asked him how he had come to this decision.

"Well it's pretty obvious from the reading we did. I mean I've lived most of my life in Plattsburgh, so that's all I really know, so that's what I should be writing about."

I asked him if he had formulated some idea of the plot or characters. Then the revelations began.

"There's something I have to tell you," he said. "But I don't want to offend you or upset you. But since we're working on this novel together" — indeed, the effort almost seemed to be a co-operative one now, although it would always be Alan's novel, not mine — "I think there's something I should tell you about myself." Ahh. Something about himself. I had known that for the novel to be true, for the creation to be profound, this eventuality might occur. "But I'm afraid if I tell you you'll get mad at me."

This was a typical remark. What was I to make of it? Such cautions were annoying because they predicted my response, and had a tendency to defang it. In other words, *how could* I even be angry with him after he had confided his fear that I might very well do so? I said the only thing one can under the circumstances. "Of course I'm not going to get mad at you. Have I ever gotten mad at you?" Up to that point, I hadn't. "What is it. What do you have to tell me? What?"

"It's something personal. I guess I don't think you'll be mad at me, I think you'll just disapprove of me because —"

"Go on. I'm sure I won't disapprove."

"I was molested." His manner and voice were remarkably businesslike and matter of fact. "I want to write about it in this novel and I think I can write about it, because it's something I know. But just because I was molested I don't want you to think I'm crazy or fucked up. Some sort of . . . damaged goods."

Damaged goods. I remember how sweet I found that phrase to be.

He then gave me a look of childlike, petulant concern. This was the most emotional energy that he had directed my way since we had met. I resisted the urge to hug him.

"Of course I wouldn't think that. Abuse is abuse," I said. "It's not right to blame the victim."

"I know," said Alan, "people say that, but it doesn't matter. It still changes the way people think of you. And I want you to respect me."

Well how could I resist this urgent heartfelt appeal? I indicated to him that of course I respected him, and assured him that the fact that he had been the victim of some criminal's cruel and violent act would never change that. I asked him if he would be comfortable telling me about the incident.

His manner was remarkably calm and collected.

"It was in a toilet in Plattsburgh. At a Fourth of July celebration. There was no one around and this man dragged me into one of those Johnny-on-the-spot type toilets. He did stuff to me." Alan didn't show any discernible emotion, but I couldn't imagine that it didn't upset him to talk about it. I reassured him that I didn't disapprove of him or hold him responsible. How could I? He had been ten years old at the time.

Since Alan was obviously frightened that I might judge him and his experience, I thought it best not to pry from him any more information concerning the incident. Abuse was something that he most certainly knew, the experience would be forever branded in his heart. I encouraged him to write about it and to bring the pages to me.

Alan continued working during the day, only now he was less forthcoming about his progress. At first this concerned me, then I realized that if he was to tackle the emotionally difficult material, he would most certainly need some privacy. I continued to read him *Oliver Twist* in the evenings, though, conscious of the appropriateness of the novel which, in its own way, deals with Victorian child abuse.

My decision was finally rewarded. A couple of weeks after his confession Alan came to me with some pages that he asked me to read. He was all trepidation. I knew to match this with my own stern, yet loving, critical acceptance of whatever he had to bring to me. Because of its importance to the developing relationship between Alan and myself, to the process of Alan's writing, and to Alan's primal emotional trauma, I have decided to reproduce the pages here.

It was to be a no-school day for Benjamin. All he could think about (being ten) was the Town Common. There would be a wonderful party for Firecracker Day, with booths and red, white, and blue curtains. Benjamin loved the way the sun made his legs and arms feel. There would be games and races.

He decided to wear a special outfit without telling his mother. She sometimes nixed his fashion choices. One day he tried to wear a red kerchief. He had only been trying to look like a spaceman. Benjamin's mother said it looked embarrassing. "Besides," | 197
she said, "spacemen don't wear kerchiefs!" "Who says?" thought Benjamin.

Benjamin decided on his favourite overalls. He also decided not to wear underwear. The idea of being buck naked under his pants appealed to him. Wrestling had something to do with it. Benjamin enjoyed watching the Worldwide Wrestling Federation channel on tv. Sometimes he would get naked to watch the show — but only when his mother was out. It was very stimulating. The idea of wearing overalls without underwear made Benjamin think of wrestling. Benjamin's mother was at work, so he could wear anything he wanted.

When Benjamin left the house he knew he was being bad.

His house was only a block away from the Town Common. He could hear the marching band, the cheering, the fun. It was too late for the Sack Races. Since he had no father to enter the Father and Son races with, Benjamin decided to stand with his friend Wallace and his father. Wallace's Dad bought Benjamin and his son cotton candy.

He was a very nice man.

After the cotton candy Benjamin had to pee. Wallace's Dad

said that he had to pee too. "Cotton candy has that effect on me," he said. He took Benjamin by the hand and led him to the Johnny-on-the-spot under the trees at the side of the green. There was a lineup. When it was Wallace's Dad's turn, Wallace's Dad saw Benjamin pressing his knees together. "Why don't you go with me?" he said. The idea of peeing with Wallace's Dad scared Benjamin. Wallace's Dad would find out Benjamin wasn't wearing any underwear. Benjamin didn't know what to do.

He said, "Okay."

The inside of the Johnny-on-the-spot was very small. Afterwards, Benjamin remembered the smell of it. Wallace's Dad took his thing out. He looked at Benjamin and said, "Go ahead, don't be shy." Benjamin undid one side of his overalls and the flap fell down. He tried to pee. Wallace's Dad's thing was big. It made Benjamin feel small. He couldn't pee. Wallace's Dad said, "You're pee shy. I get pee shy sometimes, too." Wallace's Dad saw Benjamin looking at his thing. "What are you looking at?"

"Nothing," said Benjamin.

Wallace's Dad told Benjamin he could touch it. "Do you want to play 'Hide in the Hood?'" he asked. Part of Benjamin thought it was wrong to play a game like that, but he did.

Wallace's Dad moaned softly.

Someone knocked on the door and said, "Hurry up in there before I burst my bladder!" Benjamin still had to pee, so Wallace's Dad told him he could go behind the church on the other side of the park. But Benjamin said no. They left the Johnny-on-the-spot. The guy waiting pushed his way into the toilet after them, looking very annoyed. Benjamin stayed with Wallace and his Dad for a while. Then he began to feel sick. He told them he had to go *home. On the way home Benjamin started crying. He thought it must be his fault for wearing overalls.*

As you might imagine, I was in a state of shock. It was by no means the recounting of the actual molestation itself that I found so appalling. Two aspects of the story were unsettling to me. First, there was the very lean, spare (shall we say parched?) style. The lack of adjectives, adverbs, and conjunctives struck me as a forced | 199 and unnecessary pose. Second, the content was deeply problematic. It seemed to me that the narrative (perhaps unintentionally) suggested that the boy might be responsible for tempting his abuser by choosing not to wear underwear. It's hard to say which element I found to be the most offensive. Even before I confronted Alan with these issues, I had a pretty good idea of what he would say. He would defend his style by citing Hemingway (most young writers adore Hemingway), the master of the unadorned sentence. I would then point out that Alan was, sadly, no Ernest Hemingway, and suggest that a hapless reader might require a few more signposts, and simple connectives (an "if," "so," "and," or "but" might be helpful now and then).

And then there was the much more troubling issue of the guilt of the child. Of course the child was not guilty of any crime or indiscretion. That the ten-year-old Alan would have thought that not wearing underwear might implicate him in his own molestation I found deeply touching. But as a valuable (and indeed the only) advocate for Alan's work, I felt it necessary not to let my emotions hold sway. Alan's chosen attire on the day of the abuse was a resonant personal detail, but there were obvious political reasons for not including it in the story. It was again the old case of something in the writing that personally means so very much to the author but which may have unforeseen effects when included in the final draft.

I had a lot to say to him, and he knew it. Alan sat on the couch at an angle to the La-Z-Boy recliner which rests so appropriately beside my window. His little hands were folded in his lap, and his lips were pursed expectantly. His impeccable button-down collar gently grazed the skin of his precious neck as he moved one hand to straighten the pleat of his khaki pants. He might easily have been at church. But instead, I knew that he was experiencing one of the most vulnerable moments of his young life.

I will not pretend that I was at a loss for words. I had sat just like this before many students, and countless times I had read their papers as they waited, and offered critical analysis on the spot. But this was not the same. I had so much invested in this particular student — in fact I was developing a deep (though chaste) love for him — that I was acutely aware of his sensitivities. I knew how very much this precious creation meant to Alan, and I did not want to hurt him. On the other hand — and this other hand was terribly important — there was the writing itself to consider, as well as Alan's future career. Would I be doing the boy a service if I stifled my honest response simply in order to spare his feelings? Indeed, what did feelings matter where art was concerned?

I have found that in these pedagogical situations, asking the student questions often serves as the most tactful approach. "So, I'm wondering, Alan, why you chose to write in such short, brutal sentences which are nearly stripped of adjectives, conjunctions, and qualifiers?"

He looked a little miffed. "I used adjectives."

"Well, perhaps now and then. What you don't want to do is engender exasperation or even anger in your reader. You don't want to alienate him or her."

This didn't seem to intimidate Alan. "Why not?"

"Well if you anger your readers, you are likely to lose them."

"But I understood that the job of the artist was to lead."

This was something new. I had never heard this idea (or anything like it) from Alan before. "I don't know if I would entirely agree," I said. "It seems to me that the job of the artist is to communicate. How can you communicate anything through a style which is lean to the point of starvation, and lacks variation and rhythm?"

"I don't think Allen Ginsberg would agree with you."

I looked at him, sitting rigid and a little hot under his prim colour. But he still managed not to stir from my couch.

"Pardon me?"

"Allen Ginsberg. He thinks that the artist's job is to lead. And that sometimes the artist might leave the audience behind. But that's okay."

I could tell that Alan was very, very upset, but as usual he didn't really show it. He looked at me with a persistence that I would have most certainly — if I had noticed it in anyone else — labelled stubbornness.

"Where in heaven's name did you get advice from Allen Ginsberg?"

"In Plattsburgh."

"Allen Ginsberg was in Plattsburgh?"

"At the State University there. He came to give a lecture. He talked a lot about style and alienating the audience. And he read one of his poems called 'Howl' which he said didn't have any punctuation, because it was meant to be a cry from the heart. 'Howl' made a lot of people angry. Allen Ginsberg didn't seem to care."

Well this was certainly manipulative. Was I to be pressured into accusing him of not writing from his heart? I most certainly could not do that. But I could mention something else.

"Well," I said, leaning back comfortably in my La-Z-Boy, "I find it quite ironic that you would quote Allen Ginsberg. Why haven't you mentioned him before?"

"I thought it might upset you."

This really was getting infuriating. I bounced up out of my chair and started to pace the room.

"Alan, I have to say I'm beginning to find your attempts to always spare my feelings very annoying. Do you know how many times you have said to me that you didn't tell me something because you were afraid it would upset me? This is getting to be a habit with you."

"But look at you now. You're getting upset. You got out of your easy chair."

"Alan, I'm *not* upset with you for telling me about Allen Ginsberg. I *am* upset with you for withholding that information from me to spare my feelings, which is a very different thing. Besides, it's not *my* feelings your sparing, it's *yours*. Because it's not just my reaction, but the effect my reaction will have on you, that you're really afraid of. So here, I'm angry now. Is that such a big deal?"

Alan almost smiled, a little uncomfortably. "No," he said.

"Good. I just hate being painted as some sort of frightening emotional bear, or a volcano ready to blow. You can tell me things. I'm you're friend. You shouldn't be afraid of me. That's not a good friendship. Do you understand?"

"I understand," said Alan, quietly, meeting my gaze.

Only I'm not entirely sure he did.

"And let me tell you a little bit about Mr. Allen Ginsberg. You may not be aware of this, but Mr. Ginsberg, for whom you seem to have so much respect, was something of a boy-lover himself."

| 203

"I know that," said Alan. "He flirted with me."

"He *what*?"

"He flirted with me when he came to read. I went up to him to get my book signed and he told me I had beautiful eyes."

"That's disgusting."

"What's disgusting about it? Why can't he admire my eyes?"

"If you can't see what's disgusting about it, then I'm certainly not going to tell you. You might remember that the man is nearly four times your age."

"So?"

I was beginning to realize that underneath the sweet little-boy exterior was quite a feisty young man. I decided to pull out the heavy ammunition. "You may or not be aware, Alan — and I think you should give me a little credit for having seen a slight bit more of the world and for having a little more experience than you. You may not be aware that when I say 'boy-lover' I am speaking quite literally. Now, I don't know if he's actually been arrested for pedophilic activities, but I do understand that his lover is much, much younger than he is, and that the two of them actually engage in the practice of luring young boys — via the device of marijuana — into their bed. And to top it all off, have you ever heard of NAMBLA?"

"Yes." Alan looked at me with what I knew was a hint of defiance.

"Well as you know then it is the name of the North American Man/Boy Love Association, and it is a perverted, disgusting, morally corrupt organization. These people actually encourage men to molest boys. Now, Allen Ginsberg is a card carrying member of NAMBLA. I am not one of those people — despite my disinclination to march in Pride Parades — who takes politics lightly. Nor do I think that politics lacks a relationship to art. I have found it quite impossible, for instance, to enjoy Ezra Pound's monumental *Cantos* after discovering he was a Fascist. No. When I discovered that Allen Ginsberg was a pedophile, I exorcised his books from my library (just as I exorcised Woody Allen's videos from my collection when I learned of how he had treated poor, suffering Mia). Now, of course you may or may not share my opinions, but I would doubt that you have even thought about the issue. But never mind, let's put my opinions of Allen Ginsberg aside. It might be important for you to take note of an interesting contradiction in your position. Here you are, taking the advice of Mr. Allen Ginsberg, the opinion of a known boy-lover, on aesthetic principles, and applying them to your piece which is, ironically enough, about the molestation of a boy. Does this not seem like a contradiction to you?"

I had worked myself up into what must have seemed quite a frenzy by this point. But I felt strongly about the issue. Whatever

Alan's feelings were for me, I don't think they were very fond ones at that moment.

"I suppose so," he said.

"You suppose so. I would think very much so. And that is my problem with the piece, outside of the syntactical difficulties I have with it. Now, don't get me wrong, the piece comes from sincere feeling, and that is its strength; you are obviously writing about what you know. But don't you understand how corrupt it is | 205 even to suggest that the boy might be guilty of having brought on his molestation by not wearing underwear? This is certainly the thing women's libbers have finally hammered into our reluctant brains, if nothing else: we can't and musn't blame the victim."

"But I'm not," he said. "That's the point. I'm just making the reader aware that the boy blamed himself, even if it was the wrong thing for him to do."

"But it's the idea that the boy wore no underwear that day because he was wanting to feel sexual or to flirt or something — I mean that's what you're suggesting isn't it?"

"I don't know what I'm suggesting . . ." he looked down at the couch and started to pick at a piece of lint.

"I'll tell you then. You're suggesting that a little boy is a seducer. And that's wrong. Surely you must understand that it certainly was the other way around."

He stared at the couch for a very long time. Had there been an old grandfather clock in the room, we would have heard it ticking. Instead, I could very clearly hear the beating of my heart. Finally he looked up at me. He looked very, very tired.

"I suppose you're right," he said with a sigh.

At the time I believed him and imagined that he truly accepted my point of view, but now I'm not so sure. I needed to be honest with him for his own good. But of course I didn't want to discourage him from continuing with his novel, so I told him what I liked about the scene and suggested he work on a new draft. I recommended that the style be a little less lean, and that the boy's guilt be minimized. Alan agreed to work on a revision. In retrospect I realize this was a watershed moment, for this discussion signaled a change in our working routine. No longer would I hear a daily, detailed report on his writing. Alan explained to me that he needed some creative privacy — in order to allow the concept and the writing itself to bubble a bit before it came to a fruitful boil. So, ironically, it was after reading his very first effort that I became less involved with his writing. I was perturbed. (Of course, it was very irritating that he felt compelled to inform me of his decision in the guilty-little-boy manner that was proving to be his trademark.) I *tried* to see it as an advance in our relations that he was confident enough to cross me at all. But I couldn't help thinking that our vacation from creative collaboration was a bad thing. And it wasn't just that I was losing control. I am not a control freak. Not at all. I made him aware that I had boundless confidence in him. As a result, Alan continued working happily each day, and the readings of Dickens continued each night.

Looking back on what happened, all this may not have been such a good thing.

Because we spent less time discussing his novel, we had more time to venture into other areas. Alan told me a little more about his family life. He told me that his mother worked at the local school as a cleaner. His father had simply not been around. Alan wouldn't tell me why; he was very secretive about his Dad. His relationship with his mother had not been a good one. In fact, he had left the house (and Plattsburgh) mainly because of the fractious nature of that relationship. (His sister's move to New York City several years before was also prompted by the difficulties with their strident mother.) I found his background fascinating but also a bit repellent. It seemed that Alan's mother was a very bitter person who felt the need to tear him down constantly. His personal history was completely alien to mine — my mother had always been (and still was) loving and very supportive of my creativity and career aspirations, and my father, before he died, had been quietly encouraging. It was hard for me to imagine what it would be like to have almost no parenting on the paternal side, and a bitter, critical mother to boot. These revelations made me feel very sad for Alan, who was, I was beginning to see, a bit of an emotional have-not.

I don't think it's surprising that Alan awakened the nurturing parent in me.

Which brings me to music.

I have always believed in the healing power of music. So now that we had more time in the evenings, I decided to use it to further Alan's education, and at the same time provide him with a sort of spiritual balm.

The night after I read that very first passage from his work-in-progress was also the night when we began Alan's musical education. I am not one of those gay men who is so ignorant as to praise the American musical as the pinnacle of art, without understanding its not-so-humble beginnings. Indeed, Stephen Sondheim's work, especially the acclaimed *Sweeney Todd*, cannot be understood without a grasp of the subtleties of opera.

That night we set sail on our journey through the history of music. Our first stop on the trip was a visit with Giuseppe Verdi and his warhorse, *Rigoletto*. The venerable Joe Green (as my Italian music teacher used to call him) is a much maligned and misunderstood artist, whose brilliant and subtle compositions have been plagiarized to provide background music for stage and screen. *Rigoletto* is not only the perfect opera to inaugurate any musical education, but one which I knew would provide fertile ground for discussions of Alan's work. It was fascinating to watch Alan's face as he listened to profoundly beautiful music for the first time. He knew nothing of opera or musicals, having been raised on boy bands and Madonna. Like any budding operaphile, Alan was quite visibly bored at the beginning. (Even though he tried to be *polite*. Ever the little gentleman, Alan always tried to be *polite*.) He remarked on the unnatural, acrobatic nature of the vocals, the trills and vibrations. He nearly jumped out of his seat upon hearing "*Caro Nome*" for the first time, and was very pleased to identify the infamous "*Woman Is Fickle*" aria when it came along. I attempted to make him understand that there is a right way and a wrong way to listen to the world's best music. It's not enough to wait around for a pretty tune that you've heard before on television, and then replay it again loudly and hum along. I explained to him that the genius of this very special opera lies in the fact that it can be understood without a knowledge of Italian, indeed without ever referring to the libretto at all. This is Verdi's genius: to have written melodies that so perfectly mirror the characters' feelings that you can tell, simply by listening to the musical notes, what specific emotions the characters are experiencing. When we came to Gilda's aria after the rape, for instance, I asked him what she was feeling. He said, perceptively, "She's defiant, she's trying to prove something."

Which is, of course, true. I explained that Gilda had just been abducted and ravished by the Duke, and that she was now attempting to convince her father that she had enjoyed the experience. I tried to make him understand that this was the one flaw in this otherwise perfect opera, the conceit that a young girl might actually take pleasure in being raped. I told him of Queen Victoria's disapproval of this scene and how proper young ladies in New York City were required to turn their backs to the stage for this particular aria until at least the year 1930. Though I did not make any specific reference to *his* molestation story, I assumed that he noticed the similarities — and the corresponding problems in themes. Though Alan insisted for quite a while (indeed all through his musicological education with me) that he was bored with opera and only really liked the tunes, I couldn't help fantasizing that, somewhere deep inside, the music was having its healing effect, and revealing profound things impossible to put into words.

| 209

Now I must take you, the reader, into my confidence.

For what happened a couple of months after this was so heart-wrenching and traumatic that it requires thoughtful exploration. Indeed, it demands an intense investigation of the inner reaches of the human soul, and, I think, has more than a little relevance (if you have been wondering where all this has been leading) to my interpretation of the importance of the J.M. Barrie–Michael Llewelyn Davies letters.

Alan didn't bring me any work and we didn't talk about it for nearly three weeks. Then, just as I was beginning to champ at the bit and require from my hardworking little angel some sample of work, he came to me with a revised version of his molestation story.

I won't bother to reproduce the revision here. Suffice it to say that he followed my suggestions to the letter. The new version was more stylistically fluid, and contained not even a hint that the little victim was complicit in his own deflowering. I was satisfied with the draft and congratulated him. I was a little concerned, however, that it had taken Alan so very long to rewrite something that was barely a short story. When I tactfully mentioned the amount of time that had passed since he had shown me written proof of his labours, he informed me that he had reached a painful impasse, and that for the past couple of weeks he had been unable to set pen to paper due to nerve-wracking indecision.

"Where should I go next?" he said.

I gave him the advice I always give: to write what you know.

"I know that. But what do I know? That incident happened in my life, it was real, but then it didn't really have much effect."

"What do you mean?"

"I mean I was really upset about it at the time, mostly ashamed, but then I went on and lived my life."

"And what happened in your life?"

"Nothing happened. I lived it."

"Things must have happened to you."

"Well I went to school, my mother bitched at me, and I got bored with life, until I decided to write about the prom for the school newspaper and then come to stay with my sister in New York City."

This was so typical of Alan. I was beginning to realize how

easily he could slip into a sort of emotional desolation, a flatness, a kind of bored, not even ultimately desperate vision of his own reality. Again I realized that we had moved forward in our relationship, because I could not have imagined him being so frank with me when we first met. But (as so often happens with people) it was only after Alan took me into his confidence that I began to realize how unmotivated my beautiful young soul could be. But Alan still had not caused me to be disillusioned. I would always see him as the incarnation of the immortal bard's sonnets, as a perfect youth, inside and out. His exterior was merely the pond, a glacial reflection of his inner sweetness. This I believed then, and still believe. I thought of T.S. Eliot's bank, of Proust's bedchamber, and even of James Joyce's working-class, sluttish, and insensitive wife (Nora Barnacle — how aptly named — she stuck to him all his life). But out of each of their dull realities these consummate artists had crafted seemingly effortless arcs of immortal prose. I had faith in my child prodigy. I knew that there were depths to be plumbed, even if he was not cognizant of their presence. So I persisted.

|211

"Surely there was something. Didn't you have any special friends?"

"You mean boyfriends?"

"Perhaps. Anyone with whom you formed a special relationship that you could write about?"

"Well, there wasn't anyone special at all, really. I always pretty much kept to myself. I've never been a really social person. Sometimes I think I'm a bit agoraphobic. I don't really like going out to bars or anything unless I'm drunk."

"Well, we have to rack our brains."

"I mean there wasn't anybody special except . . . Well, I guess there was someone. But it was stupid."

This was too tempting to resist. "Tell me, what!"

"There was . . . the iceman."

The *iceman*. The word was absolutely dripping with poetry! Now we were onto something. "Who was the iceman?"

"Oh just this guy who used to deliver ice to the corner store every week. I used to hang out in the back of the store with Wallace and smoke cigarettes."

"You didn't tell me you smoked."

"Well I don't hardly ever anymore." He paused. "That's how my father died. Lung cancer."

"It's good you don't smoke then."

"No, I hardly ever do."

"You don't?"

"No I — I don't."

I made a mental note to be more aware of suspicious smells and to keep an eye out for telltale cigarette ends in the apartment. Could he be sneaking cigarettes during the day when I was off at school? I recoiled at the notion of acting the spy, but out of concern for Alan's health I now realized I would have to be vigilant. I settled into my easy chair.

"So, tell me about the iceman."

"There's nothing to tell. He was this really nice guy. But . . . simple."

"Not very intelligent?"

"He was intelligent enough, I guess. But just a simple, not very complex person. Easy to be with."

"A sort of . . . father figure?"

"Well I don't know. He was the right age to be one, I guess."

"Well what was your relationship like?"

"He used to smoke with us, and sometimes I'd help him load in the ice. Some days he took me around in his truck. On weekends he took me fishing."

"Well that certainly sounds like a relationship. Is it possible you were working out something with him? Some feelings about Wallace's father, perhaps? Or your own?"

"I *suppose* so. But the thing was, he didn't talk very much. That's why I liked him. We had sort of a silent friendship. He was someone I could be silent with. I didn't have to *be* anything. That's why I liked him."

I knew we were onto something. But Alan seemed to be taking a perverse pleasure in setting obstacles in his own way, and then musing, glumly, on the inevitable, depressing block on his creativity. Was this persistent defeatism the result of his hopeless upbringing? I realized that it was important to move to the next stage of my "write what you know" philosophy, and rescue him from this funk.

"Well it seems to me," I said, "that whether or not you're completely aware of it, what was going on was a kind of redemption."

"Redemption?" he said.

"Yes. You'd had a very bad experience with an older man, and you found, in this friendship with another older man, a way to redeem that traumatic relationship."

"I guess so, but we didn't really have any sort of deep friendship or anything. I mean, you tell me to write what I know, but the thing is, Manny, what I know is not very much."

He really was making this very difficult.

There was nothing to do but plunge in, head first, and hope for the best. I leaned forward. "I think you may discover that there is someone else in your life who has responded only to the very best in you, someone with whom you are working on a kind of *redemption*."

"Who?"

"Think about it for a minute."

Really, could he possibly be so dense?

"Well no there wasn't, I mean —"

"Think later in your life, much later. After the iceman. After you moved to New York, maybe?" I was having to paint the picture for him.

"Oh, you mean . . . you mean . . . you?"

I sat in my easy chair, eyeing him with pleasure which was not unedged with wariness.

"But I don't get it."

"What don't you get?"

"You want me to write about you?"

"No, I don't want you to write about me, but I think it might be an interesting idea to take the experience that you are having with me — something that you know — and the experience that you had with the iceman — which is also something that you know — and put them together somehow to describe what might be a very bruised and battered young man's redemption."

Alan looked at me tentatively. I can honestly say that I absolutely did not then have any idea what he was really thinking. "That's an . . . interesting idea." he said.

"Think about it." I said. "Let it stew and gurgle and bake and maybe even burn. Something might happen."

"Yes," he said, very slowly, "something might."

And that was the end of that. I congratulated myself on my brilliance, on my ability to turn a dire artistic (and personal) situation into a productive one. But what really happened that day? Was my suggestion that he utilize our relationship as a source of inspiration for his novel hopelessly self-serving? Was it a sad attempt at self-aggrandizement? I was merely trying to help. As soon as he mentioned the iceman, the word seemed so redolent — |215 not only the imagery of coldness, of the cold man, of the cold hands that had touched a boy in a public lavatory — but also of *melting*, of the possibilities for warmth between a younger and an older man. Certainly the word "iceman" has its precedent in American literature — think of *The Iceman Cometh*, for instance. I must admit that I imagined Alan might see his way to a new understanding of our relationship through his novel. But that's not why I suggested it to him. I was only thinking of the future of his novel. I was only thinking of him. A boy in a small town, molested, dejected, forms a redemptive relationship with the old iceman (for I could see now that the character of the iceman would have to be old, in wisdom and in years). How touching it all might be. The situation was ripe with profound possibilities.

What I discovered, in due time, was that this was not what Alan would write about next.

All the following month Alan avoided talking about his work. He assured me that he was slaving away during the day. At night we listened to music. We were moving backwards to Donizetti, which I thought was only proper, and would soon arrive at Mozart. We had almost finished reading *Oliver Twist*.

I came home from work early one day, having neglected to tell him of the change in my schedule. I had quite forgotten that the students were going on a field trip to the Whitney with their art teacher. It was a brisk December afternoon. I remember that I had begin to fantasize about Christmas. I had never been able to stop myself from buying a Christmas tree (much to my mother's chagrin). I made a clear separation: Hanukkah with her, and my own little tree and presents for myself. Well this year, I realized that it would be a tree for two. Perhaps Alan and I would even pick one out together. And of course it might be appropriate for him to gather with my mother and me around the menorah. Alan would be introduced to all her aches and pains, her garrulous personality, all her fascinating, endless melodramas. I couldn't help thinking that it would be a good thing for him to witness my affection for her. Observing a healthy, loving mother–son relationship at close quarters would doubtless have a positive influence on him. Perhaps we would invite his sister over for Christmas morning and then visit my mother after? Or would we decide to spend that very special morning alone?

I was having visions of the presents that I would buy him as I hurried up the steps, hugging my coat around me, turning up the collar against the cold. I remembered wondering, on that gay afternoon, if it would be appropriate for me to buy him a pair of silk boxer shorts. He had taken to wearing his underwear to bed as the weather got colder. Perhaps it was time for Alan to graduate from those sad little boy's underpants to something more suitable for a young man about town. As I fumbled with the lock in the cold, I anticipated, with some pleasure, coming upon him when he was working. It was all too much like something from *Doctor Zhivago*. I would open the apartment door (he had probably already heard my key), and he would just be rising from his desk, dragging himself out of the intoxicating hypnotism of the creative effort, running his hand through that mop of shining, platinum hair; I knew that I would have to keep myself from hugging him.

But I was the one who was surprised. When I entered the apartment I was greeted with a deafening silence. Alan was not there. I shouted for him and searched every room. I thought that he must be taking a short break. He must have gone out for a coffee. I searched the computer and the desk for a sign of his creative efforts. I had warned him repeatedly to make hard copies of his work, so I assumed that if he had been writing, there would be a page or two in the printer or near it.

There was nothing.

It was a little after noon, and certainly what I had always imagined would be the heart of his creative day. Had he perhaps gone out for lunch? The longer he was away, the more suspicious I became.

Then I saw it.

I don't know why, after all, I hadn't seen it earlier.

There was a loft bed in the study, which I didn't use as a bed at all, but instead as storage for books and odds and ends. Underneath the loft was a dark, underused area, which housed a filing cabinet and a pile of garbage bags filled with old clothes that I had inexplicably never been able to part with. It was a corner of a vast apartment that was rarely disturbed. I felt rather guilty that I had never cleaned it up.

Sitting in the dark between two garbage bags was Alan's typewriter.

I did not move towards it immediately. I stayed on the other side of the room. It was as if I was suddenly sharing a narrow cage with a wild animal. In the typewriter was a piece of paper and there was something written there.

I didn't want to read it.

First of all it was written on his typewriter, which we had long ago agreed was a useless old contraption, but which I had allowed him to keep on the promise that he would never use it again. It wasn't so much that Alan had dared to disagree with my advice; he had lied to me. And of course, the pretty picture I had cherished (as I sipped coffee on my morning break at school) of Alan at home at *my* desk, at *my* computer, *creating*, was destroyed.

But of course it wasn't about the typewriter or the computer at all. It was about the writing.

Tentatively, I approached the typewriter, and lifted it from the floor. I searched around in a sudden panic for a place to put down the machine so I could remove the piece of paper. I turned towards the living room, and decided on the couch — the same couch where Alan always sat when we discussed his work. I put the typewriter on the couch and sat down beside it, rolled up the page and read.

In the very night of afternoon. All around me sweet with love. Is it love? They swarm, loiter, and mull. They are watching me. The door opens and he's looks attractive. I'm drunk. Maybe he's too old and I'm so drunk it doesn't matter. I take a drag on my cigarette and smile my come-on-in smile. He's on the floor. That's where he's most happy. On his knees. He pulls down his pants and it's all there. That's what God gave him. He's sucking my cock. He keeps falling asleep. His eyes close slowly and then he nods off. He sways to and fro like a tree in the wind. Or something. Then he wakes up again. Slowly, his eyes open. He can see my cock and he wants it. He starts to suck. What drugs is he on? It seems like hours. I sniff poppers and it seems all right. He wants me to squirt in his mouth. Should I? No. I'm not going to come in the mouth of some guy who can't even keep his eyes open long enough to suck me. Why am I here? I'm just looking for the same old thing. Never the same, but still

|219

And that is where it stopped.

I don't know if I can describe what I experienced at that moment.

My first reaction to this brutal text was physical pain mixed with revulsion. It was as if someone had kicked me in the gut and I was going to be sick. Then came the quivering hands. Tears began to well in my eyes.

I knew exactly what I had read, and who had written it.

My little angel was not really an angel at all.

I must admit that my initial reaction was a visceral response to the brutal text itself.

Now, as you may have surmised, I am not a fan of smut. I have never found it necessary to help satisfy my base physical needs. I will never understand why others must utilize it. When I do feel the need to pleasure myself, I find that the pictures I am able to conjure in my imagination serve the purpose. In other words, I need no pornographic aids. The piece that I had discovered was pornography of the most blatant and pernicious variety. There was nothing edifying or uplifting in the text. It was even blasphemous ("what God gave him"). What is most upsetting about pornography — of either the violent or the sexual kind —

is that the images continue to haunt one. I can completely sympathize with those who theorize that pornography is dangerous and
drives people to violence; I can see how it can work on someone
who is mentally unbalanced. This is why such garbage should and
must be censored — and in some cases destroyed.

For instance, there was one word which I simply couldn't
get out of my brain: the word "squirt." For some reason I could
not stop thinking of that appalling verb. It seemed to reduce the
possibilities for the act of human lovemaking to the romantic
necessities of a common garden hose. The idea of a human organ
"squirting" is so disgusting to me (as I'm sure it is to you) that I
almost lost my lunch. I do not want to read that text, see that
image, or have it repeated over and over in my consciousness.
After my relationship with Alan came to a very messy conclusion
(which I will recount in due time) I embarked on a period of complete abstinence which has turned into a more ordinary celibacy.
(When I talk of my celibacy I have in mind the original French
word *celibataire* which means "to be alone." Celibacy, for me,
includes masturbation. Abstinence does not.) I have no doubt that
my initial dramatic retreat from the sexual arena had much to
do with that horrible word and the unwelcome images it brought
to mind. This is why we find pornography so repugnant. It forces
us to confront images which we never, ever wish to see or hear,
and all against our will. It is a kind of spiritual rape, and I will
never understand those who collaborate in its construction.

That explains the sickness. Now I will talk of the sadness.

What was even more upsetting than the words themselves was
where they came from. I didn't want to believe Alan had written
the piece, but there was no escaping it. This was why he had kept

his writing secret. Of course he could never have shown me this passage himself. I felt deeply, achingly, horribly betrayed. For the last two months I had nurtured him like an injured colt. What a fool I had been to trust him! He was nothing but an evil boy! And evil is as evil does. Never before had I been confronted with such a situation.

As much as I hated the words, I couldn't stop rereading them. Like a car accident or a plane crash, they held me with a kind of morbid fascination. And soon it was the style of the piece that upset me nearly as much as it's content. Why in heaven's name would anyone deliberately set out to write in such a vague, staccato, inarticulate manner? (I knew what Alan was *capable* of; it was not this.) Besides "squirt," the passage "like a tree in the wind. Or something" nearly drove me mad. I kept staring at it, in disbelief. I realized of course, that this writing (if it could be called that) was most likely a first draft — after all it was not finished properly (surely a piece could not properly be meant to end in midsentence) — but that didn't excuse the slapdash use of words. The English language provides us with countless rich metaphorical possibilities, and "like a tree in the wind" — as inadequate as it might be as a phrase to describe someone nodding off during the act of sex — nevertheless did not need "Or something" tacked on to make it more clear. ("Or something" is not even a sentence.) After all the time we had spent talking about a flowing style, and the proper use of adjectives and adverbs! The fact that Alan had produced this pornography that, on top of everything, was sloppily written, made me feel that I had been a failure as a teacher, and that I was, quite simply, a fool.

This was my initial reaction; as thoughtless and irrational as most initial reactions are. Then, after reading the piece over and over (perhaps a hundred times), I came to a more profound and less selfish conclusion. I could not help thinking of the phrase I had hammered into Alan's brain for the past month and a half: write what you know. Of course it's true that Alan had blithely jettisoned most of my editorial advice in this effort, caring nothing for style, and ignoring my suggestions for content. Was it possible that he had bypassed a much more fundamental notion as well?

I knew in my heart that he had not.

Where else could this scene have come from, if it was not from his own life? The first phase-cum-sentence was particularly chilling. "In the very night of afternoon." So this is how Alan had repaid my generosity! He had been using his free time to cruise seedy hot spots. It was difficult to discern the exact location; was it a toilet, an old warehouse, or a dirty video store? Let me tell you that it offered me no reassurance to think that Alan might have taken my most important piece of advice to heart. And as much as I might have liked to think so, the work could not have been simply the product of a fertile imagination. Why in heaven's name would anyone invent such horrors? (Even the Marquis de Sade's baroque, licentious scribblings were based to some extent on actual experience, and not merely the result of an over-libidinous imagination.) To assume that Alan had written about the facts of his life would save me from a more terrifying thought — that he had made it all up, that this depraved sexual fantasy was something which he *wished to be so.*

And then another idea came to me. Perhaps Alan had written an honest, unexpurgated, desperate plea for help, a cry of the heart from a lonely, neglected, but still gifted child. Perhaps he had, consciously or unconsciously, left this very revealing writing for me to see. Regarding the passage as a coded message I examined the text with a cooler, critical eye. I noted immediately that he mentioned poppers. Historically, poppers were prescribed by medical doctors to young ladies in the form of smelling salts, and to sufferers of heart disease as a restorative, until some enterprising salesman decided to market the substance in little bottles to homosexual men as an aphrodisiac. Rampant popper usage has significant psychological implications. Ultimately, there is nothing more boring than tricking with a new partner every night. But the use of poppers, with the momentary loss of consciousness and almost poetic quickening of the heart, turns the pathetic climaxes of the homosexual male into something that resembles romance. (Poppers also have the same addictive properties as that most sublime of human emotions.) If Alan was using poppers, then he was trying to blot out his real feelings, his loneliness, his longing for love.

| 223

Then there was the question, "What drugs is he on?" This phrase completely takes for granted the notion that drugs are an ordinary part of life. Well, for many gay men, they are. Ecstasy, crystal meth, uppers, downers, and poppers are as common as a daily glass of wine for the promiscuous homosexual. But how could Alan be a drug addict without my knowing it? I knew that he smoked cigarettes, but this was much, much, worse.

I began to blame myself. Had I made a mistake by tutoring him poorly, by neglecting to watch him more closely? Was it my own fault that he was so depraved? I remembered that first night in my vast bed, as we lay entwined, spoon fashion. Though my actions toward him were chaste, there had been moments when I experienced lust for him. In my hysteria, I became obsessed with the idea that Alan somehow — through some extrasensory perception perhaps — had gained knowledge of my most private urges. My shock and fear for him propelled me into a downward spiral of fantasy. Had my base desires corrupted him? Had he somehow, intuitively, divined that my feelings for him were not pure? Had the suspicion of my lechery brought out a similar lechery in him?

I could feel myself rapidly disintegrating; soon I would be back in the humiliating state I was in when I first read the passage. This would not do. After all, I had to get ready to confront Alan, who would arrive any minute. I attempted to take control. I said to myself, "Therein madness lies." Surely Alan couldn't read my mind. Surely all that passes between people, all that can possibly pass between them, is what can be perceived by the senses. Surely one could not be guilty by thought. Wasn't that the whole idea of religion, that we are imperfect creatures with base bodies and vile emotions who must nevertheless learn to control ourselves? Isn't this what I had done? Was I to hold myself responsible for feelings that I had successfully suppressed? Surely not.

And then a thought cleared my mind and focussed my anger, and left me free of humiliation. With it came the most hope of all. Assuredly, Alan had been not only under the influence of drugs, but influenced by someone who lured him into taking drugs. He could not possibly have discovered the drugs himself. Even after all the abuse in his early life, how could he turn to drugs when he had me, here, living with him, encouraging him? No, someone must have led him to it. An evil man. There was no doubt about it. In the pornographic passage Alan had described a nameless sexual partner, but there must have been someone else: someone who had educated him into these ways, after having recognized the vulnerability of a young man and (this was too horrible to imagine) after molesting him. As I thought about Alan's seduction, about his manipulation at the hands of a Svengali, a picture emerged, one I didn't want to look at, but forced myself to see. It was of an older man, perhaps in his early fifties, riding in one of those horrible gigantic army-issue jeeps (Hummers) that have | 225 become so popular lately for well-heeled Chelsea gentlemen. He would have a goatee and a shaved head. On the surface, he would appear to be handsome, but on closer inspection, his skin would have that slightly saggy quality that typifies aging gay men who spend too much time at the gym. Alan would be sitting in a café somewhere on a fall afternoon, worrying about his writing, and this horrible creature would drive up. He would sit down beside Alan. He would flatter him. This monster, of course, would be possessed of enormous pectoral muscles, and a facile, superficial wit. He would take Alan back to his apartment and introduce him to drugs and mindless sex. This relentless pervert, this bloodsucking vulture would demand that Alan accompany him on his jaunts to sleazy toilets and orgiastic parties. The boy would be swept up in it all, and unable to resist the compliments, the sensual delights and the sparkling glamour that typifies the gay sexual underworld. He would become infatuated with it, and all because of the evil ways of an aging homosexual whose technique for keeping boys interested in him was to feed them a diet of drugs and illusions.

When I thought of it, yes, Alan had been losing weight.

I knew men like Alan's seducer. I had met them with Ronnie. They were hideous, sad, desperate creatures, but the young men they latched onto didn't know that. They only saw the huge biceps, the trim waists, the washboard stomachs, the expensive diaphanous shirts opened to the waist, and the obscene bulging crotches. It seemed to me that it had to be true that Alan was influenced by such a person and this would explain his addiction, and the composition I had found in the typewriter.

I shuddered at the thought, unable to believe how far this fantasy had taken me. But it seemed perfectly, completely real.

226 |

I cried.

I realized, finally, what the "gay" life really was. It's a religion of sex. It causes men to debase themselves in the pursuit of pleasure. The intense promiscuity that defines gay culture only leads to humiliation and death from addiction, loneliness, and AIDS. That same culture can be as irresistible to young men like Alan Peche as it is to older men like me. I had wrestled with that promiscuous lifestyle since coming out to my mother at age twenty-five. Forget for a moment about the propaganda called Gay Liberation. Think of the evil men do to boys in the name of homosexuality. Think of the ageism, the body fascism, the superficiality, the depression, the quiet sleazy desperation of gay lives.

I was seized with a hatred of my own kind that was so intense that it far surpassed anything I had ever felt before.

I mean, the sad, tasteless absurdity just goes on and on.

I thought of gay men going off with lovers, moving out of perfectly charming bachelor apartments into drafty lofts, changing their opinions, acting irresponsibly — young dizzy boys and ones old enough to know better — rejecting their old friends, wearing bizarre exhibitionistic clothing, getting tattoos with each other's names, turning their lives and jobs upside down, happily screaming, "I've found LOVE!" I thought of them opening up silly businesses together in Soho, then having "open relationships," threesomes, wild parties, going off to Palm Springs together, getting their entire bodies shaved, claiming to have safe sex when God knows what they're actually doing. I thought of all the times when such men had phoned me begging for money for hopeless spousal benefits campaigns, and imagining they might one day deserve the privilege of adopting children, only to see them them sniffing poppers and wearing trendy tight shirts and showing off their disgusting love handles at discos. I thought of gay men sporting Armani spectacles and getting all excited about the latest gay book, then greeting people at gallery openings and introducing their rapidly ageing young lovers with nauseating self-satisfaction. I thought of them marching in endless Pride Parades in their matching vile drag and leather outfits, so obviously *pretending* to be happy together, *desperately* trying to convince everyone they were having a great time and an exciting life when it was so *obviously* not true. I thought of how ridiculously unaware they all were of the peril they have placed themselves in, and that when they *finally* got sick, how they would invariably call me up for money for their AIDS charities — which of course I never gave to because they so obviously brought the disease on themselves. I thought of all the times I'd been accused of being a stick-in-the-mud, how such gay men always criticized my fashion sense simply because I wore an old sixties relic of a paisley shirt that was a bit too tight around the middle. I thought of them telling me I didn't understand camp, of them waving their arms, effeminately and infuriatingly while flirting with the new young dry-cleaning clerk after I'd been waiting in line for an hour. I thought of them then

| 227

expecting me to support their offensive art, dismal parties, and ridiculous lifestyle simply because I'm a fellow homosexual.

Because I am, after all, a gay man. That's what it all came down to, and why I was in this situation. Never mind all my academic aspirations, all my hard work at Robert Kennedy High School. What was I, after all, but merely *a homosexual*? And what did that mean? It meant a dreadful, deadening sadness, like a dull thud in the heart, night after night of searching hopelessly for love in dirty corners, dark bars, and sweaty steam rooms. It meant rejection. It meant a disrespect for fellow humans that was so enormous that an encounter with another living being was reduced to the mechanical actions of a genital organ. And it meant laughter — the laughter of the female impersonator, the campy boy, the bitter, tired old queen — that piercing ring, that heartless shriek, like bells jangled at mass rung by a hallucinating hunchback. It shattered everything good, everything pure, every dream of honesty and idealism.

I realized how important it was to rescue Alan. If he had learned evil, he could unlearn it; if it had always been a part of him, it was housed with so much goodness, so much purity of soul (I was sure of it) that it could be frightened out. At that point I made a decision which has stayed with me until this day. I felt much the same as a parent whose child has become a mass murderer. We've all seen such mothers on TV. They stare out at us bravely, clutching a handkerchief or a faded summer dress, pleading, "He's a good boy. I know in my heart of hearts he's good." I knew that Alan was good. How did I know that? Because *I decided it was so*. Because I was convinced that I knew Alan even better than he knew himself.

I still wonder sometimes whether that knowledge is just wishful thinking. But you know what? *It doesn't matter.* We must believe in other people. It's through our belief that we create them, and ourselves. Alan and I were both victims — victims of the gay lifestyle — only Alan was younger and more vulnerable to its temptations. I owed it to Alan to expect the best from him. I would love him always, and forgive him anything, because my love could transform him. By the time I had gone through all this, I sat in my favorite chair waiting, not with conflicting emotions, but inspired; my whole being was infused with a euphoric calm. At all costs, I realized that I could not and simply would not abandon my faith in Alan's goodness, whatever the cost, even if he had abandoned it himself.

| 229

I sat in that chair for what seemed like hours, and then the door opened.

Alan said hello, and set his keys down on the little table beside the door. His hair was dishevelled and his cheeks were red from the cold. He carefully removed his pathetic winter coat. (It had fake fur on the collar. I had made a promise to buy him a new one and never kept it. Well, after our little discussion, I vowed to keep my promise.) He looked at me, and I could tell that my energy unnerved him. "You're home early."

"Yes, I am. The kids went on a field trip."

I looked at him, waiting for him to notice the typewriter on the couch. I wanted to see his face as it was transformed by the realization that I had found his writing.

Alan glanced at the couch, because I was looking there. I know the very moment when he realized that his typewriter was sitting there, but amazingly all that happened was that he looked at me with a dreadful little-boy seriousness. He pressed his lips together and his eyes hardened. It was clearly a pragmatic moment for him. It was, "Well, I've been caught, and now I have to talk my way out of this."

"What's my typewriter doing there?"

I looked at him very levelly. "I might very well ask that question myself."

"What do you mean?"

"I mean, I found it under the loft in the study. And there's a piece of paper in it, too."

"I can see that." he said.

"I read it."

"You read it?" He actually looked hurt. Could he really be hurt? Or was he acting?

"Yes, I did."

"Why did you do that?"

"I did that because the typewriter is in my house. Because it's your writing and I'm supposed to be your teacher, your helper, remember? You haven't brought me anything to read for a month so, naturally, I —"

"How could you do that?"

"How could I do what?"

"Read it without my permission."

"I told you —"

"But that was my writing. My private writing. What I was working on."

"I thought we were working on this together."

"That still doesn't give you permission to read my private writing."

I hated that term "private writing"; it suggested an exclusion from Alan's affairs, from his very self, that I found intensely hurtful. But I pressed on.

"So, do you want to know what I think of it?"

"It's not ready yet."

"What do you mean?"

"It's not ready for you to read yet. I haven't got it to the final draft . . . um, stage." He was clearly fumbling now. He was nervous, losing ground.

"I have a few opinions about what I read this afternoon."

"I don't want to know." And then, unbelievably, he made a mad dash for the typewriter, and attempted to grab the piece of paper. His plan didn't work, however, because I managed to bound up from my easy chair and pull the contentious page from the roller. Then I stood up, waving it in his face. I could see that Alan was very upset. Oh yes, yes, he could be very brazen, couldn't he? Talking of his so very *private* writing. But when it came down to it, my opinion mattered a great deal to him. So much that it was no longer simply just his writing; it had become ours. He knew that; I knew that. Who did he think he was kidding?

"Give me that piece of paper."

"No, Alan. I'm not going to give it to you. I need it as a reference point, if I'm going to give you my opinion."

"But I told you I didn't want to hear your opinion."

"Oh, but I think you do."

"No, I don't."

I felt very powerful all of a sudden, and confident. I could tell that it mattered very much what I had to say to him, and I was going to use that fact fully to my advantage. It was my only hope.

The only lever I had to keep him, to change him, and make him mine again.

"It doesn't matter. I'm going to tell you anyway. You know what? When I found this I was deeply hurt that you would have abandoned that project altogether, the project that we were working on."

"How do you know I abandoned it?"

232 | I gazed at him, shocked. "Surely you don't expect me to believe that this —"

"How do you know that it isn't part of a larger . . . project?" He was fumbling again.

"Well, I would say that a disgusting little bit of pornography — badly written, I might add — has absolutely nothing to do with what we were creating together, and what I understood you were working on."

"Well I'm sorry you feel that way."

However far he had moved from me, to whatever perverted sexual universe, I still knew how to hurt him. I was sure of that. There were tears in his eyes. I thought of that old fifties song "Who's Sorry Now?" I decided to let him have it with both guns blazing.

"Yes, I do. Not only do I feel that this is a worthless, senseless piece of crap, but I feel very betrayed by the fact that you have accepted my kindness and indeed my charity while every day you were out cruising street trash. How do you think that makes me feel? Here I am offering you friendship, respect and support, and all you do is throw it back into my face. I've tried to educate you about opera, about art, about culture. I thought you were truly interested. I thought that you understood that in order to be an artist you have to gain some appreciation of the finer things in life. But no, you would rather fritter away your afternoons on carnal pleasures and your mornings writing — well I don't know if I can even call this writing."

Then I did what I'd been wanting to do since I'd found that horrible piece of paper: I ripped it into little pieces and scattered it on the floor.

I don't think this mattered much to Alan. I could tell that he | 233 was pretty devastated by my words. I decided to go in for the kill. "I'm beginning to wonder if my confidence in you has been misplaced, Alan. I had thought, since my first talk with you, that you were an intelligent, talented young man with a lot of potential. Now I'm not so sure. I'm beginning to question your fundamental intelligence, and your potential for growth as an artist. A writer with that special spark doesn't waste his time and creativity pursuing mindless sex and scribbling about it in diaries." I saved my favourite comment for the last. "Who do you think you are? The Marquis de Sade? Well I'm sorry, but your debauches aren't as interesting, and at this point, you can't even write as well as he could. And he was, if I do say so, a pretty bad writer."

I had a brief flash of the incongruity of it all, as one does at such moments. This was the boy I loved, the person I cared more deeply about than anyone in the world. What was I doing hurting him like this, lacerating him, ripping his guts apart? For that was clearly what was happening. A huge sadness threatened to overwhelm me. But I steeled myself. For what good was my beautiful boy to me when his soul had been corrupted? He was no good at all to anyone unless I could bring him back and save him.

What Alan did at that point was very unlike him, and something which I didn't expect at all. Of course I didn't know what to expect, I had never confronted him so severely before. But usually, he was subdued and cowed by any negativity which I directed towards him. Now he stood looking at me, quivering with rage and hurt. And then he spoke. It was still his little-boy voice, but it sounded otherworldly, like the voice of the little girl in *The Exorcist*. It was the voice of a stranger: "You're disgusting." And then he ran out the door.

I was shell-shocked by his response. What stopped me in my tracks was not so much that he dared to oppose me, for there had certainly been hints of stubbornness before. But why did he use that word: disgusting? Why?

And where was he going? How I wish I had run to the window to at least get a glimpse of him rushing down the steps into the street, but I couldn't move. This I will forever regret, for at least I would have had some idea in what direction he had set out. My gut reaction was to wait the amount of time that it might take him to march to his sister's apartment (nearly a half an hour) and then call her. I called her for the next six hours. There was no answer until late in the evening. When I did finally reach his sister, she told me that Alan was not there.

Where did he go? This question plagued me. I continued calling his sister's apartment for the next week, until she became rude.

And that was the beginning of the rest of my life, because I never saw Alan again.

One afternoon in the New Year (I had spent a torturous holiday season alone with my mother) the doorbell rang just moments after I had arrived home from school. At first I thought it was Alan. Who else had such an intimate knowledge of my daily schedule? But when I pressed the intercom, it was a deeper, grown-man's voice that spoke.

"Hello. My name is Juan. I've come to pick up Alan's things."

Juan.

Juan!

This was it, this was the moment I had been both hoping for and dreading at the same time: some connection, any connection, with my beloved boy. I pondered asking the voice (how could I call | 235 him Juan?) why Alan hadn't returned for his things himself. But of course I knew. Alan found me disgusting. I didn't want to hear that nauseating word again, and certainly not from a stranger.

I buzzed him up on the intercom and waited for the knock on my door. It didn't occur to me to start packing Alan's things. Not that Alan had owned so very much. He had brought nothing with him but his typewriter, a few books, and some clothing (including a few sets of his undersized underthings). I waited, certain that my worst fears would be confirmed, and that the person would be the vile, manipulative, shaved, Hummer-driving, older homosexual I had imagined.

Well, what was waiting for me was far worse.

I opened the door and Juan was standing (or perhaps I should say, leaning) there. He was *not* an older man. In fact he didn't look that much older than Alan. But his overall appearance raised very real fears which quickly eclipsed the imagined ones.

Now, keep in mind that this was the very middle of winter, and the temperature was below zero. I remember because earlier that day I had chosen to wear my least fashionable but most practical parka to school.

But silly realities like the weather had no such effect on Juan.

The young man leaning on the doorjamb was about six feet tall, which wasn't much taller than me, but he was certainly much taller than Alan. He was wearing the least amount of clothing I have ever seen anyone wear on a bitter winter day. His pants hung low around his hips (but were tight from there down) and he wore a leather vest that was open (yes, open), revealing an ample, muscular body. From the flat, muscled stomach to the defined chest there was very little to cover his olive skin. (One weighty pectoral was covered in tattoos of naked women, or mermaids, or something.) Oh yes, there was a very long, rather ugly, multicoloured scarf wound loosely around his neck and tossed casually over one shoulder, and there was a sort of a navy-blue pea jacket, the kind sailors wear, somewhere behind it all. Juan's pants had holes in the knees (not from poverty, but as a nod to fashion) and his snakeskin boots had *spurs*. I vaguely glimpsed the flash of a piercing in his furry navel. There was an astounding bulge in his pants. It was all there. I usually do not notice such things, but in this case, since Juan had obviously made an effort to show off the gifts that God gave him, I felt it was my duty to examine them closely. For Juan was blessed with a gigantic member (one that rivalled Leslie's). As for his face, well the black curly hair and deep brown eyes (I thought of limpid pools) were certainly appealing, as were his thick lips. On his head was a sort of Australian bushman's hat decorated with a feather. The word "pimp" came to mind as soon as I had processed the overall picture. He was — according to cultural signposts at least — the gayest thing I had ever, in my life, had the displeasure of encountering.

His smile quickly faded, and was replaced with a kind of perfunctory energy which suggested that the smile had been business related, and that he had, in fact, been having a somewhat trying day.

"Hi," he said.

"Hello," I said.

"Alan's stuff," he said, almost apologetically, but not quite apologetically enough.

Determined not to show bad manners, even under this, the most horrific of circumstances, I invited him in.

"Won't you come in?"

Then he did an extremely irritating thing. He stretched out his dark, thick, handsome neck and peered into my apartment, gave it the once over, and then, not quite approving of what he saw, he withdrew his head to an upright position and smiled that perfunctory smile again.

"No thanks."

I made a rather unpleasant mental observation that he was chewing gum.

"All right then. It will just be a minute while I gather things together. I had no idea you were coming."

"Oh yeah, sorry." I realized that for him, this was being polite — an alarming thought. I left the door open and collected Alan's clothes from the dresser (in all hopefulness, I had not touched them since his departure), put his typewriter in the airline bag in which he had brought it, and collected his books. When I brought the two bags to him, Juan said, "Thanks," and then to my profound discomfort, proceeded to rummage about inside the bags, obviously checking to see if everything was there. He looked up at me. He smiled. This time the smile seemed strangely warm.

"I think maybe there's something missing."

"Pardon me?" I assure you, I was almost apoplectic.

"Umm, well you know, Al mentioned some papers or something ... I don't know ... papers?" He looked at me in a not unfriendly manner, one unoccupied hand gesturing vaguely.

"The writing?"

"Yeah, yeah," he said, as if finally hitting the jackpot. "That's right. He told me to pick up his writing."

"Tell Alan that if he wants his writing, he can come and pick it up himself."

238 |

I suppose I must have been shaking, or at least betrayed some emotion in a vocal quaver. Juan seemed slightly (but not very) perturbed by my response.

"Okey-dokey. Well then. I'll tell him. Thanks a lot, old buddy. See ya."

He hauled both bags over his massive tricep and started down the hall. I slammed the door behind him, and it echoed with a resounding bang.

Well.

When I was sure Juan was gone, I sat down and had a good cry. Somehow I knew that Alan would never contact me again. And I knew that, in order to keep my mind and soul together, I had to move on.

What put the final nail in the coffin of my relationship with Alan was the fact that Juan had called him *Al*. For me, this tiny word spoke volumes. How could anyone call my dedicated protégé *Al*? For me he would always be Alan, in a button-down shirt sporting a shy smile, inquiring eyes, and an enormous potential. For me he would always be a curious, intelligent boy, poised on the precipice of deep learning. *That* was Alan. *Al*, on the other hand, was a drinking buddy, a sex partner. *Al* was simply a "fun guy." That was certainly how Juan saw Alan, and thus I was pretty sure this superficial being was what my precious boy had become. After spending three months with Alan it had become painfully evident to me that he needed an enormous amount of encouragement and support if he was to continue to pursue a career as a writer. I certainly couldn't see him getting that from *Juan*.

It helped me to understand what had caused Alan to curse me in disgust. I realized that Juan, though he fell short of the shaven-headed, Hummer-driving nightmare I had imagined, was something far worse. He was a living, breathing, gay-porn fantasy. The vast, unbreachable disparity between our physiques and our mental capacities said it all. Juan was achingly handsome; in fact, it was hard to imagine that such a gigantic, sexy boy could actually be flesh and blood. I, on the other hand, if my physical attributes were to be placed under a camp and cruel eye, was nothing more than a balding, pot-bellied "old buddy" (Juan's parting dagger did not go unnoticed). Although I am no academic star of Leslie's variety — I am nevertheless an intelligent man with an inquiring mind, whereas Juan seemed barely capable of speaking without running one hand through his perfect hair, or scratching his muscular ass with the other. But of course, in the homosexual world, the externals are all-important. Because the hot man, the sexy man, the hunk stands for one thing and one thing alone: sex. This explained Alan's demoralizing curse. I was disgusting because I was not perfectly muscular and beautiful like Juan, because I was not a sex object or a sex fantasy. Because I was, instead, a real and imperfect man.

I began telling you the story of Alan Peche so that I might shed some light on the Barrie–Llewelyn Davies letters. Our contemporary friendship shares more than a few similarities with the Barrie–Michael relationship. Barrie was much older than Michael, and I was much older than Alan. Barrie loved him as an adopted son, with a love that, I posit, was without physical manifestation. I loved Alan Peche with a chaste desire. Michael was a talented young writer, and Barrie encouraged him. I did the same for Alan. Michael became involved, probably sexually, with a series of destructive boys. Similarly, Alan was involved with dangerous, promiscuous sex. I offer his writing as proof.

In both cases, there was a mystery.

Here we come to the heart of the question.

What is there about sex that causes people to lose their minds and cast precious things aside? Surely we have all been in the situation that James Barrie and I found ourselves in — of offering a selfless love only to be rejected by someone who is in the thrall of sexual attraction. Why? What is there about sex (other than the fact that, I admit, it can be a convenient release of tension) that causes people to spurn those they really love and need for other, less satisfactory individuals?

So far, I have only interpreted one of the most enigmatic of the Barrie–Llewelyn Davies letters, the one in which Michael writes to his beloved uncle of the boys returning after a long voyage. I noted this letter contained a coded reference to Massenet's opera *Werther* and that Michael wrote it to warn Barrie that he and Rupert might commit suicide.

I believe that some, if not all, of the other letters are also written in code.

In one of the most problematic final letters, Michael wrote of meeting a dark-haired, dark-eyed girl. I wondered why girls might suddenly catch Michael's fancy after he had ignored them for so many years. In the next surviving letter, Michael quotes one of Shakespeare's most famous sonnets ("My mistress' eyes are nothing like the sun"). He also quotes from G.E. Moore in praise of friendship and the appreciation of art and nature. I set out to discover the connection between the passage from Shakespeare |241 and the enigmatic quote. Michael mentions that the girl may very well smoke, and may very well be a suffragette. These are symbols (remember we have barely reached the 1920s here) of the fallen woman. If one examines this strange "dark lady" letter closely it's plain to see that not only does Michael neglect to provide details about the girl he has supposedly just met, but his description of her does not sound like the description of a real woman. For instance, he says that her eyes "beckon one" (not *him*, but *one*). I don't in fact think there is any evidence, or any likelihood, that Michael had met a dark woman at all. I believe he was trying through code to convey to Barrie something which he could not express in ordinary words.

But what?

If I could discover the meaning of the dark lady of the sonnets, then perhaps I could also discover why Michael made reference to her. What struck me specifically, were Michael's twinned questions: "But how can you argue with a placid lake on a sunny day? Or with a sonnet by Shakespeare?" The fact that he chose to yank these two images together seemed to me significant, since the image of the placid lake brings to mind the bathing pool where

Michael and Rupert lost their lives. Could Michael have been suggesting a connection between the dark lady of the sonnets and suicide?

I spent hours ploughing through various scholars who attribute a real identity to the dark lady. I read the famous Lucy Negro book which theorizes that the dark lady was a black woman (known to Shakespeare). I do not so much reject this theory as find it less rewarding for my own personal quest. I know that's not a scholarly reason for rejecting anything (and perhaps that goes some distance in explaining why I prefer teaching high school). But I felt, in my heart of hearts, that Shakespeare was not writing about a specific woman. Late one night, while pouring through relevant scholarship in the library of New York University, my eyes lit upon a curious title, a title which I felt powerless to resist: *Renaissance Magic and Hermeticism in the Shakespeare Sonnets: Like Prayers Divine* by Thomas O. Jones. It was a thin volume published by Edwin Mellen Press. It seemed to be little more than a vanity publication of a doctoral thesis, but I didn't let this put me off, because indeed, I had always felt that Shakespeare's sonnets were, to some degree, divine prayers.

I worked my way quickly through the early parts of the book, those concerned with the analysis of Renaissance magic in reference to famous Renaissance magicians Giordano Bruno and Frances Dee. Scholars have only recently begun to explore the relationship between Shakespeare's work and magic. (Another esteemed scholar, Miss Frances Yates, has written many rewarding volumes about the bard's plays and their relationship to occultism. She advances the theory that Prospero is a portrait of Dee, and that *The Tempest* is in fact an elegiac homage to the great

Renaissance wizard.) It is nearly impossible for us to understand the nature of this ancient magic today.

It all has to do with the divine language of angels.

Towards the end of Mr. Jones' book I found the most important clue to Michael's letter. Here Jones talks about the possibility (and his arguments, citing Plato, make perfect sense to me) that Shakespeare's dark lady sonnets are not about a specific woman at all, but are actually a veiled reference to the act of sex.

My first reaction was to throw the book in the vertical file. As you know, I'm impatient with postmodernists who have replaced decent scholarship with vague theories about tearing down boundaries and notions of *the real*, only to replace them with questionable notions about that most predictable of human functions.

But I kept thinking of the line in Alan's pornographic passage: "In the very night of afternoon."

Now, I can't say that I agree with all these sexually based theories about the bard. But suffice it to say that it became clear that Michael Llewelyn Davies probably had some understanding of the significance of this Shakespearean figure. And when writing about the dark lady, he was attempting to discuss the unmentionable subject of sex and his very dark attraction to Rupert Buxton with his prudish uncle. Michael was telling his dear uncle, in code, that he had discovered a very dark and attractive world, and hoping that the older man would somehow recognize his dilemma and help. It was only natural that young Michael, a budding poet, would turn to heightened language to express his deepest feelings.

But why did Michael, in that infuriating, enigmatic letter, juxtapose the quote from the dark lady sonnets with a quote from G.E. Moore? Well, as hard as I worked researching that one,

I could find no connection between the two. G.E. Moore was a philosopher who was much lionized by the Cambridge Apostles. Indeed, that seems to be his claim to fame. Today Moore is pretty much ignored, perhaps having been eclipsed by a much more celebrated Cambridge contemporary, Ludwig Wittgenstein. To be sure, Moore's work is to some degree a kind of warmed-over Walter Pater, a kind of aestheticism that extols the virtues of beauty and the life of the artist.

244 |

Then upon returning to Barrie's response to Michael's enigmatic epistle, I hit the jackpot. I noticed that in his dismissal of the Apostles, he called them "a kind of programmatic Freemasonry." There are very few sources about the Apostles. Most books refer to them as a mysterious society and offer little detail, but I found two formal, historical accounts of the group. Apparently the organization has a long history, starting in the 1820s at Cambridge. One of the first members was Samuel Taylor Coleridge, the romantic poet, mystic, and drug addict. The Apostles were centred at St. John's College, and were named in reference to the Apostles of Christ. They were a debating society but they also were associated with some iconoclastic figures, particularly with a very radical socialist, Comte de Saint-Simon, and his disciple Barthelemy Enfantin. Apparently Enfantin was — in the middle of the nineteenth century, believe it or not — an advocate of free love.

The second book delved a little bit more deeply into the secrets of this quirky group. Apparently, the budding young poet Alfred Tennyson was involved with the Apostles and formed an alliance with a young man named Arthur Hallam, who was an atheist and a homosexual. It was rumored that they may have had an affair. Though the business of the society was to deliver papers to each other, by firelight, every Saturday (from the start these papers were often on radical, atheistic, and homosexual themes) mysterious formal rites were also on the menu. The rites involved, apparently, cursing. The group also had their own language, which was very biblical — the higher, older, most learned members were called "angels" after taking "wings." The secret records of the society were called the "ark." Lytton Strachey and Maynard Keynes became involved with the group during the early part of the twentieth century, at precisely the time when Michael was introduced to them. Through the Apostles, Strachey and Keynes propagated a philosophy called "Higher Sodomy." Higher Sodomy was essentially the idea that homosexual love was better than heterosexual sex, and that the love that had dared not speak its name was something everyone should aspire to.

|245

This philosophy I found shocking and appalling. It was evident that in this tiny ancient Cambridge organization at the turn of the century lay the seeds of what would some day be labelled gay liberation. I have found very little evidence anywhere else of the notion that homosexuality is actually a higher (spiritual or physical) form of love (or sex) than heterosexuality — at least not until the sex-crazed pre-AIDS era. Indeed, throughout the latter part of the nineteenth century homosexuality was treated essentially as a medical condition, or a scientific category. Edmund Carpenter extolled a sort of gay spirituality, but he still presented homosexuality as a pleasant alternative to heterosexuality — different but equal. It is from Lytton Strachey's Apostles that we hear the first stirrings of the arrogant and quite repulsive notion that homosexuals may actually be a more highly evolved segment of society.

Of course Barrie would never have used the term Higher

Sodomy. (I myself have some trouble writing it down.) But the fact that he referred to the Apostles as a "programmatic Freemasonry" fascinated me. I must say that I'm not entirely certain that Freemasonry itself was not associated with homosexuality — at least historically — at its core. Of course the Freemasons, as we know them today, are an antiquated fraternal male organization which is famous for having built various temples in Northern Europe and North America. Like the Apostles, it is very difficult to find reliable information about Freemasonry, or even to discern whether or not the organization still functions. But during my research I came upon the notion that Freemasonry had its origins in the Knights Templar.

246 |

It was with the discovery of this seminal group that all these little clues finally began to fit together into some sort of coherent whole.

In a book about the Templars there is a photo of a medieval coin on which the Templars are pictured. The image is of two men riding the same horse — something that would certainly be an uncharacteristic practice during the twelfth century! It struck me that the men appear to be embracing each other. I may be accused of Leslie's homophilic scholarship here. Indeed, the explanation usually given for this image (it may very well be the correct one) is that the Knights Templar were, during the early years after their founding, a very poor order, and thus the engraving of the two knights on one horse aptly symbolizes their poverty. But that image holds personal meaning for me. It reminds me poignantly of my personal relationship with Alan Peche; for this is the position in which we cuddled every night during the first month that he slept in my bed. We hugged spoon fashion, my arm encircling his tender boy belly. The coin also brings to my mind the two boys clutching each other in Sandford Pool. Not, of course, that I have any evidence that Michael and Rupert held each other in this fashion (they could even have been facing each other). But, for what it's worth, the engraving on the Templar insignia will always be, for me, an affecting reminder of those two lost boys.

I decided to further research their tragic deaths. I knew that articles in contemporary newspapers implied suicide and that Nico Llewelyn Davies is quoted as saying that there may have been a homosexual relationship between Michael and Rupert. | 247

As the story goes, two mill workers, Charles Beecham and Matthew Gaskel, were regulating water for the mill, when they heard shouts and saw two people having difficulties in the pool. Neither of the two workmen was able to swim, but they did throw a life belt to the drowning boys. The men went to get help but the help sadly arrived too late. This story seems to run contrary to any notion of suicide. Why, after all, would the boys shout for rescue if they had made some sort of pact? On the other hand, since only Michael was unable to swim, why did they drown, especially if they had a life preserver?

I continued to dig, this time trying to find out anything I could about Sandford Pool, where the drowning occurred. I discovered that there had been two drowning incidents prior to the one involving Michael and Rupert Buxton. There is a memorial at the site of the pool to the people who had drowned there, one which would have been known to the two boys (and to which their names were eventually, and tragically, added). I also came across a curious quote from *Three Men in a Boat*, a book by Jerome K. Jerome (a very popular late Victorian playwright and humorist).

This book would again, most likely, have been known to the two boys, as it was one of the most popular comic tales of the period. Anyway, in this book Jerome K. Jerome states, "The pool under Sandford lasher, just behind the lock, is a very good place to drown yourself in."

What could be more transparent? The boys died in a place which was a death pool, so whether they shouted for help or not (surely we are all allowed to change our mind, especially in matters of life and death), they must have known, consciously or not, what brought them there.

Sandford Pool, and the land surrounding it, (at that time called Sandford Manor) was donated to the Knights Templar, Cowley Chapter, in the twelfth century. Thomas Sandford who originally owned the land on which the pool was located, was himself a Templar.

My research into the Knights Templar led me to a fascinating book by Lynn Picknett and Clive Prince called *The Templar Revelation: Secret Guardians of the True Identity of Christ*. I can't say that the book is truly scholarly; indeed, if anything, the authors have an occultist agenda and have written elsewhere about the Turin Shroud (which they believe to be a forgery by the Freemason Leonardo da Vinci) and the paranormal. But the authors draw on much reliable historical material to bolster their thesis, which is, to put it simply, this: that Christianity, far from being a sexless religion of love under the leadership of Christ, was, in fact, a cult of sex, related to the Egyptian cults of Isis and Osiris. The leader of that cult was not, in fact, Jesus Christ, but a very sexual John the Baptist and his wife, Mary Magdalene.

It is perhaps possible for myself, as a Jew, to maintain a skeptical, or at least a somewhat open-minded view of Christianity. We were always taught that Gentiles were a little crazy and certainly suspect. I'm not maintaining that Picknett and Prince are correct in their theories about the origin of Christianity, but they do present a convincing argument that the Knights Templar — who were obsessed with St. John the Baptist — may very well have been sexual occultists, and leaders of a religion that advocated free love and blasphemy. (The accusation of sodomy was hurled at the |249 Templars when they were exterminated by the inquisition in the fourteenth century.) Picknett and Prince claim that the true origin of Christianity was obscured by the Apostles and St. Paul.

The *Apostles*. Again, we come full circle. I don't think it is by chance that the secret, blasphemous, homosexual society at Cambridge originated at St. John's College, or that they took as one of their leaders a nineteenth-century advocate of free love, or that they called themselves Apostles.

I'm not necessarily suggesting that these two innocent boys, who drowned themselves at Sandford Pool, necessarily knew all the history of that place, or were involved in the secret rites of the Apostles at Cambridge, or were necessarily knowledgeable about the secrets of the Knights Templar. But there are so many strange elements, so many coincidental links, that it all starts to dovetail. The one thing that I am certain of is that the brilliant young Michael did have some inkling that in his sexual games with Roger Senhouse (and in his obsessive mystical romance with Rupert Buxton) he was embarking on a dark path, a dangerous journey. What I am suggesting is that Michael *did* understand (whether intuitively or in a more scholarly fashion) the very important concept that there is an inevitable link between sexual obsession and death.

I am convinced that the key to the mystery of Michael Llewelyn Davies' suicide lies here, in an exploration of the bizarre connection between sex and death.

We all know that love and marriage will produce children. This is why Shakespeare urged the young nobleman of the sonnets to woo and marry and thus multiply the human race. This is also why Barrie, despite his own difficulties with the opposite sex, urged Michael to form healthy relationships with girls. Sex that is not related to procreation is more than simply a wastage, a spilling of seed on the ground. It is a dark libidinous journey of pleasure and forgetfulness. Sex is a drug, and all drugs are oblivion; all drugs are death. As soon as people (and homosexuals are most guilty of this) begin to pursue sex for the sake of orgasm alone, they risk becoming addicted unto death. An obsession with sex, or sexual love, is a tendency to want to "lose" oneself — in the other person, or in dark nights of sex — a similar impulse to the desire to kill oneself. It's no accident that the French term for orgasm means "a little death" — *le petit mort.*

I am convinced that I lost Alan, and Barrie lost his beloved Michael, to the disease of sexual obsession. Alan had been hypnotized by promiscuous sex, this was obvious. And what, in this age of AIDS, could be more suicidal? I was quick to notice (like most observant readers, I'm sure) that in the pornographic fragment that broke my heart, Alan mentioned nothing about condoms. Now if the piece was actually written as pornography, condoms would be irrelevant; they might hinder a perfectly arousing depiction of the sexual act. But the fact remains that it is irresponsible in this day and age to depict sex of any kind, in any sort of films, fiction, or poetry, without the attendant prophylactic device.

Thus you can see that my concerns over Alan's lifestyle were not merely puritanical. I was worried that it all had become a matter of life and death. Meeting the inarticulate-piece-of-meat-named-Juan simply confirmed the notion that Alan was on a road to self-destruction through the oblivion that is mindless sex. This pursuit is all about erasing the self, forgetting day-to-day life. Non-procreative sex is death.

Michael Llewelyn Davies knew that. Which is why he dreamed about kissing boys without mouths on smoking battlefields. That's why he went to die clutching his lover in his arms.

Barrie's greatest disservice to his adopted son is that he may have unwittingly encouraged his depression by babying him and pampering his obsessive nature. When Barrie finally realized that Michael was suicidal, it was much too late. He ineffectually offered the services of a psychologist who was dedicated to filling up his patients with food and giving them shots to nullify their animal urges. This would not have been enough, in any case. What he had not taught the boy, and what every child must learn, is the virtue of "blocking."

Blocking may sound like a negative thing. But, as far as I'm concerned, it is the most productive psychological technique we have at our disposal. It quite simply refers to the act of blocking from consciousness those thoughts and ideas that are upsetting and destructive. Freud taught us that repression is not necessarily a negative thing, but can be a tool for emotional survival. Unfortunately, during the free love era of the 1960s, repression got a bad name. So for the purposes of clarity I will use my own term: blocking.

The opposite of blocking is spiralling. This is what happened to Michael, and clearly to Alan. The emotional spiral is a condition that will be clear to anyone who has ever experienced an anxiety attack, drug or sexual addiction, obsessive-compulsion, or intense worry. Everyone, to various degrees, spirals. We obsess over this or that thing, a promotion, a love affair, whatever. This is normal and controllable. We all find that we are able — by refusing to think about these petty concerns — to get back on track; to sleep, to work, to function. Because, after all, it is *reality*, and the *function of that reality*, which is ultimately important. But there are those of us who become so wrapped up in one idea or another, that it takes over our entire lives, and we are incapable of working, loving, or creating. An obsessive-compulsive will spiral over and over again around the fantasy that his house is filthy. Someone like Alan will find themselves overwhelmed by sexual ideas and become addicted to promiscuity. They are unable to stop, to say no, to repress, to block. And those like Michael will become so hypnotized by the twin attraction to and repulsion of sex and death, that they become paralyzed by an emotional whirlpool that is the psychological equivalent of the eddying waters of Sandford Pool.

It is no accident that young Michael's opera of choice was Massenet's *Werther*. I would not go so far as to condemn the opera in the manner that Barrie does. In fact it has proved to be a perennial favourite with audiences because the music is compellingly, hauntingly beautiful. But the work's libretto — it's the story of a man who commits suicide after being rejected by a married woman — is a hopeless one. Young Werther is a classic case of the spiralling mentality: a person who is held in the grip of a destructive obsession, helpless and unable to stop. In fact, if you wish to hear the musical equivalent of an emotional spiral, listen to

"Prelude to Act Three" of Massenet's *Werther*. (It was the perfect soundtrack for Michael's doomed young life.) As you will hear, the music swirls deep and deeper, and through progressive key changes becomes an ever-widening, dangerous, yet strangely enervating, vortex of depression. I have never heard, in music, such a perfect representation of the downward journey of a mind turned in on itself, eating itself alive, doomed to inevitable oblivion and death.

Of course Michael would not have been able to bring himself to go to war and for one reason only: he was unable to block. It is evident that his night-terrors were symptomatic of this deficiency, too. For him, there was no possibility of repressing upsetting thoughts and getting on with his life. For so many men in the trenches were evidently and horribly — and with foreknowledge — marching directly to their own deaths. In order to march into death (the honorable, important, necessary death — the death of a gentleman serving his country) it is important to block, to repress. That's all bravery is: the blocking of fear, the repression of unpleasant thoughts. The kind of sensitive, childish soul that lived inside Michael Llewelyn Davies would forever run from war, spiralling in fear, only to find that fear replaced with an overwhelming obsession with doomed love. He never confronted his spiralling mentality; he never blocked; in fact, he wallowed. He could not fight, nor be a man, nor function in the real world. He could only plummet, drown, suffocate, choke. We have two choices in life. We can block and act, and live. Or we can become helpless victims of emotion and passion, and as a result, die.

I decided to burn the Barrie–Llewelyn Davies letters.

I think that the reasons for my celibacy will now be clear. I have watched others die from devoting themselves to pleasure. I have seen, all too clearly, the glint of passion for death in Leslie's eyes, and in Alan's writing.

I'm still not certain whether these letters should be read by anyone. Least of all by the young. They are too potent a mirror of what is dangerous inside us all.

EPILOGUE

by Alan Peche

                                         I was born in Plattsburgh, New York. My family lived in a white clapboard two-storey house on Lawn Avenue. My relationship with my mother was terrible. My father was not part of my life. My father killed a man. He got into a drunken fight, slugged a guy who never got up again, pleaded guilty to manslaughter, and went to jail for five years. He's been out of jail for fifteen years now. He's bitter because he wasted his life. Now he's dying of lung cancer.

I am a diagnosed manic-depressive. I take lithium to prevent manic episodes. For a long time I didn't tell anyone about my symptoms: they start with a burning in my head. A spot on my forehead gets hot. I get anxious. I can't be around people.

I've also been diagnosed with a Body Dysmorphic Disorder. The only symptom of this illness is that I hate my body. I think I'm ugly and fat. The lithium takes away this symptom, too.

The molestation I wrote about for Manny Masters actually happened. My friend Wallace and I went to the Fourth of July festivities at the school. His father took me to the Johnny-on-the-spot to pee. Something no ten-year-old needs help with. In the toilet, he undid his belt and pulled down his jeans and boxer shorts. Wallace's Dad saw me looking at his dick and he asked me to touch him. I did.

Manny made me change my story; he wanted me to take out the details. He claimed that he didn't want the boy to appear be complicit in the molestation. But it's true: I didn't wear underwear that day, because it felt sexy. Manny wanted me to say that being molested changed my life, that I went through a lot of pain, and that I was redeemed. But the experience wasn't particularly painful or redeeming. Did the molestation have something to do with my homosexuality? I'd had sexual fantasies about men before I was ten. Being molested could not have made me gay. I am gay. Period.

Remember the guy that I used to help with the ice? Well after I helped him with the ice I'd give him a blow job. In return, he helped me with some pocket money. He wasn't my idea of a boyfriend, but I figured I wasn't going to find one in Plattsburgh. He was just a nice guy with the kind of physical equipment that made it a pleasure to get twenty dollars. There were other guys in town who I used to help out in the same way.

Manny didn't know me. He was in love with his imaginary Alan Peche. My relationship with Manny was just like the relationship between James Barrie and Michael Llewelyn Davies. Did Michael tell Barrie all the details about his relationship with Roger Senhouse? No. He knew that if he spilled the beans he wasn't going to receive presents: the car, the holiday on the private island, or money for school.

I didn't know Manny was in love with me. When I first met him I was very vulnerable. I was living with my sister, and feeling lonely. I was also desperate to make some connections in New York City's literary world. When he held me while we were sleeping that first night, I liked the affection. Later, I tried to make him understand that he had to stop touching me. I thought Manny knew there was not going to be anything sexual between us, and that there was no point in him falling in love with me.

The trouble between us started after Manny made me change the molestation story. I worked hard to rewrite it. He told me that I should base the iceman on him, and write about redemption. I couldn't write about my childhood anymore after that.

Around that time, I started having lots of sex. Then I started to write about it. Allen Ginsberg was at the back of my mind. I was also reading a lot of poems by Frank O'Hara and Pier Paolo Pasolini. I started going out in the day and cruising the docks. Most of the Lower West Side has been renovated, but there are still some places where you can find like-minded men. I found them. I had a lot of good sex. I was never kidnapped by a guy in a Hummer with a shaved head. I did poppers and some pot. I met a lot of sad and sorry losers and a lot of perfect, beautiful guys.

After the breakup with Manny I met Juan. Juan is a very cute, shallow waiter. I moved in with him and then moved out in a period of two weeks. We had fun for a while, but it was no big deal.

Soon after that I was wandering around Soho and I walked into Keith's gallery. He was sitting behind a desk. One thing led to another and we went back to his loft. After a couple of months I moved in. Keith is an art dealer. He's a lot of fun and he understands that I need to have my own life. He also looks very good in a suit, which turns me on, for some reason.

A few months after I had moved in with Keith, I got the news that Manny was dead. Keith's cellphone rang and it was Manny's mother. How she found Keith's number or knew to call there is still a mystery to me. She was civil. She told me Manny had written a book, that it was dedicated to me, and that he wanted me to have it.

I picked it up on a hot and sunny summer day. Mrs. Masters' apartment was in one of those huge buildings on the Upper East Side facing the park. I took the old elevator to the seventh floor. I knocked on her door. It opened a crack. A bitter cold came rushing out at me, slamming me in the chest so hard it almost hurt. I could hardly see into the dark. A tiny woman stood on the other side of the door. She looked very strange. She had dyed blonde hair and was heavily made up. Like a drag queen. There was a cigarette hanging out of her mouth. I could see she was having trouble holding the heavy wooden door. I pushed it gently open a little more. "I came for Manny's manuscript," I said.

"Just a minute," she said. She did not invite me in, but turned and walked away. I stood there holding the door, trying to get used to the cold air. The apartment was dark. The TV was playing *The Price Is Right*. A heavy curtain moved in the breeze from the air conditioner and a shaft of sunlight burst through, spilling over a chair. I caught sight of a brocade couch and an ornate lamp. The couch was covered in plastic that glinted briefly in the sunlight.

Mrs. Masters came back with the manuscript. I felt very sorry for her, thinking that she looked like a monkey. A skinny, gnarled, little old monkey wearing lipstick with hair done up like Ann Landers. She handed me the brown paper-wrapped parcel. I thanked her. She said, "Goodbye, young man." And she let the door slam hard, right in my face.

"Young man" seemed like an accusation.

Manny had written me a letter. It was attached to the first page of the manuscript.

Master Alan P.,

> *This book is dedicated to you. A very fine young man in a crisp white collar with the soul of an angel. Please read it, and take its message to heart. I have faith in you, and all the beautiful possibilities that life has in store. I will always love you, as a father loves a son.*

> *Yours, affec.*
> *Manny*

How did Manny die? He was hit by a garbage truck one Tuesday in June after walking out the front door of his apartment building. It wasn't suicide because Manny wasn't capable of suicide.

When people think of older gay men and boys together they wonder if the older man is buggering the younger one. But the evil that the older men do is much worse. They don't see the boys. They don't understand that they are people too. Do you know what it was like to sit every night in that dusty old apartment while Manny read me Dickens? And then listen to his opera? Look at his last letter. He calls me "a fine young man in a crisp white collar with the soul of an angel." Nothing could be further from the truth. I wear crisp white button-down shirts because of my body dysmorphia.

Barrie treated Michael the same way Manny treated me. In his eyes, Michael could do no wrong. Meanwhile, the kid was romping around with boy after boy right under his nose. Manny thinks that Michael was brainwashed by Roger Senhouse, Rupert Buxton, the Apostles, the Knights Templar, the Freemasons, and everyone else. He thinks that sex destroyed Michael, and that obsessive sex is involved with death. But sex and death are opposites. I don't think Michael Llewelyn Davies and Rupert Buxton went to Sandford Pool to commit suicide. They went there to have sex.

260 | Are sexual obsession and suicide connected?

When I go out and have sex, I go out with two different approaches. Basically there are the nights when I go out just to have fun. I feel good about myself, and the body dysmorphia pills are working. I get laid, and the guy is usually cute. Then there are what Keith calls my "black" nights. On those nights I get stoned And despite AIDS, I sometimes fuck without condoms. I know that's unsafe. But I still do it. Sometimes I feel guilty for being a survivor. All these guys are dead from AIDS. Why not me?

Ronnie Connaught is still alive. He looks pretty bad because of all the protease inhibitors he has to take.

Once he tried to pick me up.

I didn't have sex with him. I didn't find him attractive.

There is one last letter from Michael Llewelyn Davies to James Barrie. Manny wrapped it with a special ribbon. He gave it to me, with this book, along with special instructions: "For Your Eyes Only." This letter is dated on the very day of Michael's death. Why did Manny hide it?

19th May, 1921
Dearest Uncle,

It is going to be the most lovely day of all!
And how do I know?
Well.

Do you remember us, dearest uncle, standing at the edge of Round Pond, our fingers high in the air, our serious little noses pointed into the wind? But surely Uncle you must! There is no child in London who has never worried at Round Pond whether or not it was a pleasant enough day to play. For as you so famously said: all perambulators lead to the Kensington Gardens.

There was a day once, when you told us that it was far too windy, and that our stickboat would most surely capsize. You told us, too, that on windy days, our intrepid little schooner was much more likely to be overrun by Pirates — though Pirates were terribly exciting for us, and I daresay you must have known that. But little Nico tugged at your coattails. He was always the most charming one of us — since one of us, on any given day, was required to be thought the most charming — and you knew that, in baby language, he was insisting. Lo & behold you let him launch the stickboat, and the moment it hit the water everything suddenly became very still. We were so frightened! Would the boat ever move? But of course the sails went up . . .

And then it was a perfect day.

Sandford Pool is beckoning. Rupert stuck his finger out the dormitory window. He said that there are moments when the wind is high, and then, strangely, moments when there is no wind at all. And then he said a very odd thing. (But not odd at all, because he is so terribly deep and serious.)

"This is the still point between love and desire!"

I'm afraid I don't know what it means, for I rarely know what Rupert means. In fact, I mostly don't understand him at all.

But when we chase what we don't understand — some solitary truth obscured by love — the dark is light enough. I see this letter has quite unintentionally turned into a poem, and quite a serious one at that.

So please ignore this letter, with my apologies, for it must be forgiven, and forgotten. I beg you to forget! Or better yet, lose it, let it fall, deep into Round Pond, on a very windy day.
Let it be lost!

For then, dearest Uncle, I promise I shall be your loving nephew forever,

Michael